# BEATRIX POTTER'S TALE

D1332399

# BEATRIX POTTER'S TALE

## A FICTIONAL PORTRAIT

· 

### ELIZABETH BATTRICK

*Ellenbank*
*Press*

Published by Ellenbank Press
The Lathes, Selby Terrace, Maryport, Cumbria CA15 6LX

First published 1993

The moral right of the author has been asserted
All rights reserved

Copyright © Elizabeth Battrick 1993

Designed by Linda Blakemore

Typeset in 10/11pt Plantin by Deltatype Ltd,
Ellesmere Port, Cheshire
Printed and bound in Great Britain by Athenaeum Press Ltd,
Newcastle upon Tyne

British Library Cataloguing in Publication Data
A catalogue record for this book is available from
the British Library

ISBN 1-873551-06-1

05795402

| LANCASHIRE LIBRARY | | | |
|---|---|---|---|
| LL | | LM | |
| LK | | LH | |
| LA | | LC | |
| LW | | LB | |
| LS | | LE | |
| LZ | | ML | |

# PREFACE

—— • ——

The main facts of Beatrix Potter's life are fairly well known, but the trouble with facts is that they can be interpreted so differently. As I live in the part of the world she loved, have written a book about Beatrix's association with the Lake District and the National Trust and have contributed to the study of her life and art that went with the Tate Exhibition of her work, I have had plenty of opportunity to hear many different interpretations. Some of them sounded to me so wide of the mark, I felt a balanced assessment was badly needed. To my mind, the only way to present a true picture of Beatrix Potter's life was to write a fictionalised version of it.

Having decided that fiction was the best medium, the next question was whether the book should cover all of her life or a part. There seemed no need to include the long years of childhood and adolescence, a grey London environment for three-quarters of the year, with a governess coming in and always mutton chops for lunch, and the blissful escape to Dalguise House by the River Tay in Scotland, with woodlands, wild flowers, wild creatures of every kind, for three months each summer. Equally, the years of marriage, the building up of a big agricultural estate and increasing the tally of property to be finally bequeathed to the National Trust, seemed a fulfilment, a completion. It was the years between that were full of conflict, passion, tragedy and a final happiness: surely the stuff of fiction.

There were too many minor characters, friends, relations, acquaintances and domestic staff, to include them all in the narrative. In the end I selected those who had real influence, who altered the fabric of Beatrix's life during those 'between' years. The few fictional characters were introduced to depict the contrasting life of the 'below stairs' Victorian household.

Naturally it was Beatrix's parents who initially influenced her character. Her shyness, her reluctance to meet people and her lack of self-confidence resulted at least in part from their ideas on the upbringing of their children.

Rupert and Helen Potter were both Lancastrians, from wealthy cotton families. Rupert's father, Edmund, had made a considerable fortune as a calico printer with his own works in Glossop and Helen's father had been a prosperous cotton merchant in Stalybridge. So there was money enough for Rupert to read law and for Helen to learn the ways of a lady of means.

After beginning their married life in Upper Harley Street, the couple moved to No. 2 Bolton Gardens in 1866, when Helen was expecting her first child, Beatrix. Bertram was born six years later. Both parents enjoyed life in London, Rupert becoming a member of the Reform Club where he met his fellow Liberals and Helen holding elegant dinner parties for her husband's friends.

The children were largely confined to the nursery suite on the fourth floor of the narrow London house, and after Bertram went away to school Beatrix was left there alone with her many pets – bats, lizards, mice, rabbits – and a succession of governesses. This was not an unusual pattern of life for middle-class Victorian children, but was more marked in the Potter household than in most. Mrs Potter did not include her daughter in her social life even when Beatrix reached her late teens, nor was she greatly encouraged to meet or stay with her many cousins.

Beatrix was sixteen when the family took their first summer holiday in the Lake District, at Wray Castle on Windermere. Dalguise House had been reclaimed by its owner, a devastating disappointment to them all, and Wray Castle was thought of as a temporary expedient.

It was here that Beatrix met Hardwicke Rawnsley, then Vicar of Wray, later a founder of the National Trust, and was introduced to the countryside round Sawrey, which she was to describe as 'the most pleasant countryside in the world'. It was also here that she began to form her own opinions, to become a person in her own right. By the time she was thirty years old her strong sense of duty was being assailed by her equally strong spirit of independence. This is when *Beatrix Potter's Tale* really begins.

It would have been impossible to write this book without assistance. I am most grateful to Judy Taylor, whose careful research has thrown so much light on Beatrix Potter's life and times, and to Dr Mary Noble for her help with the Scottish side of things and the complicated life of what Beatrix called 'funguses'. Thanks are also due to Irene Whalley and other friends and family for their prompt response in times of need and for their continued encouragement.

# CHAPTER ONE

On fine winter mornings, crisp with frost and a hint of blue above the trees, Beatrix could tolerate Bolton Gardens. There was a sense of established order, proper commitments, cleanliness being next to godliness and all being right with the Potter family. Foggy mornings were different and there were a lot of them in the late autumn of 1896. On foggy mornings Bolton Gardens bared its soul, becoming disembodied and unreliable. Beatrix found Bolton Gardens most unsettling in a London fog and this one, on 14th November, the day chosen by Uncle Harry for their meeting, couldn't have come at a worse time.

She unbolted the front door and opened it a crack to see if the day was improving. Not at the moment, or ever by the look of it. Well, there was no going back now. Arrangements had been made and she had to leave the house before Papa and Mama were up and about.

She went out quietly, shutting the door carefully behind her. Then she crossed the road, trying to ignore the startled recognition of next-door's housemaid, and came up rather hard against the opposite railings. She followed them round into Bramham Gardens – with no more mishap than stumbling over a kerb – and looked at her fob watch. It wanted ten minutes to eight o'clock and she was meeting Uncle Henry at nine. She would have to walk round the gardens for nearly an hour.

Was she wrong, she wondered, beginning her perambulations, to want her work to be acknowledged? It seemed to be causing a lot of trouble and there was little sign of progress. It was nearly six months since Uncle Harry had first taken her to Kew to meet the Director, Mr Thiselton-Dyer, a thin, elderly, boastful gentleman who puffed on cigarettes all the time. Apart from agreeing that she should have a student's ticket and taking a desultory look at her drawings of fungi, he had appeared to forget she was there and conversed solely with her uncle. She did wish she was a little taller and had more confidence in her own abilities.

Then she had met Mr Massee, a desiccated old gentleman

who regarded her vaguely over the top of his spectacles and looked through her portfolio so intently he had given her high hopes that something might be made of the fungus drawings. Of course in the end it had turned out that he was just short-sighted. He had told her, in the kindest manner, that though they were pretty her method of laying out the drawings was not professional and therefore they could not be used in a properly scientific paper. Not any of the four hundred or more studies she had made.

A wraith, which Beatrix had thought to be a bush, suddenly developed arms and legs and began to move very fast in the opposite direction. She wasn't sure whether she or the tramp had been the most startled. The trees were dripping on her hat and she put up her umbrella.

So now she was thrown back on her study of lichen, fungus and alga and there was the need to know if anyone else had considered the germination of the spores of fungi. This was indirectly the cause of this very damp early morning walk. Perhaps she should have told the maids of her plans before she left. She wondered what was happening at No. 2.

The Potters' housemaid Elizabeth, who had a lively imagination, was sitting on the battered kitchen couch drinking a cup of tea in the hope that it would do something for her nerves. She'd seen Miss Beatrix slipping out of the front door and in the last half-hour had invented a dozen dramatic reasons for such an early departure.

'What's up wi' you?' asked Norah, stirring the porridge as though she had a grudge against it. Planted solidly on the rag rug, the latest in a line of hearth-rugs she never stopped making, she reminded Elizabeth of a wooden Mrs Noah she and her sister Dorothy had played with as children.

'Slept badly,' Elizabeth said. She used this excuse for almost everything. Norah was not to be trusted.

'Time for the Master's shaving water,' Norah said. She associated sympathy with being 'soft' and she didn't believe in being soft. Filling a copper jug from the brass tap on the range, she thumped it down on the scrubbed table.

Elizabeth stood up, settled the cap which always worked backwards on her soft, light-brown hair, and reluctantly lifted the steaming container.

'Best be sharp,' said Norah, whose sly eyes were roving over Elizabeth's person looking for unfastened buttons over the plump bosom or badly tied apron strings round the slim waist. She was disappointed. 'Master don't like being kept waiting.'

As though I didn't know after all these years, Elizabeth thought, burning her fingers on the jug as she pushed through the green baize door into the hall. That castor-oil plant looked down in the mouth; it needed water. She plodded automatically up the stairs.

The water was safely delivered to the Master's dressing-room and Elizabeth had got back to the top of the stairs when the worst happened. A deep, husky voice with a brisk northern clip to it brought her to a sudden halt.

'Elizabeth, send Miss Beatrix to me at once.'

Elizabeth turned, taut as picture wire. Mrs Potter, hair scraped back, morning wrapper held tightly round her, stood in the bedroom doorway.

It wasn't that she was large; she was quite a short woman really, not even fat. Perhaps it was her eyes, small and black and blank with puffy grey flesh padding them from below. Or her mouth, the lower lip protruding beyond the upper in perpetual discontent, with her apology for a chin tucked into her neck. Whatever it was, she terrified Elizabeth.

'Good morning, Ma'am. I'm afraid Miss Beatrix has already left the house.' What else could she say? Elizabeth waited for the storm.

Mrs Potter began to swell, like a toad when poked with a stick. Fascinated, Elizabeth watched the edges of the grey wrapper move perceptibly apart on the flat bosom. Then a dark mulberry flush began in Mrs Potter's neck and washed upwards to mottle the leaden skin of her face.

'She can't have gone, she has no right. I'm ill, I was up all night. I need her at once. Where is she and why has she gone so early, without a word to me.' She stamped a foot, choked on a breath and waited for an answer.

So you couldn't get your claws on her, you cranky old bitch, Elizabeth said silently.

'I don't know I'm sure, Ma'am,' she said aloud.

Mrs Potter's angry eyes rested on the maid for a moment, then she backed into the bedroom and slammed the door. Elizabeth went downstairs clinging to the bannisters for support.

At a quarter to nine, just after breakfast had been taken up and the gong sounded, the area door was pushed stealthily open from the outside, letting in a bitter breath of foggy air. Elizabeth

9

and Norah looked up from their porridge to see Miss Beatrix, after a quick look round, come in and close the door quietly.

They stared at her in astonishment. Dressed all in brown, like a sparrow, her coat and hat were covered with rime, her skirt soiled round the hem and her shoes dark with moisture. Her pale face, oval, with a straight nose, blue eyes and a firm mouth and chin, was pinched and purple with cold. She took off her gloves, put them carefully on the table and turned to Elizabeth.

'Well,' she said, quite composed, as though she did this every morning, 'have I been missed?' Only in her gruff little voice did she at all resemble her mother.

Elizabeth didn't know whether to be glad or sorry that her dramatic flights of fancy were, as usual, wrong.

'Madam has asked for you, Miss Beatrix. It would seem she wants you with her today.'

'There now, just as I thought. I knew if I was in the house it would be fatal! I'm meeting Sir Henry in ten minutes, so if I could just have a cup of tea I'll be out again before they've finished breakfast.'

She drank her tea and ate a piece of bread and butter standing by the range, gradually beginning to glow a little with both warmth and triumph.

'If anyone asks,' she said to Elizabeth, 'I'm spending the day with Sir Henry and will be back this evening.'

Elizabeth nodded and saw Miss Beatrix's knuckles go white on the back of the Windsor rocking chair as they all heard a deep voice shouting in the hall above them. It was followed by the sound of wood crashing on wood, as of a chest lid being dropped into place. Miss Beatrix shot out of the back door like a disturbed partridge.

'Did you hear what the Mistress said?' Norah asked excitedly.

'Not to make out the words.' Elizabeth wasn't going to discuss it.

'Devil's child, devil's spawn. That's what I heard.'

Elizabeth sighed. It was going to be a bad day and Miss Beatrix with one of her colds at the end of it.

After breakfast was cleared Elizabeth went upstairs. The bed-rooms were the under-housemaid's job but Lily was at home in Hastings with a sickly mother. Miss Beatrix had said she was to stay as long as she was needed.

She started on the principal bedroom on the second floor which had tall windows overlooking the Gardens. She opened the bed, throwing back the linen sheet, two blankets, blanket cover, eiderdown, eiderdown cover and white Durham quilt to air in the muggy atmosphere. The windows remained closed in the winter. Then she reached under the brass bed, knobbed like one of the tombs in Westminster Abbey, for the chamber pot.

It was a pretty sea-green colour and glazed. It was also half-full and needed careful managing. The Master had a commode in his dressing-room. She took the pot to the housemaid's cupboard on the landing where there was a sink and gave the contents a thorough inspection before disposing of them. So much for the Mistress being ill; her water was pale, clear and healthy. She was putting it on, as usual.

She finished the bedroom, did the Master's dressing-room and went up another flight of stairs. This brought her to the floor where Miss Beatrix and Mr Bertram had a bedroom each and shared the old nursery as a sitting-room, menagerie and museum. Not that Mr Bertram spent much time at home.

Miss Beatrix had the back bedroom, stuffed with large mahogany furniture and staring out at chimney pots. The bed was already made, with the cold, white honeycomb quilt smoothed down. Elizabeth absently realigned the quilt and felt something wriggle under her fingers.

She snatched her hand away with a silent scream; with only one exception no one made loud noises in this house. She stared transfixed as something made a sort of tunnelling movement under the quilt like a miniature mole under grass. Then she remembered Miss Beatrix telling her to keep a look out for her lizard, Henry, who had escaped from the nursery. It looked as though she'd found him.

The problem was how to catch him. Not even for Miss Beatrix was she going to handle one of those nasty, wriggly, creepy creatures. Not since the day she'd picked up Henry's predecessor and his tail had come away in her hand.

She looked at the dressing-table for inspiration. The hair-brushes and mirror, silver-backed with cherubs? No, she didn't want to swat the blessed Henry. Button hook, glove-stretcher – ah, glove-stretcher. The thin ivory arms that stretched the fingers of kid gloves could also be used like tongs. She could put him in the hair tidy used to store hair combings.

Elizabeth caught sight of herself in the mirror, brown

11

morning uniform, plain cap sitting crooked on her smooth plait wound like a coronet round her head, large uneasy brown eyes and a small nose she could twitch like a rabbit. She put her cap straight – always look tidy for big-game hunting – and picked up the glove-stretcher.

The wriggler was now a tiny bump near the foot of the bed. Suppose it was a poisonous snake, like the one in *The Speckled Band?* Elizabeth encircled the bump with her left hand and then bravely turned back the quilt. Ah, it was Henry. She approached him with the ivory tongs, as though she was going to serve a portion of fish. He made a final bid for freedom and she only caught his tail; to her relief it stayed put. She shovelled him into the bag and pulled the mouth shut with the draw-strings. Now to put him back.

Breathing a little fast, she opened the door of the old nursery, but nothing seemed to be moving. In her opinion it was the only comfortable room in the house, in spite of its occupants.

It was big and square with a view over dripping trees reaching their branches into thinning fog. The large table was covered by a shabby red chenille cloth missing several bobbles and a cheerful fire was reflected in a high brass fender. There was also the usual feeling that she'd interrupted a colloquy between the various occupants who now regarded her with bright eyes.

'Good thing it's only me,' she told them. 'If it was the Mistress you'd be for it.' Not that Mrs Potter ever came up here, which was just as well.

Elizabeth shook Henry into his box under the window, averting her gaze from the caged mice on top of the old toy cupboard and the mounted bat skeleton set like an ornament on the cabinet. She looked disparagingly at the little messes growing in a collection of saucers on the windowsill and then went over to exchange greetings with the rabbit in his hutch by the coal box. Mice were one thing, rabbits another, and she rather liked Peter. He was more intelligent than that old Benjamin. She twitched her nose and made squeaky noises at him and he whiffled his whiskers in return. He even let her tickle him under the chin.

There was a drawing of Cinderella's coach being pulled by rabbits on the table. Miss Beatrix would have done it for that card firm that took some of her drawings. All the rabbits looked like Peter.

'You'll make her famous one day,' she told him, not meaning it.

12

William Beckett, coachman to the Potter family, timed his morning visits to No. 2 for the day's orders very carefully. It took a few minutes to walk round from the mews where the horses were kept, fifteen minutes or so to drink his tea, and the drawing-room bell rang on the dot of 9.30. It was now 9 o'clock.

He checked the angle of his high-crowned bowler in the broken mirror on the tack-room shelf and ran a hand round his fleshy, clean-shaven jaw. Horses, he had decided long ago, didn't like beards.

'I'll be off now,' he called to the new groom, busy with shovel and wheelbarrow.

In contrast to the foggy outside world, the kitchen at No. 2 was warm and cheerful. Norah had his tea just poured and Lizzie came down the basement stairs as he lifted his mug. She looked pink and dishevelled and tasty. She was a good sort, even when he teased her by calling her Lizzie.

'Miss Beatrix driving today, Lizzie?' he asked. He'd made a good job of teaching Miss Beatrix to drive her own phaeton, though he said so himself.

'No more she is, Mr Beckett. She's gone for the day,' Elizabeth said. 'And don't call me Lizzie.'

'How's Mrs P. then?' Mr Beckett knew the ways of the household.

'Not pleased.' Norah's mouth was tight. 'Complaining about the leg of mutton they had last night and wanting to see the butcher's bills for the month.'

Mr Beckett considered this as he got on with his tea and buttered scone. Mrs P. was quite capable of taking her bad temper out on him and the horses if she felt that way out. Lizzie must have made the scones; they were too light to have come through Norah's heavy hands.

There was a clanging above their heads and all three of them looked at the indicator board, though they knew perfectly well which bell had rung. Mr Beckett was conscious of a faint flutter of apprehension where his middle button rested.

Mrs Potter was sitting where she always sat, in the cane-backed upright chair beside the little walnut desk she called her davenport. She was wearing a morning cap with flapping earpieces, reminiscent of blinkers, and had her eyes on her folded hands. He'd still be a poor man if he'd had a guinea for every time she'd looked him in the face. There was a crackling feel to the air around her. Mr Beckett straightened his back.

'Well Beckett,' she said, addressing her hands, 'I shan't be needing the carriage this afternoon and really the carriages are used so seldom I have decided there shall be some economies. We can sell Miss Beatrix's pony. There's no need for her to have her own phaeton when we already have the landau and the brougham. Please arrange for the sale of the animal immediately. I believe the zoo gives good prices for plump horseflesh.'

Mr Beckett felt the muscles round his jaw tighten. The reason the carriages were under-used was that Mr Potter would only allow the horses to be taken out once a day except in emergencies. Mrs Potter was revenging herself on Miss Beatrix for escaping from her leading rein. Well, sell the pony before he spoke to Miss Beatrix he would not, even if it meant giving his notice. Zoo indeed!

He found he was staring at the bowed head that so parodied the portraits of Queen Victoria. He grunted wordlessly, turned on his heel and marched out of the room and down to the kitchen. Lizzie was going to hear about this.

Beatrix arrived home before six o'clock, infinitely tired but not unsatisfied. Uncle Harry had been very sprightly all day and she'd had to help him with the parcels. There had been enough of them to take to his house at Woodcote, but coming back there had been eight to bring on the train, including a hamper containing a goose and a bunch of gigantic chrysanthemums, though perhaps the most awkward had been the two large band boxes. These had inspired Uncle Harry to announce loudly on three different occasions that he was travelling for a milliner. With his twinkling eyes and commanding presence, he could easily have been taken for an actor-manager; Beatrix sometimes wondered if the world of the stage would have suited him better than that of chemistry. She found playing up to his lead quite exhilarating.

This was not to say that the day had been wasted. Uncle Harry had written a 'fishing' letter to Mr Massee at Kew, the one member of staff who seemed at all helpful, to ask for the name of any book that could help him with a totally fictitious piece of research in Beatrix's field. The note was in her pocket ready to post.

Now she had to face Mama, but first she must find Elizabeth to be forewarned of any disaster. She found her in the dining-room setting the table.

'How have things gone today?' she asked, then sneezed, twice.

Elizabeth hesitated; there was no doubt about that cold. She looked tired as well. 'It could have been worse, Miss Bea,' she said at last, 'but it's not been an easy day, one way and another.'

This was not encouraging. Beatrix found a clean handkerchief in her pocket, blew her nose firmly and went into the drawing-room.

# CHAPTER TWO

Mr Massee provided an author, Dr Oscar Brefeld, and his book, *Botanische Untersuchungen uber Schimmelpilze*, to come in fifteen parts, of which so far only twelve had been finished. As was to be expected, it was written in German.

In an effort to bypass Brefeld, Beatrix drove over to Kew in her phaeton and confronted Mr Massee with her problem. He had been studying fungi in little glass covers and she couldn't help feeling he had passed through several stages on the way to becoming a fungus himself.

He was sadly ignorant on the subject but took the line that Beatrix's experiments might serve to confirm Brefeld's theories – hardly what she had in mind. He was also disparaging about the slips she had taken from samples she was growing in the nursery. Finding herself flatly contradicting him, she had given up and driven home in a light drizzle which did not improve her cold.

Later in the day Uncle Harry called on Beatrix and was cheerfully optimistic about her chances of having researched spore germination before Brefeld. He clowned round the old nursery and frightened the mice. Beatrix was more worried about him being optimistic than if he had been depressed. She felt sure now that Brefeld had studied spore germination. Then Uncle Harry said she must get something 'written out' to show to Mr Thiselton-Dyer, and gave her a note to his former assistant at the Society of Preventive Medicine to get instruction about slips.

With Uncle Harry taking such pains, there had been no avoiding this expedition, so she'd arranged to go on the Wednesday. Mama, she knew, could not object to something arranged by the one titled relative they possessed, but she hadn't allowed for Papa. Despite his reluctance on account of the risk of contagion, he thought it his duty to accompany her.

'It would seem odd to the assistants if you arrived on your own. They would get a bad impression,' he said when she mentioned her plans.

Considering that she was now thirty, Papa's concern seemed

altogether over-paternal. And it was with some foreboding that Beatrix went to put on her hat on Wednesday morning. She found Papa pacing the hall in a fine taking as his ulster had been mislaid. Elizabeth located it in the kitchen where it had been sent to be dried, but of course now they were going to be late, with Papa's face choleric behind his fringe of grey whiskers and not a cab to be seen.

They found one eventually, by which time Beatrix was feeling sick. Great Russell Street was busy; then, at last, they were there. The Society of Preventive Medicine was housed in red brick and full of long, tiled corridors. Beatrix handed in her note only to be told that Mr Lunt, Uncle Harry's old assistant, was out. A Dr McFadden kindly took them under his wing and up the stairs. Papa, earning several curious glances, had his bushy eyebrows drawn together and his high-crowned hat pulled down over his ears as a form of protection from contagion. The laboratory was at the top of the building.

Dr McFadden was most obliging and carefully demonstrated how to prepare a slip for the microscope, but Beatrix was distracted. Papa kept wandering off and regarding with evident horror a dishevelled boy dabbing dots of madder jelly on to petri dishes. She later found that Papa had suspected the jelly to contain an infection of smallpox.

On Friday Beatrix let a microscope lens roll off the table and on Sunday discovered the glass was missing. The carpet had been swept by then, so the morning of Monday, 30th November, found her in the paved area of No. 2 sifting ashes from the dustbin through a riddle. Fortunately the weather had improved and a weak sun was drying the paving stones, but it looked as though it would be a long job.

The door into the area opened and Elizabeth walked out purposefully with cabbage leaves for the dustbin.

'Why, Miss Beatrix, what . . . Can I help?'

Beatrix straightened up, dusting ash from her skirt and blowing a stray lock of hair from her nose. She laughed at Elizabeth's shocked face.

'I feel like Cinderella,' she said, 'all among the ashes. I've lost a treasure, a lens, which must have landed in your dustpan. It'll be a week before I get through this pile, so you'd better let me get on with it. But you can do something; help me carry the microscope to Becks in Cornhill this afternoon to get another

17

lens. I need to have a new one fitted, I can't wait until I find this particular one.'

Elizabeth hesitated for a fraction of a second and Beatrix was immediately sorry she'd ever mentioned the matter, afraid that it might have sounded like an order.

'If there's something else you must do, don't worry, I can manage.'

'No, of course not. I'll be glad to help you carry that heavy thing. The Mistress'll have the carriage with it being fine and you can't take it on your own in the train.'

'I'll be ready at two o'clock, then.' Beatrix went back to her ashes, glad there was one person in the house who didn't need everything *explaining*.

When Mr Beckett arrived for orders, Elizabeth had instructions to ask him to go up and see the Master in the study. He was not surprised; he'd been expecting it for a week. He was sorry for the Master, a nice enough man if a poor judge of horseflesh. He'd warned against the grey, but the Master would have it as being well-bred. In-bred he'd have said, if he'd been asked. It would go down soon, and then, once more, they'd need another horse. He knocked on the study door with a confident rap, bowler in hand.

Mr Potter was sitting behind his desk with a pensive expression on his face. The spray of whiskers on each side of his clean-shaven chin drooped in a depressed fashion.

'Ah, Beckett.' There was the usual note of surprise, as though Beckett was the last person he expected to see. 'Now there was something, yes. Mrs Potter tells me that a decision has been made to sell Miss Beatrix's pony and that you were going to see about getting a good price for him. How are you getting on?'

'Well sir, I'm not, so to speak, getting on at all. For one thing, I needed your word on the matter and for another, now I've got your word, I have to say I'm not going to do it. I could give you reasons, one or two, but I think it better just to give you my month's notice.'

Mr Potter leaned back in his chair and Mr Beckett had to endure his hard, blue glare for quite half a minute. It didn't bother him; he knew it only meant the Master was thinking, hard, how to get out of this predicament. And he knew all about the predicament, which boiled down to the fact that if Beckett left the Master would not only need a new coachman, he would have to tell Miss Beatrix her mother had decided the pony had to go and then arrange to get it sold. The Master couldn't do that any more than he could himself. Give him his due, he was fond of his daughter, which was more than could be said for the mother.

'Don't you think you should reconsider that decision, Beckett?' There was a pleading note in the deep, rather pleasant voice.

'No, sir, I don't. T'will be best for all concerned if I go at the end of the month.' It would mean Miss Beatrix would keep her pony, because that old besom Mrs Potter never did anything directly if she could help it. It would mean they'd have to keep the groom on for the moment, a nice enough lad, and it would also mean a change for himself, which wouldn't hurt. They weren't in a tied cottage and he could have his pick of the many jobs about for a good coachman, perhaps find one where he could at least advise on the choice of horses. He might come back after a bit; he'd done all this once before when he was groom and Reynolds was coachman, just to prove a point, and he'd come back to the coachman's job. He'd married again, on the strength of that. He thought of his second marriage, at St Mary's, The Boltons, earlier this year, and sucked on a hollow tooth.

Mr Potter stood up, levering himself to his feet like an old man with the help of the desk top. Of course, he'd been ill not long ago.

'Well Beckett, I can see you're going to be your usual stubborn self about this. I would give you a reference of course, but if you'd wait a bit I'll take some advice. After all, Mrs Potter only wants to make the stables more efficient and there may be a better way. Leave it with me.'

If the Master wanted to deceive himself like that, who was he to undeceive him? 'Very well sir, I'll do that then.' He nodded gravely and left the study, his dignity unimpaired.

Beatrix came downstairs at 2 o'clock hugging the microscope box to her chest. Elizabeth was waiting in the hall. She was wearing a green tweed costume and a Lovat green felt hat with a tuft of pheasant's feathers tucked into the ribbon. The hat was tilted slightly forward on her coronet of hair and Beatrix hardly recognised her, she looked so elegant.

'Why, Elizabeth, how nice you look,' she said, and then wondered at herself for making such a condescending remark. Did she expect Elizabeth to come to Becks in her afternoon uniform?

Elizabeth had picked up the clothes brush from the hall stand and was batting at the traces of ash still marking Beatrix's skirt.

'My sister Dorothy, she lives in Liverpool you'll remember, is a tailoress. This costume was refused by a client and she kept it for me. Oh, goodness Miss Bea, I'm afraid your petticoat's showing.'

Beatrix obediently went back upstairs to remedy the matter.

The day was more like September than late November. Elizabeth carried the box, in spite of Beatrix's protests, and things didn't begin to deteriorate until they reached South Kensington station. Here, Elizabeth caught her heel in the steps going down to the platform and went sprawling head-first, not being able to use her hands as they were taken up with saving the microscope box. Once stopped, she managed to pull herself up to sit on the steps. Beatrix sat down beside her holding the green felt hat and taking the box, ignoring the startled looks of other passengers. Someone nearly fell over her and she found herself giggling.

'I'm sorry Elizabeth, I shouldn't laugh, but I couldn't help wondering what Mama would say if she could see us now. Are you hurt?'

Elizabeth was rubbing her head where it had hit a railing and painfully stretching her legs.

'No, I'll be all right in a moment, Miss Bea. I'll just put on my hat.' She put it on her head by touch, tucking in wisps of hair. Then she too started to laugh. 'She'd have put her head down like an ostrich and pretended not to see us, Miss Bea,' she said.

They both sat giggling as people stared and the train came in.

During the journey Beatrix felt it was only fair to tell Elizabeth why she needed the new lens so urgently.

'You've been so good about coming, Elizabeth, and about not dropping the box, I really must tell you what it's all about.'

'There's no need. Please, Miss Bea,' Elizabeth protested and looked unhappy when Beatrix insisted. She listened with a worried frown as Beatrix told her how Uncle Harry, Sir Henry Roscoe, was now the Vice-Chancellor of London University and in a position to help her with her Paper on Fungus Spore Germination. She seemed relieved when they reached Cornhill.

Becks was one of those superior places, all mahogany counters and a young man in a tail-coat pouncing from behind the optical instruments, telescopes, binoculars, microscopes, viewfinders and concave and convex mirrors which made Beatrix feel dizzy. To her private amusement, she was ignored and Elizabeth was asked her pleasure. This was sorted out and a new lens purchased, with higher magnification than the one that had been lost.

Once outside, Beatrix found she was not as calm as she had thought. She dropped a florin and it rolled down a grating. Not wishing to make an exhibition of herself, she assured Elizabeth it was only a shilling, and saw her cowardice was going to profit a ragged lad propping up the wall who was clearly going to fish for it when they had gone.

Once on the train, Elizabeth asked a strange question.

'Where will it get you, Miss Bea, if Sir Henry does get your Paper read to this Society?'

'Well, it won't, as you put it, "get me" anywhere. My Paper would be read at a meeting of the Linnean Society and, if accepted, my name would be associated with the discovery.'

'Would you read it?'

'Oh no. Gracious, what an idea. Naturally women are not allowed to attend meetings of such an important Society!'

Elizabeth evidently didn't think it a laughing matter. 'So there's no money in it?'

'No, no money, but considerable prestige.'

'If I know anything about men,' Elizabeth said with asperity, 'they'll soon see about the prestige. You watch it, Miss Bea. They'll turn it down and then rediscover it for themselves, what a surprise, in a year or two. Sir Henry excepted, of course.'

'Oh, I can't believe that, Elizabeth. I have the greatest hopes all will go swimmingly. Sir Henry is convinced I have a clear field. And Sir Henry is well respected. The *Lancet* called him one of the greatest scientific men of our age. They can't turn down something he supports.' Beatrix wondered which of them she was trying to convince.

Elizabeth looked at her pityingly.

Later, as Beatrix put the microscope away, she thought about what Elizabeth had said. She seemed to think Beatrix was wasting her time. Surely, though, one should try? She supposed it would be as well if she told her parents what she was trying to do.

Later still, when she had changed her dusty skirt and wondered, after her experience that afternoon, if it was perhaps time she had some new clothes, she was stricken with guilt. She remembered it should have been Elizabeth's afternoon off.

The consequences of Beatrix telling her parents she was writing a Paper on the *Germination of the Spores of Agaricineae* were apparent during the evening meal. Elizabeth, forced to listen as she waited at table, worked off her exasperation by banging the fire irons about when she made up the drawing-room fire.

The Mistress confined herself to telling Miss Beatrix that she'd only give herself brain fever worrying about things that didn't matter and she should give it up at once. The Master was not concerned with what the Paper was about, as though anything written by his daughter was of no consequence, but worried that she might disgrace his brother-in-law Henry Roscoe with incorrect grammer. He wanted to read the whole thing to make sure Beatrix had got it right.

'Grammar is important,' he was saying when Elizabeth left the room. 'Fetch me a pencil and we'll go through it together. You know you always used to get commas in the wrong place.'

Elizabeth stumped down the basement stairs in one of her sudden, short-lived fits of temper. 'It really is too bad!' she said to Fred. 'Poor Miss Bea, they never give her credit for anything, not even knowing where to put a comma, and after all those governesses too!'

Fred was a peeler – a policeman. She used to give him cups of tea when Bolton Gardens was on his beat. Now he got rather more when he called. Sometimes Elizabeth thought she loved him, sometimes not.

'Now, now, 'old your horses,' Fred said in reply. 'She's their daughter isn't she? What's she done, anyway?'

He was sprawled across the kitchen table reading *Reynolds Weekly* and looking very much at home, which for some reason annoyed Elizabeth all over again, even more than his assumption that daughters were for doing what you liked with.

'She's made a scientific discovery, something to do with those fungi she's always collecting and drawing. She's that clever and they treat her like a fool. The Mistress is a tyrant, like Napoleon was.' She sat down suddenly and blew her nose.

Fred folded his paper. 'Now then Lizzie, don't take on so. Miss Beatrix'll be all right. She's not one of them flibberty gibbets that can be put off by somebody saying them nay. She's got bottom. That's what my old mother used to say, every tub should stand on its own bottom, and that's just what she does. Come on now, cheer up and give us a kiss.'

Elizabeth looked at him as she put away her handkerchief.

He was a beautiful man, there was no getting away from it. Over six foot, well you had to be to be in the police, with wide shoulders and a strong neck, and as if that wasn't enough, he looked like one of them Greek gods. He was fair, with brown eyes flecked with gold, a nice-shaped mouth that smiled a lot and a little moustache that just made a kiss interesting without making a pincushion of your face. He also thought he could charm the birds off the trees just by whistling.

'How's your wife?' she asked him, to bring him down a peg.

'Now, Lizzie!' Fred put up his hands as if to ward off an attack. 'We did agree – oh, she's in fine form, nagging at me up hill and down dale to move out of our cottage into one of them new model homes. She says it's her due, now I've been made sergeant, an' one of these fine days I might give in, in spite of the garden, just to have a bit of peace.'

'You'd never!' Elizabeth was diverted. 'And don't call me Lizzie,' she added automatically.

'I won't, promise, if you'll give me a kiss.'

Fred kissed beautifully. Elizabeth's breathing grew deep and her knees trembled. She found herself on the hearth-rug, something that often happened when Fred called in after Norah had gone to bed, undoing the stiff buttons on Fred's tunic. There was a longish interval, greatly enjoyed by them both. At one point Elizabeth found herself wondering what Norah would say if she knew the use to which they put her handiwork.

'Lily still be away next Monday? Fred asked, buttoning his tunic and preparing to go.

'Depends.'

'Oh, well.' Fred was philosophical. 'See you then anyway.'

Elizabeth had a return of her earlier irritation. Men always took you so much for granted. 'I'll see how Miss Beatrix is,' she said. 'Things are chancy just now.'

# CHAPTER THREE

——— • ———

Just before Christmas Beatrix was suddenly taken ill. Lying in bed, shivering and sick, she thought it was odd how they all had their particular maladies. Papa suffered from attacks of the gravel and sometimes gout; Bertram got pleurisy, always had since school days; Mama went down with influenza, some bouts more imaginary than others. Her own speciality was bilious attacks, not the best of choices. She thought this one had been brought on by allowing herself to be dragged down by this wretched business with the *Agaricineae*.

Elizabeth had been proved right. Mr Thiselton-Dyer had no time for her. When she had first tried to see him, after she had got something written out and typed, he kept her waiting so long she had found it more than she could bear and had fled out into the Gardens where there was ice on the ponds so all the ducks were skating. She had tried again four days later, going to Kew by train and determined to sit it out. Mr T. D. once more kept her an interminable time in the outer office, where she sat watching a clerk slowly cut snippets from a pink newspaper and paste them on a foolscap sheet headed with the Royal Arms. When Mr T. D. finally condescended to see her, he said at once that he wasn't going to look at her drawings and her whole theory was a mare's nest. He recommended her to the University of Cambridge.

Dizzily clinging to her pillow as though it were a lifebelt, Beatrix remembered her temerity at this point in the interview. She had told Mr Thiselton-Dyer that he could ridicule a small, shy person as much as he liked, but wait a few years and what she had discovered would be in all the biology books. She had left the office in a fit of nervous giggles, to the consternation of the clerk.

After a lapse of a week, Uncle Harry had received what he told her was a rude and stupid letter from Mr T. D. He wouldn't show it to her, but it must have said she should be sent back to school instead of trying to instruct her elders and betters on matters about which she knew nothing. This had the effect of annoying Uncle Harry so much that he had told her not to worry, he would see her Paper read to a full meeting of the Linnean Society if it was the last thing he did in this life. His face, as mobile as that of a clown in spite of his Roman nose, had taken on an expression of determination. It was probably this promise which had weighed her down to such bad effect. Or perhaps it was the fact that Papa intended to buy her all twelve volumes of the record of Dr Brefeld's researches.

She drifted into sleep and dreamed she was struggling up a slope with the help of an alpenstock that wavered and bent but she was not surprised as it was a stick of liquorice. She was suddenly at the top, confronting a rock formation in the shape of a lion, but then it was a lion and roaring ferociously.

'Beatrix.' It was Mama's voice. 'Wake up.'

Mrs Potter had a draconian approach to illness: she believed the more drastic the medicine, the better the cure. Seidlitz powders and calomel were what she gave Beatrix for bilious attacks. She stood by the bedside, head bowed and fingers busy pinching the skirt of her black silk dress, until they were swallowed.

'Really,' she said to her daughter, 'I'm at my wits' end to know what to do with you, staying in bed on the smallest pretext. I've given orders for albumen water, but no solid food until you are better. I'm about to go and call on your Aunt Clara; you should be with me.' Then, to Beatrix's great relief, she rustled impatiently out of the room.

Elizabeth arrived next, light hurrying footsteps and no albumen water but a dish of calf's foot jelly instead. She sat by the bed with a spoon in one hand and the bowl in the other.

'Come on, Miss Bea, you must have something. It'll slip down so's you'll hardly notice,' she said.

'I don't think I can lift my head, Elizabeth, without undesirable results.'

Elizabeth wasn't deterred. 'Never mind your head, Miss Bea, you look just about ready to lift into your coffin,' she said frankly. 'Took me forever to make the jelly and it's very good. Just one spoonful?'

'Oh, very well.'

Elizabeth propped Beatrix's head up with another pillow and the first offering went down without disaster.

'Mr Bertram's back. Came in for lunch,' Elizabeth said chattily, then slipped in another spoonful when Beatrix opened her mouth to answer.

She swallowed. 'How is he?'

'Looks a bit so-so. Sort of on edge.'

'He's bored, that's what's the matter with him. He should do some proper work, but he just dabbles.' She was surprised to find herself accepting more jelly. Elizabeth was right. It was good.

'Said he was going out; might be back for supper. Perhaps he'll come and see you then.' Elizabeth put the empty bowl on the night table and removed the extra pillow. 'Now you try and sleep, Miss Bea, and I'll be up again later.'

Sleep proved elusive and after a time Beatrix thought about the nursery fire, which Peter Rabbit had to himself. She felt better enough to get up. She had no idea that calf's foot jelly was so reviving.

When Elizabeth climbed the stairs again Beatrix was sitting at the nursery table wrapped in blue flannel. Her folios, in their patchwork covers, were spread out in front of her.

'Look at this,' she said. '*Boletus luridus*. I found it in a wood near Smailholm Tower, not far from the farm where Sir Walter Scott used to stay. If you break a bit off the cap it turns blue. Turn you blue too if you ate it.' She grinned at Elizabeth's expression.

'It's pretty,' said Elizabeth, looking doubtfully at the drawing of the buff and crimson fungus.

Beatrix found there was a cup of steaming beef tea placed in front of her.

'It's not meant to be pretty, it's a study. I've done hundreds, but now I'm told they're "not technically correct", so I shan't do any more.' She closed the folio with a snap and tied the tapes and for some reason picked up the spoon.

'Never mind those old mushrooms, Miss Bea. Your animal drawings are ever so much nicer. There's those picture letters you do for the Moore children and things like this.' Elizabeth pulled out the pen and ink sketch of Cinderella's coach from under the folios. 'Look at those rabbits, lazy as anything. Just like Peter, aren't they young man?' She twitched her nose at the rabbit, sitting on the hearth-rug with his ears raised as though he understood every word.

Beatrix was hardly listening. She'd gone suddenly sleepy and stifled a yawn as she put down the spoon. She'd finished the beef tea.

'Perhaps if I'd decided to be an artist, fate would have insisted I be a scientist,' she said. Her eyes were nearly closing.

26

When Elizabeth got back to the kitchen she found Norah waiting for her, wearing an expression of malicious satisfaction.

'Where've you bin? They were asking for you?' She saw the bowl and her elbows went akimbo. 'I thought so. You've bin making special little dishes for Miss Beatrix, when the mistress said she was to have nothing but albumen water.' Her rough Northern voice rose. 'And you went and put brandy in that there jelly when they're all abstainers. I saw the bottle, the one you keep in your cupboard. Setting yourself up as knowing better than they do what's good for that high and mighty little Miss.' She was hissing like an angry gander. 'You want to watch it, Lizzie, you're heading for a fall.'

Elizabeth thought of the dejected figure upstairs and didn't even try to control her quick temper.

'High and mighty indeed! She's no more high and mighty than I am, and she's more sense in her little finger than the rest of the family in all their noddle heads. They all depend on her, even Mr Bertram, and take less care of her when she's ill than if she'd been that silly spaniel Spot they used to dote on. Brandy's what she needed and someone's got to have some in this house. Go on, tell them what I've said! Have yourself a real good tittle-tattle. But think on that I might have things to say too. What about that cherry cake that did a vanishing act last week? Could it have gone off with our friendly milkman whose bills go up every month and who slips you a backhander when you pay him?'

Norah turned purple with frustration and fury. Words failing her, she fell back on the last resort of the slow-witted and looked round for a weapon. She'd been sitting in the rocking-chair pegging a rag rug. She snatched up the pegging hook and went for Elizabeth's face. Elizabeth put the kitchen table between them. Norah made a dash for her. Elizabeth hopped on to the old couch and from there to the table top. Braced, ready to defend her mountain citadel, she heard someone clattering the latch of the back door. It opened and a face peered round.

'Dancing is it? Doing the old can-can, what? Now I ask you, ladies, is that the way to go on in this mos' wespectable of households?' It was a light voice, slurred, like warm jam, well known to Elizabeth.

'Why, Mr Bertram!' She descended sheepishly, adjusting her skirts. 'Was there something you wanted?' Norah had plonked herself in the rocking chair, face like a wild winter sunset and eyes popping. She was pretending to get on with her pegging.

27

Mr Bertram didn't look entirely himself either. His long, almost pretty face with its perky little moustache was flushed and his rather deep-set eyes, the only Potter feature he'd inherited, were hot and bright. Elizabeth used to have maternal yearnings over Mr Bertram when he was a boy, that was before Fred, wondering what it would feel like to run her hands through his thick dark hair. Nowadays she took him as he came and decided that at the moment he was what Fred called 'pixilated': not so drunk as he didn't realise he should avoid his parents by coming in at the back, but not so reliable all the same.

'Jus' coming in without any fuss, tha's all, me an' my little friend.' Bertram slapped the bird cage he was carrying on to the kitchen table with such force that the door flew open and its occupant, a jay in iridescent plumage and with a predatory look to its blue eye, stepped delicately out and flapped like a dark thought on to the back of the couch.

'Damn it all, what did you do that for?' Bertram looked accusingly at Elizabeth. 'Got to get him back in his cage. Find a lure, that's the ticket. Nice dead mouse, Bea'll have one. Always got nice mice about. You go. Don't want to meet me'mother.'

Bertram was too late. The door from the hall opened and Mrs Potter looked down on them. She was back early from her afternoon calls.

'What was the reason for that unseemly noise?' she asked, looking at Elizabeth.

'Mr Bertram frightened us, Madam, coming in by the back door.'

That brought her son to Mrs Potter's attention. 'Oh, there you are, Bertram. We had expected you earlier.' Bertram, for all his failures, was still the favourite child but she couldn't help being querulous even with him. 'Are you coming up?'

Elizabeth was turned to stone by an attack of indecision. Should she faint or something to prevent the mistress seeing Bertram's condition, or should she let matters take their course?

In the event, sacrifice was not required of her. Sandy the cat had woken from his afternoon nap on the couch to see a bird in miraculous reach. Unnoticed by the jay until almost too late, he uncoiled his length and sprang. All he caught was a tail feather. With harsh, unlovely protests the bird flew up to the mantelpiece, teetered on the edge in a puff of dust, then launched himself forward in a shallow dive. His trailing claws caught the top of Mrs Potter's upswept coiffure and he rose again, wings batting, trailing some of her hair and leaving a bald patch in its place.

For one freezing moment Elizabeth thought Mrs Potter had been scalped, but almost immediately saw it was a hair switch, used to conceal the lack of natural tresses, that the bird had caught up. She took a quick deep breath that sounded more like a whoop.

Bertram was suddenly cold sober, as though dowsed with a bucket of water, and set about catching the bird. Norah's jaw dropped. Elizabeth took her hand from her mouth and snatched her scarf off the hook on the door to drape over the denuded head. Mrs Potter was standing with her eyes closed and her fists clenched.

'That bird' she said, still with her eyes closed and her voice clotted with anger, 'must have its neck wrung immediately. See to it, Bertram.' Even holding the scarf and moving at double speed, she made a dignified exit.

The next day was Christmas Eve. Questions on religion had never been encouraged, but close observation had informed Beatrix that Mama and Papa's religious convictions were unusually perverse even among Unitarians, so tomorrow, Christmas day, would be more of a penance than a feast. Bertram would be sullen and get out of the house as much as he could. She might, as she felt so much better, visit Uncle Harry to get moral support for a final effort to get her germination theory accepted.

Elizabeth joined her in the nursery for some of the morning, washing and drying Mama's switch.

'I really didn't know, Miss Bea. I thought she'd been scalped,' she said, as she brushed it dry in front of the nursery fire.

'I knew, and Mama knew I knew, but it's one of those many things we never mention. Anyway, I'd better be the person to return it, though I'm afraid there'll be some rubs. Mama does so hate any loss of dignity.'

Beatrix was sketching Peter, who lay fast asleep on his back in a blanket-lined box by the fire, one front paw raised to his ear and the other relaxed across his chest.

'Well, you can leave it until you've finished your drawing.' Elizabeth sounded bossy this morning. 'The mistress came down to breakfast in a white lace cap that hardly showed her hair at all: she'll probably wear it through Christmas, until she feels better about the whole business.' She pulled the brush slowly through the long, almost dry chestnut-coloured tress, so that the hair crackled and curled at the ends as though it was alive.

'That's electrical energy,' Beatrix said, watching. 'It's a funny thing about energy, it's said to go on for ever. I was thinking a while ago, something to do with weight-lifting, about what happens to spare energy. For instance, what happens when Peter Rabbit stamps? That's one of the most energetic manifestations of insignificance I have ever seen. What do you think?'

Elizabeth looked at the unconscious animal, relaxed in sublime dreams.

'There's no saying, Miss Bea, unless,' she frowned heavily in an effort to make her meaning clear, 'unless, you being his nearest as it were, what he gives out in energy is picked up by you.'

Beatrix felt jolted, as though Elizabeth had said something important, which was ridiculous.

It was well over three days before Mr Potter sent for his coachman again, but William Beckett was not an impatient man. Besides, nothing much in the way of another situation had shown its face yet. When he was once more standing in the study, and they had gone through the charade of his arrival being a surprise and the matter to be discussed having to be brought to mind, it was to be told good news.

'I think I've found a reasonable compromise with the carriages, Beckett,' he said. 'One that solves another problem too. Hiring a Victoria when we're on holiday is getting more and more unsatisfactory: these open carriages are expensive and unreliable and they give Mrs Potter the toothache. I've been consulting one or two people and I think we should sell our brougham and have a landaulette built that could travel north with us by train. We'll need Miss Beatrix's phaeton for use in town without the brougham, so there's no point in selling the pony. What d'you say?'

Mr Beckett thought it might do. Miss Beatrix would keep her pony, and there was something in it for him too. If there was one thing he did appreciate about this job, it was the three-month-long summer holidays the Potters took in Scotland or the Lake District. When he was needed his family went as well and it was good for the two boys to be in the country. Now, of course, he would always be needed to take the Potter horses to go with the Potter landaulette. He thought his new wife would enjoy the summer break away from London very much.

'No complaints, sir. That would be just right.' No reason to labour the point.

Mr Potter leaned contentedly back in his chair. 'We're going to that place near Keswick this summer. Ling something. Lingholm, that's it.'

After Christmas Elizabeth was concerned to find that Miss Beatrix continued to dash about, first to see her Uncle and then to Kew. She was hardly at home – most unlike her – until well into January. When she was at home, she spent her time in the nursery studying foreign books that had been delivered to the house from Sotherans. Elizabeth began to have forebodings. When Mrs Potter felt neglected, influenza had been known to strike.

The news that the brougham was to be sold and replaced with a landaulette was no help. Mrs Potter had liked the brougham. Elizabeth watched for the signs out of the corners of her eyes.

On the last day of January Mrs Potter complained of aching bones, on the first of February she also felt faint and dizzy and generally weak. Mr Potter's suggestion of sending for Dr Aikin was spurned but the following day she couldn't lift her head from her pillow. Influenza, no possible doubt. Norah looked to her stock of arrowroot and ordered an old fowl for chicken broth. Elizabeth counted clean sheets. Mr Bertram went back to Scotland. Miss Bea cancelled all engagements in order to look after her mother.

# CHAPTER FOUR

It wasn't until April that No. 2 Bolton Gardens pivoted towards capricious malevolence again. What with one thing and another, Mrs Potter's influenza lasted well into February and imposed an iron routine. March was devoted to her convalescence. Beatrix's life, for the tail end of the winter, was aloof from hail and sleet, howling gales that rattled the casements and early spring sunshine. It had a consequent lack of fresh air and entertainment that made for a lowness of spirits. She found herself looking forward to the Easter holiday in Weymouth (not something she usually did), as a change of wallpaper if nothing else.

Then came the expected letter from Mr George Massee F.L.S., who signed himself as Principal Assistant, Royal Botanic Gardens, Kew.

The first thing Beatrix understood was that Mr Massee had, as agreed with Uncle Harry, presented her Paper on *The Germination of the Spores of Agaricineae* to the Linnean Society on 1st April. That must mean he'd read it; why didn't he say so? He went on to inform Miss Potter that the paper was well received, but that both Mr Thiselton-Dyer and Mr Murray, Keeper of Botany at the British Museum (Natural History), had presented communications after he had spoken. The result of this was that he felt it necessary to advise Miss Potter to allow him, at the Council Meeting to be held on 8th April, to withdraw Paper No. 2978 on her behalf in order that she might bring her researches to a more advanced stage before publication. He was her very obedient servant.

So that was that. Miss Potter the eminent botanist was a figment, a mere flippancy, to be whisked into oblivion. She saw herself, skirts all anyhow, being hoisted into a cloud. Of course this was what she'd known would happen, that Mr Thiselton-Dyer and friends would never allow it to be published, but it was like expecting the water to be cold and then actually immersing oneself.

She turned to Peter, warming first his stomach and then his

back at the bright fire, a rabbit on a spit. 'There, you see, just as I told you,' she said. 'Very obedient servant indeed! No spunk. Couldn't stand up to his superiors who didn't want it printed, though I suppose he was afraid of losing his job, poor little worm. April 1st indeed. A very nice April Fool's joke to play on poor Miss Potter!' Peter looked at her with his bright eyes and thought he was being given a command. He did a somersault.

The Potters returned from Weymouth in a heatwave – Beatrix feeling a bit tight-lipped after being complimented by her father on not losing the luggage on the journey – to find London in the grip of Diamond Jubilee fever. Everything that could be decorated was being decorated. Flags were strung round every lamp-post, banners floated over every street. There was a flutter of festivity in the air and there were to be competitions for the most festooned district. Even before she'd properly seen the luggage into the house, Beatrix found that she was expected to provide a string of loyal flags and lengths of red, white and blue bunting to loop across the facade of No. 2. It would, she thought, look like mutton dressed as lamb.

That night, when they were in the drawing-room, the theft of the Chelsea fiddler was discovered.

An unlocked Sheraton mahogany cabinet held the best china pieces: Worcester jugs and vases, cups and saucers and some little figures in Chelsea ware, oddments of Derby china and two flamboyant Coalport vases from which Beatrix generally averted her eyes.

Mama was the first to notice he had gone. Getting up from her cane chair by the davenport desk to come over to the fire, just after Elizabeth had come in with the nine o'clock tray, she stopped by the cabinet with a little cry.

'My Chelsea fiddler's gone,' she said. 'I wonder if someone's moved him or if he got broken?'

Beatrix had always liked the fiddler, who seemed to view life as seen from his shelf with a gentle irony, but she only noticed him when she occasionally dusted the cabinet. Mama then suddenly and unusually lifted her head, resting her emotionless gaze on Beatrix.

'No Mama, I haven't moved him. There's been no reason.'

Papa had been in the middle of regretting that they hadn't arranged to go to Keswick this month instead of next, so they could have seen the lighting of Mr Rawnsley's Jubilee bonfire on top of Skiddaw. He didn't like being interrupted and rose from

33

the sofa, where Elizabeth was trying to serve him his Indian tonic water, to prove his wife wrong. He peered shortsightedly at the cabinet shelves but failed to find the fiddler.

'Mystery to me,' he said shortly.

Mrs Potter turned towards Elizabeth and stared with her unblinking eyes. She didn't say anything, just looked.

Beatrix could see Elizabeth getting flustered. She put the tray on the pierced ebony stool and wiped her hands down the side of her skirt.

'Well Madam, it was there when I last dusted and I certainly didn't break it, nor hold it even. I'd no reason to open the door of the cabinet.'

'When did you dust last?' Mama asked.

'Three days ago,' Elizabeth said. It sounded to Beatrix more like a question than an answer. The room would have been shut up once it had been spring-cleaned.

Mrs Potter drew her little finger along the top of the cabinet, leaving a disdainful line in the dust, then wiped her finger on her lace handkerchief.

'You may go now, Elizabeth,' she said.

It was two days before Elizabeth saw Fred again; two days when no one mentioned the Chelsea fiddler to her, but she felt suspicion pressing down from the ceilings and draping itself round the doors. Miss Beatrix did have a word with Norah when she came down for cabbage leaves, but Norah, giving her the ones she had been going to throw away and Miss Beatrix too worried to notice, had been adamant.

'Not been in the drawing-room for weeks, Miss Beatrix. Why should I?'

When Fred tapped on the door in the late evening he was tired after policing the Jubilee celebrations, though he needn't have sounded as though he'd done it all single-handed. His lazy voice, flavoured with his native Sussex, went on and on about the thanksgiving service in St Paul's and the crowds, and the procession of colonial troops until Elizabeth could have screamed.

'Good thing it didn't rain, like last Jubilee,' he said. 'I remember m'sisters taking me to see the Queen and we got home looking like water rats. Mind you, the sun brought out some real villains. Got a good haul of dippers – pickpockets to you.' He added a liberal waterfall of sugar to his mug of tea. 'Mostly outside St Paul's. Churches always attract them.' He stirred slowly and another thought struck him. 'Why the Queen needed eight horses to draw her landau beats me. It took eight crossing sweepers to clear up.'

He took a reviving swallow and Elizabeth got in a word at last. She told him about the jay first. She'd always found it was best with Fred to lead up gently to matters of importance. That is if it could be done before he got randy.

'What happened to it after that?' he asked.

'Mr Bertram let it go in Hyde Park. He couldn't kill a caterpillar, let alone a pet,' she told him.

'I thought he was supposed to like farming,' Fred said. 'Some farmer he'd make.'

Elizabeth didn't want to discuss farming.

'Many thefts apart from the dippers?' she asked. She was in the rocking-chair with her lace cap on her knee, the streamers trailing on the floor. Norah had gone to bed an hour ago.

'Some. Sneak-thieves. Why d'you ask?'

'I'm wondering if we had one like that.' She told him about the disappearance of the Chelsea fiddler. 'He must be quite valuable and Mrs Potter thinks I took him,' she finished.

Fred sat up, his lips, usually a little slack, in a straight strong line. 'We'll have to alter that idea before much more water goes under London Bridge,' he said. 'We can't have you being turned off without a character.'

This thought had not occurred to Elizabeth. She put her hand on her stomach, where there was the same sinking feeling she'd experienced once when crossing to the Isle of Man.

'They'd never, not after all these years.'

'They might, Lizzie. It's happened before on less evidence than that. She was saying you were a liar, wasn't she, over the dusting – and likely you were – but what she was really saying was that if you'd lie over one thing, you'd lie over another. We'll have to find the real thief. How about young Tom? He does the fires, he'd 'ave been in there.'

'Never! A more willing lad I never met in a month of Sundays. Besides, his mother takes our washing. He'd not risk losing her the work; his father died last year.'

'Well, if it wasn't him, and Norah's too daft even to think of it, where did it go?'

'It's what I was saying. A sneak-thief got in some way. Someone like those spring-heeled Jacks we had a time ago.'

35

'They were muggers mostly, not thieves. Quite different,' Fred said absently as he finished his tea. 'I'll see if there are any reported thefts around here, that'd be somewhere to make a start. But why just the one? That makes me think.'

He rose, all six feet two inches of him, picked her up as though she was made of feathers, nibbled her ear and settled himself in the rocking-chair with Elizabeth cuddled on his knee.

'You great lummock,' she said, rescuing her cap.

'Lizzie my girl, I'm going to have to look after you,' he said. 'You don't know enough about this wicked world. Now listen. You made an enemy of Madam Potter from the moment you took to Miss Beatrix, and don't say you didn't because it stands out a mile. Trying to make her life easier like you do gets up Madam's nose. Then the old vinegar bottle's been thwarted over selling Miss B's pony and while she's been ill she's brooded and you made things worse by seeing her without her hairpiece. That's a heinous crime, my officer says, looking at women when they're not properly dressed.' He unbuttoned her blouse. 'So maybe she's taken steps.'

Elizabeth wriggled, but in vain. 'What d'you mean, taken steps? And don't call me Lizzie.'

'Could have been one thing, could have been another,' Fred said infuriatingly, nuzzling the back of her neck and blowing a warm breath down her spine.

'Oh, give over, do. That tickles. What thing?'

'Well,' he scratched his head with his free hand, 'maybe her precious china statuette was taken by someone who got into the house without leaving a trace. It could just have happened if you lot were careless. If that was so, she don't care who it was, she's taking the opportunity of making sure you're blamed and put out of the way. More likely, she took and hid the thing before they went to Weymouth, knowing as well as I do that you're not likely to look in the drawing-room until they're back.' Fred sighed. 'You annoy her, that's what. You'll have to look out. Even if we get over this, she won't give up. I know the type, but on a different level so to speak.'

'Oh Fred! She can't be that wicked, I don't believe it.' Elizabeth thought for a moment, while another part of her mind admired Fred's lustrous eyelashes. 'Where's she put it then, if you're right?'

'That's what you're going to have to find out, my girl, and sharpish. Before she pretends to find it herself, most likely in your room. I'll come and help you look now if you like.'

'That'd get me turned off quicker than being proved a thief. Keep your hands to yourself. Where in my room?'

'Somewhere that looks as though it was you as hid it. They'll insist on a search and she'll be all righteous and sorrowful about your immortal soul and say you were just waiting for the right opportunity to get it out of the house to sell.'

'Oh Fred.' Elizabeth hid her face in his shoulder. 'What if she does?'

'I'll look after you. Don't take on. We could go and live with my sisters in Hampstead.'

Elizabeth came up for air and decided she'd better find the fiddler. She had once met Fred's sisters and she couldn't stand either of them.

It was Beatrix who first broached the idea of a search. She'd spent a sleepless night thinking about the theft and had decided, rather desperately in the small hours of the morning, that everyone except her father had some motive for taking the fiddler. Papa would have to be responsible. She went into the study straight after breakfast.

Her father expressed his opinion of the idea with a noise like an outraged walrus. 'Pshaw, Beatrix, you're talking nonsense. It must be one of the domestics. I intend to confront them later today and if they won't own up we'll threaten them with the police.'

'But Papa, I'm just as likely to have taken it to sell as Elizabeth. I'm quite unable to buy myself even a new hat. Elizabeth is better dressed than I am. Bertram has his allowance of course, but never a spare penny, and as for Mama . . .' She paused, looking at quicksand.

The study door opened and her mother came in, a noiseless glide as though she was on wheels.

'Ah, Helen,' said her father, 'you've come at the right moment. Beatrix is saying we should make our own enquiries, search every room in the house for your china fiddler. I say that's ridiculous. We must get the police in to question the staff and search their rooms. Just to make sure the piece is not already in a pawn shop.'

'Of course their rooms must be searched,' his wife said comfortably. 'I've never complained, Beatrix, about your management of the domestics, but I do feel you could have done better than to surround us with thieves, and, who knows, cut-throats as well.'

'If rooms are to be searched, then it must be all our rooms. Mine and yours and Bertram's too.' Beatrix felt unwanted laughter well up in her throat as she watched her father's face. Incomprehension changed to horror and then to uncertainty.

'My God, Beatrix, what are you saying?' He stood up in his sudden distress. 'You *can't* mean what I think you mean.' He was almost pleading with her to withdraw her words.

'You unnatural child, accusing your brother in that fashion.' Her mother sank into a chair.

'Did I hear my name being taken in vain?' Bertram came cheerfully and untidily down the stairs and paused in the study doorway. 'What's all this? A family conference?'

'Bertram,' said his father slowly and with the deepest gloom, 'if your mother and sister would leave us, there are some things I think we should discuss.'

The results of the interview in the study were conveyed to Beatrix by a furious Bertram later that morning.

'It's your fault, Bea. I can't think what got into you,' he said, standing over the nursery table where she was sketching. 'I'm leaving the house tomorrow and it'll be a while before I come back. I'll take the *Yellow Books*. Papa threatened to burn them.'

It was then that Beatrix saw he had some magazines tucked under his arm, with covers in a shade of egg yolk. Whatever had happened?

'Oh Bertram, I'm so sorry. I never thought Papa would take it up like that. I didn't want the maids to be made scapegoats.'

'Scapegoats! A goat is just what I was made to feel. He went on for hours about honour and integrity being the most important things in life, which God knows they are not, and that I should make a clean breast of it, and if it was shortage of money that had been the cause he would consider raising my allowance. Honestly, Bea, I hadn't the foggiest what he was talking about. I think he'd forgotten I wasn't there when Mama noticed the theft. Then he said if I wasn't going to co-operate, he would have to search my room.'

'What did you say then?'

'What d'you think I said? There's a bottle of whisky and some cigarettes in the cupboard. I said I wouldn't have it, of course, but it wasn't any good. He told me what it was all about then and threatened me with the police, so I had to let him search. I don't even remember what Mama had in the cabinet, never mind took it. The only lucky thing was that he went through the drawers first and found the *Yellow Books* before the whisky. I'd forgotten them altogether, they'd been there so long. Then he decided they were it, the guilty secret, and stopped looking with some relief. You know how he hates any kind of fuss. That's why . . .'

'He never argues with Mama. I know. What's wrong with the books?'

'There's nothing wrong with them, the *Yellow Book* was a perfectly respectable art journal, you could compare it with the *Saturday Review*. It's just the early ones that had the Aubrey Beardsley illustrations. I only wish I could do as well myself, but mine come out a mess. I can't get the line. That's why I bought the *Salome* too: for the Beardsley, not because it's by Oscar Wilde. He's a bit too precious for me, though *Ernest* was a cracking good show.' Bertram thrust a hand through his hair with Byronic abandon. Beatrix began to see the light.

'Papa didn't like the illustrations?'

'He went raving on about depravity and decadence until I couldn't stand it any longer. I told him he should open up his mind to what was going on in the world of art and literature instead of burying his head in tomes about the Civil War. I told him he should read Shaw and Yeats instead of Macaulay and Tennyson and look at the work of other artists besides old Millais. I told him that even his friend Rawnsley knew more about modern art than him, that Walter Crane who illustrated for Wilde was his friend.' Bertram was defiant, flushed and noisy.

'Papa met Wilde once,' Beatrix said. 'He and Mama went to a ball given by the Millais' and he was there. Papa said he was fat and merry and wore a black choker instead of a shirt collar and had his hair in a mop. He didn't have a lily in his buttonhole, but his wife had her front covered with great water-lilies. I wonder if Papa remembers?'

'He wouldn't admit to it now. Oh, I'm sorry Bea, I shouldn't blame it on you, it's really my own fault. Look, it's a sunny day and I shan't be here again for a time. Would you like to go to look at some nice animals in the zoo? That would cheer you up.'

Just as you despaired of Bertram, he would say something nice.

They arranged to go after lunch and Bertram went across to

his room to pack, leaving the little pile of books on the nursery table. Beatrix opened the top one, *Salome*, with an exploratory finger.

At first she was disappointed. The Beardsley drawings were all black and white, penny plain. Though on closer inspection they were rather striking. She found she was looking at the severed head of John the Baptist, swimming in black blood which was dripping off the edge of a dish. A rigid black arm was holding it in front of the gloating Salome, whose face expressed greed, lust and exultation in such a triumph of composition that Beatrix was quite shaken.

'Calculated to terrify young rabbits,' she told Peter.

She put *Salome* to one side and opened a *Yellow Book* at random. Nearly the whole of a page was taken up with an illustration of a woman in flowing draperies in such lines of beauty and grace it took her a moment to realise that they were totally diaphanous. Nipples, navel . . . everything was visible. On the opposite page the bodies were completely naked – young girls, young boys, some with their backs turned and one boy with the face of a satyr in a state of what Mrs Moore, when she was still her governess Miss Carter, would have called 'sexual arousement'. Beatrix certainly saw what had upset Papa. She imagined his face when he saw this picture and laughed so much she had to hold onto the table.

'Collapse of stout party,' she said to Peter.

Elizabeth had spent an uncomfortable morning pretending to get on with her usual duties but in fact spending most of it ransacking her bedroom. She found the Chelsea fiddler, wrapped up in her winter flannel drawers which she kept in her box under the bed, when she was supposed to be sprinkling damp tea leaves on the drawing-room carpet. She'd knocked over the bucket which held them as she pulled out the box and a pattern of leaves decorated the lino.

Putting the bundle on the bed, she stood and stared blankly at the dormer window that looked over the gardens, chewing a long strand of hair that had detached itself from the plait that crowned her head. After a while she sighed and wound it damply round the end of her nose.

It was no good putting it off any longer. She'd promised Fred she'd do as he told her.

'Don't be a goose and shilly-shally like you usually do,' he'd said, kissing her lovingly on her nose. 'If you find the fiddler, take it straight to Miss Beatrix, explain where you found it and that I told you to look, then leave it to her.'

So she'd better get on with it. She trotted down one flight of stairs with her bundle and put her head round the door of the old nursery.

The room was warm and sunny and smelt of mice. Miss Beatrix was finishing a letter with some drawings of squirrels. Her hair was all anyhow as usual and she had rabbit fur on the lapel of her jacket, but she was as removed from the world of No. 2 as though it didn't exist. Elizabeth hesitated, but Miss Bea lifted her head and saw her.

'Oh Elizabeth, come in. If you were wondering about letters to post, I've nearly finished this one to Noel Moore. He liked the squirrels I drew for him last summer, so I'm doing a few more. He's such a sickly little boy, I do try to take his mind off himself.'

Elizabeth admired a sketch of a squirrel on a raft, its tail spread to act as a sail.

'It's lovely, Miss Bea. The picture letters you send the Moore children are just like little books. It's funny to think of Miss Carter as a mother instead of a governess.' Elizabeth didn't know what she was doing, gossiping about Mrs Moore. She must do what she'd come to do. She cleared her throat for her speech but Miss Bea took no notice.

'There's no doubt about her being a mother. She's about to have her seventh child, and there's no saying the seventh will be the last. Her husband's due home again in the New Year.' Miss Bea focused properly on Elizabeth. 'Why are you opening and shutting your mouth like a fish and what's in that bundle?'

'I've found the Chelsea fiddler,' Elizabeth said, which wasn't what she'd meant to say at all.

Miss Bea was silent for a moment, the time it took her to return to the cumbersome world of No. 2. From being broad and peaceful, her face seemed to go thin and almost haggard.

'Tell me about it,' she said.

Elizabeth told her what Fred – she called him 'my friend' – thought was happening, that someone wanted to get rid of her, and what he'd told her to do, but she couldn't bring herself to name names. 'I didn't take it, Miss Bea,' she finished. 'What would I do it for?'

Miss Bea stood up and went over to look out of the window.

'Elizabeth, you mustn't think anyone imagines you took the fiddler,' she said, without turning round.

41

'It looks bad, with it turning up in my room,' Elizabeth pointed out. 'I don't see how I can do much else but give in my notice regardless.' She had quite decided, now, to go and stay with Dorothy in Liverpool until she found another place. She couldn't begin to count the number of times the unconscious Dorothy had nearly had to give up her precious spare room to her younger sister.

'Oh no, Elizabeth, you mustn't do that, not unless you can't bear to go on working here. That would mean justice had not been done.'

'What are you going to do then?' But Dorothy's spare room was receding into the distance again.

Miss Beatrix grinned suddenly. 'I'll give the matter my best attention,' she said. 'Hand over the fiddler but I shan't need the flannel drawers.'

# CHAPTER FIVE

Beatrix solemnly announced at breakfast that she had found the Chelsea fiddler.

'I was looking for a tube of Prussian blue on the shelf and there he was, behind the mice cage. Then I remembered I'd borrowed him before we went to Weymouth as a possible background for *Mice Dancing* for Hildesheimer & Faulkner.'

She waited.

'But,' said Papa, 'but you . . .' His voice trailed into silence.

Mama gave Beatrix a piercing look, her mouth at its most petulant, but said nothing.

'I've put it back in the cabinet. I'm sorry to have caused everyone so much trouble,' Beatrix finished, and applied herself to her boiled egg.

After a time her father began to discuss their coming holiday at Derwentwater and speculate on what photographic equipment they should take. Beatrix argued for two tripods so they could both work at the same time, she with the small hand-held camera using the tripod as a balance and her father with the large 6 x 4 plate camera.

Her mother, who, in common with several African tribes, looked on cameras and photographs as an intolerable intrusion on her privacy, went away to write letters.

'By the way, Beatrix,' said her father after the door had closed behind his wife, 'I've been going through my investments and found a small parcel of shares you might like to take over. If you sold them now they should fetch £100 – quite a profit on what I paid. We could go down to the City and get it done today.'

'Thank you, Papa, I should like to do that,' she replied sedately.

The transaction, conducted in the Royal Exchange Building with Papa's brokers, was not in the least difficult. Beatrix resisted suggestions that she should hang on to the shares because of her youth and converted them into real money.

She managed to get home and regain the nursery with

decorum, but once on her own she waltzed round the room with Peter in her arms. The feeling of quite delirious independence was wonderful. Peter protested and she sat down, breathless.

The trouble was that one could not rely on Papa to continue to be generous and he would never agree that she needed an allowance so she could plan ahead. There was nothing for it, she would have to put scientific research behind her and find a better source of income than painting cards for Hildesheimer & Faulkner.

Preparations for the holiday continued, including the choice of a supply of books. Reading matter left in furnished houses was always a source of entertainment to Beatrix, so often throwing new light on the characters of the owners, but seldom to her taste.

Her father was well on his way through Gibbon's *Decline and Fall of the Roman Empire* again, though Beatrix was convinced that by the time he got to the fourth book of seven, he had forgotten the first three. She had also told him that, as a subject to read aloud, she did not find it enlivening. Even so, he was insisting that Gibbon should go with them.

Beatrix decided on Trollope. She felt she needed someone witty and objective.

Mr Beckett was looking forward to getting his wife and the boys out of London, stifling just now, and showing Keswick how a proper equipage should look. They were a slack lot up there. But first of all there was the journey and he was not too sure about the black gelding. He'd been right about the grey – he did go down – and Mr Potter had got the black, suspiciously cheap for such a good looker, as a replacement. Mr Beckett had a feeling, and he respected his feelings, that the black had something in his past that had been well covered up at the sale. Nothing had happened so far, but he hoped he wasn't a killer.

In the meantime there was Mrs Potter's afternoon drive. She wished to call on her sister-in-law at Queen's Gate. Mr Beckett had no doubt but that she intended to invite Miss Potter to spend some time at Lingholm, probably also to bring that Miss Gentile with her as she had on past holidays. He sighed. Coachmen were supposed to be deaf and dumb, but there were times when Miss Gentile, always capable of endless and maddeningly pointless monologues, and particularly when taken out driving, had almost provoked him into bolting the horses to provide a diversion.

It was a warm and sunny afternoon. The new landaulette

looked impressive, the horses' rumps gleamed with good grooming, the harness and Mr Beckett's buttons shone with much polishing and Mrs Potter was late. She knew, the master had told her more than once, that it was not good for the horses to keep them standing in the heat, but she would do it.

The horses were sweating by the time she came down the steps, the gelding tossing his head against the bit and foaming slightly at the mouth.

She was wearing a grey dress, which had required tight corseting, and she carried a grey, flounced parasol with a long, ivory handle. Her face, except for the down-turned mouth, was almost hidden by her blancmange-shaped hat.

Young Tom had come to open the carriage door for her. Mr Beckett was single-handed these days, the groom being the one casualty of the pony incident.

Mrs Potter stopped by the nearside horse, the gelding. 'The horses don't look too comfortable, Beckett,' she said sharply. 'That bit should be loosened.'

Mr Beckett knew they'd been comfortable enough when they left the stable and there was nothing wrong with them now; that ebony limb of Satan was only playing up to pass the time. He descended and went round to the black's head. At the very moment he put up his hand to feel the bit, Mrs Potter put up her parasol. Not turning her back and putting it up slowly, the accepted method where horses were concerned, but snapping it open, aimed straight at the black's eyes.

The result was catastrophic. The horse reared, a hoof catching Mr Beckett a glancing blow in the ribs, and came down tangled in the traces. The mare, usually as placid an animal as you could wish to see, started kicking and plunging. Mr Beckett nearly had his arm pulled out of its socket trying to control both animals. Fortunately young Tom saved the day by leaping onto the box and hauling on the reins.

'Well,' said Mrs Potter when relative peace was restored, 'nothing would persuade me to go out with those two horses in their present state. That's what comes, Beckett, of having the bearing rein too tight. As I still wish to call at the Queen's Gate house, I expect you to have a hired carriage here within fifteen minutes.' She swept up the steps and indoors with regal disdain.

Mr Beckett and Tom looked at each other and were as one in the great union of men defeated by women's lack of logic. 'Women!' as Mr Beckett expressed it.

'I'll hop round to Smith's Stables, Mr Beckett, and hire a fly if you can manage to take the horses back on your own.'

Mr Beckett, suppressing a smile, looked him over. Tom was always pleasant, with his round, brown eyes and anxious-to-please smile, but not always tidy. Today he was wearing one of Mr Bertram's cast-off shirts and his trousers had no holes, so though his dusty fair hair could have done with a brush, he'd do.

'Righto, young fellow-me-lad, off you go.' Mr Beckett had a feeling young Tom might go far.

Getting the horses back to their stalls, settling them and rubbing them down, Mr Beckett considered Mrs Potter's action. For the life of him, he couldn't decide if it had been premeditated, to pay him out for the business of Miss Beatrix's pony, or if it had just been plain thoughtlessness. He might have had a better idea if he could have seen Madam's eyes, but the hat had defeated him.

'And as for you, young fly-be-night,' he said aloud, looking at the black gelding who was still inclined to sidle against the side of his stall and show the whites of his eyes, 'you've still got a surprise somewhere for us, and another do like that might have you springing it.'

Miss Beatrix was in charge of the travelling arrangements and Mr Beckett reckoned she was a paragon to have them all running as smoothly as they usually did. The Potters had a saloon coach to themselves and went earlier on a fast train. Horses weren't allowed on the fast trains and Mr Beckett had to get the landaulette, two horses and a pony to Euston Station and put them, and himself, on a train that left at midnight. Miss Beatrix booked it all and gave him the dockets. It was no good getting there too early, there was no one to help him load. Usually about an hour beforehand was about right. This year the family were travelling on Thursday 23rd July and he was to follow on the Friday, arriving in Keswick on Saturday morning.

Thursday was fine and bright and the family left in fine style, Mr Potter clasping *Bradshaw's Railway Guide* as though its very bulk ensured the punctuality of the trains. They took some of the luggage, but Mr Beckett was left with a couple of trunks to go in the horse-box. His wife and the two boys travelled third class on the same train. That was going all right at least; the boys had taken to their stepmother famously.

Friday looked threatening all day and rain began in the early evening. Young Tom was to go to Euston with him, the price of the omnibus home to be put in his righthand jacket pocket which did not have a hole in it. It wasn't that Mr Beckett felt fatherly towards Tom, he had told his wife, just that it would pay to look after him.

Euston, when they found their train, was a black cavern lit by sudden glimpses of searing interiors as fire-boxes were opened and fed. Gouts of steam spouted from boilers towards the high glass dome of the roof, porters shouted, boxes of day-old chicks cheeped and a cacophony of young calves in a crate bellowed. Tom was transfixed with amazement.

The horse-boxes were tacked onto the end of the train which was too long to be sheltered by the canopy and the rain fell steadily. The landaulette was taken in charge and put on a flat truck, though Mr Beckett was sure Miss Beatrix had specified, and paid for, a closed one. 'There ain't none left,' he was told, laconically. 'We'll fix a tarpaulin.' The horses were restless, but the pony, who had an unaccountable liking for trains, looked round with obvious pleasure as though it was Christmas.

All might yet have gone well if it hadn't been for the station master and his assistant, who had taken it into their heads to inspect the boxing of the horses. When the two uniformed men left the shelter of the canopy they both put up umbrellas almost under the nose of the black gelding.

The result, as Mr Beckett said to his wife later, was entirely predictable. The black reared, pawing the air with his hoofs and, once his legs had thudded back on terra firma, endeavoured to gallop off into the wet, black night. Tom had the presence of mind to hold the other two animals and leave the black to Mr Beckett, who was dragged off into a world of shunting trucks and hooting engines.

He escaped death by inches, or so it felt to him, halting the black almost under the wheels of a moving truck, and returned, leading the trembling horse, in as near a state of jitters as he ever allowed himself. Tom and the bunch of loaders were of the opinion that the sooner the animal was in the box, the better. The black had no intention of obliging them. He stiffened his forelegs and leaned back on his haunches to resist their tugging. He also bared his large yellow teeth and tried to sink them into any leg or forearm that came within reach.

Mr Beckett stood back and wiped the rain off his face with a massive red handkerchief. He then looked down at the handkerchief and smote himself on the forehead for a fool. Holding the black's head, he got Tom to use it to blindfold the animal, who then stepped into the horse-box as coyly as a little girl arriving at her first dancing lesson.

'Sometimes I hates horses,' Mr Beckett told the unheeding loaders.

The rest of the journey was an anti-climax. The horse-box had a luggage compartment at one end, where the two boxes shared the space with hay and water for the journey, and a seating compartment at the other. Here Mr Beckett made himself comfortable, listening to the animals threshing and complaining in their narrow stalls, three to the width of the carriage, stumbling when the train pulled out with whistles, shudders and a clanking of buffers, then settling down to the soporific long, slow rhythm of the heavy engine pulling them north.

Around 3 o'clock in the morning, when Bletchley and Reading were well past, he opened the square shutters that allowed him to feed his charges. They looked at him calmly, bright-eyed and cheerful, and accepted wisps of hay as though receiving tribute. Mr Beckett felt bitter. His ribs were sore, his arm ached, his eyes and teeth were gritty with train smoke and his head hurt.

'What I've done in a former life to deserve you lot,' he said to them, 'I hate to think.' He turned to the black. 'I suppose you enjoyed tonight's fun and games,' he said, 'but I know you now. You're a biter, that's what. Perhaps we can do something about it, perhaps not, but you're something else as well after this; you're a horse that goes berserk when he sees an umbrella. And what we can do about that in this climate I don't know. You'll be better out of my sight, the lot of you.' He closed the shutters.

Dawn and the train labouring up Shap woke him from a refreshing sleep. The rain had gone over, to expose a calm, blue sky, hills sharp against the pale background and the glint of a river in the valley below. Ah, getting near Penrith. He must have slept through Preston. The animals still seemed to be enjoying the novelty of a train journey.

The slow pull to the summit, accompanied by heavy black smoke shot with red-hot cinders, was followed by the exhilarating turn of speed reached on the descent towards the Eden Valley. Penrith was a red sandstone platform and a clanking of milk-churns, then the sound of hammers detaching the horse-box to push it into a siding ready, together with the carriage truck, for the Cockermouth train. There was half an hour to wait and Mr

Beckett got out to stretch his legs and see if there was a mug of tea going in the porter's lodge. He was lucky on this count: he got two of them, with sugar.

The LNER locomotive that ran on the single line to Cockermouth lacked the solid dignity of the monolith that had gone on to Glasgow. It puffed fussily west towards the Lakeland fells, the saddleback outline of Blencathra detaching itself just before they took what seemed like a nose-dive towards the River Greta, going backwards and forwards like a darning needle over latticework bridges. There was some water coming down; must have had quite a bit of rain last night.

Keswick was wide awake and they soon had the box and the carriage in a siding for unloading. That was all right, but Mr Beckett was disgusted with the condition of the landaulette. Not only had the rain got under the tarpaulin, but it had been no match for burning cinders. He could see a lot of work needing doing before he would feel happy to take the carriage into Keswick at a fashionable hour.

Seven o'clock in the morning being given over to trades-men's drays and sleepy night-porters polishing hotel doorknobs, Mr Beckett clattered comfortably down Station Street, the pony bringing up the rear on a leading rein, past the George and the Queen's and the Moot Hall and out of the town on the Cockermouth road towards the Over Derwent fells.

Soon he could see the old stone bridge over the river, his road to Portinscale and Lingholm, which meant only another half an hour to his breakfast. It felt quite like coming home. He must remember to tell Miss Beatrix about the black's faults and about the burn marks on the landaulette. Then he pulled himself up. Why was he reporting to Miss Beatrix instead of to the Master? He deliberated on this as the horses took the bridge and the green pools of the river came and went, and decided he'd long had a feeling that Miss Beatrix was slowly taking over. Not that any one said so, but it was her fault if anything went wrong.

Portinscale was awake now; there were even two girls on bicycles going through the village. He kept a firm hold on the reins, but the black didn't show any sign of adding to his other dislike, though the pony shied. Well, one thing was certain. Miss Beatrix was a better judge of horseflesh than her father.

Beatrix, opening up Lingholm stables to the sound of larks proclaiming the joy of a summer morning, found she too was

49

singing. It was a catchy tune and the words had a message.

'We don't want to fight but by jingo if we do, we've got the men, we've got the ships, we've got the money too.'

Whatever had put that into her head? She wasn't going to fight the Boers. Then she remembered the conversation during the train journey. She had said that ordinary people were saying there was going to be a war.

'There's no call for us to worry about what ordinary people think,' Mama had replied.

'I've never fathomed *what* ordinary people think,' Papa had contributed pettishly, sprawled like a whiskered starfish over the opposite seat. 'All they seem to want these days is some sort of excitement, like these football matches that cause such trouble.'

Beatrix wondered if either of her parents really minded what anybody thought. It seemed highly unlikely, from the way they went on. The episode of the Chelsea fiddler was as if it had never been, with no consideration for poor Elizabeth's feelings, no word of regret for Bertram's prolonged absence. She had tried herself to explain to Elizabeth.

'It's my fault, I'm afraid,' she'd told her. 'Poor Mama finds me so repugnant she naturally assumes that those who do not, such as yourself and Beckett, are sadly deluded. Though she regards it as her duty to keep me by her always, she doesn't feel the same about you. She was, in her own way, taking steps to remedy the matter.'

'Likely as not then, she'll try again in a bit,' Elizabeth had said. Beatrix had not been able to deny it, but thought Beckett might suffer first.

Ah, she could hear the horses coming up the drive. There they were, but, good heavens, talking of fighting, the landaulette certainly looked as though it had been in the wars.

# CHAPTER SIX

Aunt Clara Potter and Miss Gentile arrived at Lingholm in the middle of August. Beatrix, wisps of hair blown into her eyes by a blustery east wind as she helped Mr Beckett with their considerable luggage, viewed them as a mixed blessing.

Aunt Clara was of a nervous disposition, had a face a little like a horse and was fond of her food. Her habit of tidiness, always returning her possessions to their original box or drawer after use, also had its drawbacks. Beatrix could find herself asked three times in a day, and Lingholm was a large house, to fetch her aunt's gloves. Still, Aunt Clara was always kind, at whatever cost to herself.

Miss Gentile was quite different. She was small and dark, with a sharp nose and piercing black eyes. She had a formidable intellect and believed in speaking her mind, which made large holes in the delicate structure of social conversation. The cross she had to bear was her constipation, which she would discuss endlessly when gentlemen were not present. In her luggage would be her last resort, a small, sinister green box containing an enema syringe. Her use of this in the past, Beatrix remembered with dread, had occasioned the worst sort of domestic upset.

'How extraordinary,' Miss Gentile now said, following her luggage into the hall and picking up an object from the table. 'What a curious thing to find lying about.' She was holding a short length of damp, rotten planking from which a small mushroom appeared to be growing. She smelt it, like a dog with an unsavoury bone, and wrinkled her nose. 'Most peculiar,' she said, putting it down.

'Oh, Beatrix will have picked it up somewhere,' said Mrs Potter. 'She collects the most disgusting objects without the slightest thought of what she might be bringing into the house.' She spoke without acknowledgement that Beatrix was in the same room. 'Frogs, toads . . .' In her afternoon hat of drooping black straw, Mrs Potter looked rather like a toad herself as she ticked off the anomalous list on her fingers. 'Beetles, lizards, bats, birds, mice, rats . . . She spends her time drawing them instead of doing something useful. I throw everything away that I can, but now she's taken up with squirrels – messy, chattery, excitable creatures. You've no idea, Miss Gentile, what a time I have with that girl.'

'Squirrels!' Miss Gentile appeared amazed.

'Yes, squirrels.' Mrs Potter fidgeted, tired of the conversation. She never liked a subject to be prolonged. 'Come along Clara, surely you don't need to roll up your gloves. Put everything on the oak settle. Beatrix will hang them up later.'

'You surely don't want me to strew my outdoor clothes all over the place, Helen. Nothing makes a house look so sordid as gloves and mantles spread on the furniture. I'll hang them up myself. And Beatrix dear, I have a great fondness for squirrels.' Aunt Clara gave her sister-in-law a defiant look which Mrs Potter ignored.

'Come into the library,' she said. 'Beatrix, tell Elizabeth to bring tea.'

The library was a room which shrank its occupants. Decorated and panelled in gothic style, with a stone fireplace whose mock canopy ran up into the rafters, it seemed to Beatrix to need a caterpillar smoking a hookah in the corner and advising her what to eat to reach a comfortable size. Mama never seemed to be affected. She sat down now on the only comfortable seat, leaving her guests and Beatrix to perch themselves as they would on the massive oak chairs.

They were discussing possible expeditions when Elizabeth arrived with the heavy tray. Beatrix had never been able to understand why Mama insisted on bringing the silver tea-service with them on holiday. Elizabeth put it on a table beside Mrs Potter's chair and waited to carry cups and offer the multitude of scones. The resident cook came from across the border.

'I would like to call on Mrs Rawnsley and her husband at Crosthwaite Vicarage, if it could be arranged,' said Aunt Clara in her quiet, pleasant voice. 'She paints charming watercolours and, though he's sometimes a little alarming, Mr Rawnsley was very comforting on the subject of original sin.'

'Oh, of course.' Miss Gentile slammed the Derby cup onto its saucer with awesome lack of care. 'That's the man Miss Beezley told me wrote such an interesting book about Egypt. Imagine, he says that the natives going up the Nile on steamers often whisk travellers' side-saddles off returning steamers for their own use. The Missionary Society should be told about that – they've made a lot of converts in Egypt. Or those Cook's Tours.'

'Then you must of course call on the Rawnsleys,' Mrs Potter said with finality. 'I may be busy myself, but Beatrix can accompany you. She hasn't a lot to do.'

Beatrix, handing shortbread, was pleased to agree. It was just the opportunity she had been looking for, as she wanted to consult Canon Rawnsley on the perils of authorship. At the same time she wondered if she saw a gleam of anticipation in Mama's eye. Now what could there be in a visit to the Rawnsleys that might provide ammunition for her war against her daughter?

Harwicke Rawnsley had been a friend of the family since their first holiday in the Lake District when they had stayed at Wray Castle. A short, round, bustling cleric with a sharp eye and a cheerfully bouncing manner, he had arrived to pay a pastoral visit. Beatrix had only just passed her sixteenth birthday and had been astonished and embarrassed when he had been loudly complimentary about her paintings. Her parents had been astonished too. Papa had even come over to take a look himself at what she was doing, which was quite out of the way. Then Mr Rawnsley had been charming about her pets, writing poems to them and making her laugh, an unusual experience in her life at that time, before she had learned the value of laughing at herself. When she thought of him now, she couldn't help smiling. He did so much good in his life, with his passion for providing open spaces for the poor, and wrote enough books and articles and absurd verse to have contented two normal people. It was impossible not to like him, though someone had told her he did make enemies. Did Mama come into that category? And if so, was she intending to use her daughter as a weapon against the poor man? She'd have to take care.

The east wind and resulting thunderstorms gave way to cool, clear sunny days, and the countryside, in spite of the over-riding dark green of late summer, shone with a sleek harvest of rowanberries, elderberries, blackberries, hazel nuts and rose-hips. The day on which the Crosthwaite visit had been arranged was so warm that it was decided the hood of the landaulette could be lowered.

Beatrix was sketching a briar covered with rosehips, holding it gingerly in one hand as she drew with the other, when Elizabeth found her to say the carriage was waiting.

She looked up, feeling hunted. 'The man in the wilderness,' she told Elizabeth, 'said to me, how many strawberries grow in the sea? I answered him as I thought good, as many red herrings as grow in a wood.' She then laughed at Elizabeth's expression and got up. 'Heigh ho, the red herrings I am sent to pursue! But at least it doesn't look like rain.'

Elizabeth brushed bits of briar off Beatrix's skirt, looking anxiously to make sure there was no petticoat showing, which made Beatrix smile, and found her hat and jacket. She then went off to find Aunt Clara's shawl.

When she returned they were all settled in the carriage. Beatrix and Aunt Clara had their backs to Mr Beckett, and as neither of them was slim it was rather a tight fit, whilst little Miss Gentile sat facing the way they were going with all the room in the world. The hood was folded back in its two halves.

'There you are at last,' said Miss Gentile, as though it was Elizabeth's fault they were waiting.

Mr Beckett furled his whip and looked at the swishing tails of the horses.

'Walk on,' he told them.

Clara Potter sighed with pleasure. There was nothing she enjoyed more than a gentle drive through pleasant countryside, and Beckett was so reliable. She spread the shawl over the skirt of her gold-brown silk dress as protection against horse hairs and settled her large, matching hat.

The great beauty of Lingholm lay in its woodland and lakeside setting rather than in the barrack-like house, and the road to Keswick twisted and turned through sun-shot woods smelling of damp earth and fading leaves all the way to Portinscale and the bridge. It was preferable to sit with one's back to the horses, so there was no coachman in a top hat to impede the view and less danger of shed hair and any other equine unpleasantness. Dear Gentile understood her preferences and conducted her campaigns accordingly, sometimes treading rather hard, Clara was afraid, on other people's corns. She was now in the middle of a long description of Miss Beezley's visit to Petra and her sufferings when forced to ride a camel, which gave Clara, who had heard the story before, a pleasant respite in which to indulge her own thoughts.

'Are you comfortable, Aunt Clara?' Beatrix asked quietly, so as not to interrupt the monologue.

'Indeed yes, my dear.' Clara patted her niece's hand and smiled into her concerned blue eyes. 'Very comfortable.'

She did wish that her brother Rupert and his wife Helen weren't so demanding in regard to the services of poor dear Beatrix. It was, of course, the duty of daughters to look after their parents. Hadn't she looked after her own father and mother, particularly after father went so peculiar. She saw him, in her mind's eye, trotting naked down the top corridor at Camfield, and suppressed a giggle. But they had been so kind, so unwilling to give trouble, whilst Helen – really, Helen was getting more and more difficult. She blamed her strongly for Beatrix's shyness and social gaucherie. How could the poor child be otherwise after being hidden away in the nursery until she was nearly twenty? Bertram had been the favourite of course, but his education had been mismanaged and it was no wonder he often buried himself in Scotland with his box of paints. There was his drinking too. That would make life at home impossible. She did wonder, looking at him sometimes, if women were a problem as well, but she'd heard it said that women and alcoholism didn't generally mix. She relaxed when they clattered over the stone bridge and she was able to enjoy the river vistas north and south.

After Portinscale bridge they turned towards the town of Keswick, the skyline improved by the spire of the new Church of St John. Very high church, she'd heard, almost Anglo-Catholic. Not at all to dear Canon Rawnsley's taste, she was sure, though he never remarked upon it.

The long roof-ridge and stocky tower of the ancient parish church of Crosthwaite became visible above them through the trees on their left, with a muddle of gravestones spilling down the hill. The poet Southey and his wife were buried there, in an overcrowded grave. This contained, as far as she could remember, the body of a faithful servant, another of an ancient sister-in-law and one of an illegitimate baby, or suspected to be so. It was all most irregular.

Petra was now left behind and some inroads were being made on Miss Beezley's latest exploits in the Lebanon.

'You'll be able to talk about the Cedars with Mr Rawnsley. I believe he brought one back to plant amongst the Crosthwaite graves,' Clara said, smiling indulgently at her friend.

Now they were climbing Vicarage Hill and Beatrix had descended to relieve the horses and was toiling up behind them, getting her skirts all dusty. Clara wondered if it was Helen or

Beatrix herself who chose the old-fashioned and unbecoming clothes she wore.

Mrs Rawnsley, or Edith as she insisted old friends like Beatrix and Clara should call her, came to the door of the long, low Queen Anne vicarage as the carriage came through the gate. A small woman, delicately made, she was wearing an afternoon gown in a subtle shade of violet that excited Clara's envy. Of course there was money on both sides, Rawnsley and Fletcher.

Edith greeted them warmly and when Beckett had been directed round the back to the stables and Beatrix had arrived, she took the three ladies to the front of the house and the sunlit long terrace, which, as the vicarage had its back to Skiddaw, faced west and had a view of the Over Derwent fells. Here there were definite preparations for afternoon tea: a table covered to the floor by a heavily crocheted cloth, cups and a sugar basin in impeccable blue and gold Rockingham.

'How delightful,' Clara said.

Edith thought she meant the view. 'Such a wonderful vista,' she agreed, 'framed by the yews.' She turned her face, wide-eyed and oval like a medieval portrait, to the fells. 'Coleridge thought it looked like a giants' encampment, and you can see just what he meant.'

The ladies dutifully admired the angular outlines of the far hills.

'Something like the black tents of the Bedouin,' Miss Gentile offered helpfully.

Edith abandoned the view.

'Hardwicke will be here presently,' she told them. 'He is very busy just at the moment finishing his book on the life of Henry Whitehead, Vicar of Lanercost. The trouble is, people will interrupt him, particularly over this business of establishing a colony of Armenian refugees in Cyprus.'

'I'm afraid we too are an unnecessary interruption,' Beatrix said. 'Casual callers can so often be a nuisance.'

Clara did wish her niece wouldn't always be so apologetic.

'Of course not. He must, after all, have some tea. But we will start without him,' Edith added practically.

They had reached the cake stage, maids of honour which Clara thought could have done with a little more jam, when Hardwicke Rawnsley came out on the terrace to greet his guests.

He was not a tall man – every time Clara saw him she was surprised anew that he wasn't taller – but he had wonderful presence. He'd grown a beard and, to be objective, he'd lost on top what he had gained round his chin. But his eyes still had the same intense gleam, his smile embraced the company with a warm glow and his welcome gave the impression that they were the most delightful thing that had happened to him all day.

Clara, who was seated so she could see through the long drawing-room windows and admire the Della Robia relief above the mantelpiece, meditated for a moment or two, over her third cup of tea, on the extraordinary power of charm backed by money.

The Canon was plied with egg and anchovy sandwiches, the sun continued to shine, more strong tea was dispensed, and the company became, in Clara's opinion, a little over-excited. The conversation started with an observation by Miss Gentile on the peace to be found amongst the Cedars of Lebanon, took a small excursion into the new scientific thought as expounded by Darwin, and was then adroitly diverted by Canon Rawnsley to the new ideas on education as advocated by Dr Arnold. Edith's rather impassive face became animated at the mention of his name.

'We've met both the Doctor and his son Matthew. I remember you walked with them once, Hardwicke, from Thirlmere to Borrowdale. Matthew is a great admirer of Wordsworth. He was for a time the President of the Wordsworth Society. Do you care for Wordsworth, Miss Gentile?'

'My opinion coincides with that of the poet Byron,' said Miss Gentile. 'Are you cognisant of Byron's name for Wordsworth?'

'Well, no,' Edith said hesitantly. Her face reflected her thought that there was something not quite nice about Byron.

'Turdsworth!' said Miss Gentile with relish.

Canon Rawnsley burst into a bellow of laughter and Beatrix's face melted into mirth. Edith, not amused, watched her husband slapping his knees to the detriment of his well-cut trousers, and decided to abandon poets altogether. She turned to Beatrix, who was still chuckling.

'How are your drawings of fungi coming along?' she asked in a kindly manner. 'Hardwicke tells me you are hoping to publish the whole collection when it's finished.'

Beatrix, just for a second, looked distressed. 'The collection is increasing,' she said, trying to speak lightly, 'but I have discovered that there are forty thousand named and classified fungi, so it may take some time to complete.'

The distress had evidently not escaped Canon Rawnsley.

Clara thought that very little of that nature escaped the good Canon. He stood up and offered his arm to Beatrix.

'You've reminded me that I wanted to ask a favour of you,' he said. 'Would you do me the honour of taking a turn round the garden whilst I explain what is needed?'

The two of them descended the steps onto the lawn and strolled towards the yew walk. Neither Miss Gentile nor Clara commented.

'Well,' said Edith brightly, 'that's nice. It looks as though Beatrix has been added to Hardwicke's group of women friends.'

'Women friends?' repeated Clara faintly.

'Oh yes, he has several. There's Mrs Lyn Lynton, who used to live here, there's Lady Adam-Smith, there's – oh, I can't remember them all. They look on him as a father, you know, turning to him for advice. Then there are the older ones, who look on him as a son.' She smiled happily at her guests. 'He has so much sympathy, and there is so much distress.'

'I suppose there's also safety in numbers,' Miss Gentile remarked acidly.

Edith laughed again but didn't pretend to misunderstand. 'There's no danger,' she said. 'There was once some talk when Hardwicke was left a house and its contents by one of his old ladies, but it soon died down when it became known that he had donated the whole legacy to the Armenian Fund. Now, can I give you any more tea?'

It wasn't until the Canon had returned to his study and the two ladies were ensconced in the carriage, waiting for Beatrix to finish taking leave of her hostess, that Miss Gentile could explode into comment.

'That woman is either a fool or a saint,' she said.

'Well,' said Clara, unusually tart, 'I don't think she's either. Which makes it the Canon, certainly not a fool, who is the saint.'

'No one is a saint who writes such bad verse,' retorted Miss Gentile, getting the last word in as usual.

During the drive home Clara Potter considered her niece. She'd had a disappointment over those interminable fungus drawings which she now, it was quite apparent, meant to abandon. Probably not before time. She had a sense of humour, even if it had a common streak, which her aunt had never suspected, and she looked really pretty when she laughed, an unlooked-for asset. So there was hope for her yet, especially as she had shown no sign of shyness when whisked off by the Canon to discuss whatever it was he had in mind and had been considerably more cheerful on their return.

She thought about all this for a while and then, as they came through Portinscale and she could see Walla Crag across the lake with its weaving garland of seagulls, she made a decision. She'd change her will. As well as the diamond brooch, she'd leave Beatrix a useful sum of money.

# CHAPTER SEVEN

Some days after the family had returned from Lingholm, Beatrix, passing the half-open drawing-room door around 10 o'clock in the morning, hesitated and then stopped to listen. Mama appeared to be making a speech. She was of a very precise disposition, dividing each day into household management, reading improving books, sewing and the afternoon drive, and seldom wasted words even on reproof; certainly not on praise. Now Norah was apparently receiving an accolade!

'. . . and I must say, Cook, that I find it a comfort to have a loyal servant like yourself, who has been with the family over a number of years, in charge of the domestics,' she heard. Mama would have her eyes on her folded hands and that smug look about her mouth. 'Not all our servants are so reliable and I have serious fears as the honesty of one in particular,' the grey voice droned on, 'but we'll see what we can do on that count. I am quite satisfied, Cook, with today's menus. That will be all.'

The sound of Norah's squeaking boots approached the door and Beatrix fled upstairs to the nursery.

Well really, that was a bit rich! Having failed to label Elizabeth as a thief, Mama was now, by innuendo and encouragement, pushing Norah into the role of *agent provocateur*. The holiday in the Lake District had been no more than a pause to regroup her forces. The secrets and uncertainties of the house were to be built up again. She ran her hands through her hair and looked at Peter in despair.

'I meant to do some painting,' she told him, 'but an unquiet mind makes the colours muddy. I owe cousin Caroline a letter, perhaps I could manage that. What d'you think *she* would make of Mama and her ideas on the rights of the individual?' Peter, dozing in front of the empty hearth, raised his head in enquiry.

'She'd probably say we should quote John Stuart Mill to her to revise her thinking, but I'm afraid the task is quite beyond someone of my limited capabilities,' she answered for him and sorted out notepaper and pen from the muddle on the table.

Elizabeth was also finding it difficult to keep her mind on her work. Fred had turned up late last night when the house was quiet and they'd satisfactorily made up for their long separation. Fred had said it was almost worth doing without for so long, just to experience the glory of their reunion. Then he'd started all over again. She was standing in the middle of the kitchen tingling with the memory of their lovemaking when Norah returned from her morning conference with Mrs Potter.

'There! Just what I expected,' Norah said, very full of herself and even sharper than usual. 'Mooning around, no work getting done, thinking how to get some money for that fancy man o'yourn, with better luck than you had with that china fiddler. Younger than you, isn't he? Well then, stands to reason you need more than your pert bosom' – she pronounced it *boosom* – 'to keep him 'appy.' Norah could be very coarse when she chose.

'I didn't take the fiddler, you great Yorkshire pudding.' Elizabeth could feel her face going red with rage. 'What would I want to do that for and lose my place? Anyway I know who took it, so there.' She knew she shouldn't have said it as soon as the words left her lips.

Norah immediately leapt to an interesting, though wrong, conclusion.

'Mr Bertram! You accusing Mr Bertram of doing things like that? You want to watch it, my girl, or they'll have you up for slander. I'll . . .' She shut her mouth on what she'd been about to say, having remembered her arrangement with the milkman. 'I'd be careful if I wus you. The Mistress 'as got it in for you,' she finished lamely.

Elizabeth escaped upstairs with turpentine and linseed oil and soft rags to try to remove a heat ring from the walnut dining table. Someone had told her that rubbing with the bottoms of champagne corks worked wonders, but fat chance there was of getting champagne, never mind the corks, in this household. As she rubbed she considered her strategy for the day in order to keep out of Norah's way, which seemed advisable. It was her day for doing the brass, but that would put her in the kitchen and it was Lily's afternoon off and Norah's day for doing her ironing, as she never trusted Tom's mother to do her aprons properly.

Elizabeth thought of poor Cox, the old butler who had died rather suddenly last year. He had not been replaced and they were supposed to share his duties. As far as she could see, all he'd ever done was answer the front door and clean the silver, shutting himself up in the butler's pantry like an old turtle retreating into its shell. She'd clean the silver this afternoon, shutting herself up like old Cox used to do.

After lunch, in pursuit of this plan, she went through the kitchen towards the back premises. She skirted Norah, with her best apron spread on the ironing blanket and just changing irons. As she spat on the bottom of the new one to check its heat, she gave Elizabeth a sideways jerk of the head that said she'd just as soon be spitting on her.

The butler's pantry had a long sink under the high window and was lined on one side with drawers up to waist height and cupboards above, varnished a sticky yellow and divided by a narrow ledge. The cupboards went up to the ceiling and the top shelves could only be reached by pulling out the heavy lower drawers to use as a ladder. Since the time a former housemaid had slipped off the edge of a drawer and broken her ankle whilst putting away a set of dinner plates which also suffered, Miss Beatrix had decreed that only the very best china, never used, should be kept on the top shelves.

On the floor was a piece of carpet that used to be in front of the kitchen range, its pattern hardly visible through the grease and dirt. It had been put in the pantry for poor old Cox who had complained of cold feet and Elizabeth gave it a disgusted look. She could try beating it and washing it in vinegar, but it looked more like a candidate for the dustbin.

She pulled out the knife-cleaning drum from under the sink and found the box of Wellington Knife Powder, Cox never using any other. Why the family ever had a butler, she couldn't think; in a house where there was nothing in the cellar but some coal and a tribe of cockroaches. They said he'd died of water on the brain, not that he'd had one so's you'd notice, but he'd drunk bottles and bottles of Benger's Liquor Pancreaticus which he said was for his stomach ulcer, so you could take your choice. She decided to do the knives before the silver and put on a pair of old gloves.

Norah clumped past the door to the back kitchen and there was a crash as she dropped the flat-irons on the slate bench to cool off. She was on the rampage. Elizabeth braced herself. Sure enough, Norah stumped into the pantry, eyes narrowed, cap crooked.

'You'll be looking for a new place, then?' she grunted, hands on her hips and her lips set in a confident leer.

'Nothing of the sort,' said Elizabeth. 'Why should I?'

'Yer mean ter say you think you'll get away with pinching that bit of an ornament? The luck of the devil, that's what you've got. I've allus thought so.'

There was definitely something odder than usual about Norah this afternoon. Elizabeth put down a carving knife and looked at her. Her hair was all anyhow and her eyes suspiciously bright. Could it be drink? No, not the saintly Norah.

'What d'you mean by that?' she asked.

Instead of answering, Norah bent down and tugged out two drawers, the bottom one further out than the one above, climbed the resulting steps, opened the cupboard above her and took out a bottle labelled 'Benger's Liquor Pancreaticus' from behind a dozen-set of Mason's Ironstone dessert plates that hadn't seen the light of day for years. She also grabbed a transparent Limoges cup with a pattern of bluebirds and then teetered down to floor level.

'Naw, it's not that stomach muck, it's gin. That's what Cox allus drank an' you never the wiser. I'm using up 'is old stock, Waste not, want not, that's what Miss Beatrix sez.' She took a gulp, half the contents of the cup. 'Mother's ruin, that's what they call it, but it can't ruin me, I've never bin a mother. No more 'ave you, though I've waited long enough to see something 'appening under that pure starched apron o'yourn. Don't think I don't know what you get up to with that fancy man you keep. Devil's own luck, or something else. How d'you manage it?' She emptied the cup.

Elizabeth went cold with shock. Norah the chapel-goer, the Bible-thumper, the hymn-singer! Well, she certainly wasn't going to tell her how she managed to avoid pregnancy, that was for sure. Not that Norah couldn't have found out for herself what they sold at those herbal places besides liquorice water and orris root. Mother had told her and Dorothy what to get when they were quite young. 'Don't want either of you caught like me,' she'd said, and then kissed them both so they wouldn't feel unwanted. Dorothy hadn't any children either, though she'd been married these twelve years.

'You'd better go up to your room, Norah,' she said. 'I'll finish clearing up in the kitchen for you.'

'Thank you for nothing, you toffee-nosed little tart. It's you who should go. I'm fed up with all your airs and graces.' She reached over and grabbed the carving knife. 'There's one sure way of getting rid of you.' She lunged with it at Elizabeth's face.

The drawers were still pulled out and the cupboard door

open. Elizabeth found herself on the ledge clinging to the shelves and warding off erratic knife thrusts with her slippered feet. Her fingers curled involuntarily round a heavy Ironstone plate. She swung it down and crashed it on Norah's head. Norah staggered, dropped the knife and wavered to the floor like a rag doll.

Elizabeth climbed slowly down and stood looking first at Norah and then at the scattered green and orange shards.

'That's spoilt the set,' she said aloud and scurried off to find Miss Beatrix.

Elizabeth's arrival in the nursery in a state of near collapse led Beatrix, with thumping heart, to expect Norah's blood-stained body laid out in the pantry. Instead they found her asleep on the floor, flushed and snoring with a lump on her forehead. They hauled her up the endless stairs, where she woke up enough to protest loudly at a malevolent fate that wouldn't let her be, and she was snoring again before Elizabeth had swung her legs onto the bed and thrown a blanket over her.

'By morning she'll feel wretched enough to sign the pledge,' Beatrix said, shutting the bedroom door on the unsavoury sight and locking it. 'I have a dreadful feeling I ought to speak to you severely for hitting her with that plate. It was not a Christian action and it might be said you should have reasoned with her. I shall refrain from saying anything so ridiculous.'

Elizabeth giggled weakly; she was recovering. 'Yes Miss Beatrix,' she said.

Realising it would have to be done sometime, Beatrix thought the sooner the better and told her parents about it after afternoon tea, brought in by a subdued Elizabeth. Once on their own, Beatrix was in deep trouble.

'Are you sure what you say is true?' Mama said in a voice that indicated this would be unusual. 'It seems to me Cook was the one who was attacked, otherwise why was she lying senseless on the floor with a lump on her head? We've only the housemaid's word for it that Cook went for her with a carving knife, and as for Cook being drunk, I simply don't believe it; she goes to chapel.'

'You're talking nonsense, Beatrix,' Papa took up the thread. 'Your mother must be right. Norah is a quiet, sensible woman; it's Elizabeth who's the flighty one. I've heard her singing music hall songs.'

Beatrix fleetingly wondered how Papa identified such songs. Music halls were not, as far as she knew, a part of his life.

'It's the quiet, sensible ones you have to watch,' she

answered darkly, causing Mama to close her eyes and turn alarmingly pink.

This had the required effect, Papa having such a terror of any disturbance or violence that he would go to any lengths to avoid it. 'I think the solution is for you to dismiss Elizabeth out of hand,' he said. 'She causes trouble in this house and your mother would feel more comfortable if you engaged an older, more staid woman who would get along with Norah.'

Beatrix fished in her capacious skirt pocket and brought out the bottle labelled 'Benger's Liquor Pancreaticus'. She poured a little of the clear, oily liquid into a cup.

'There,' she said, putting it under Papa's unwilling nose. 'Gin. Besides which, Norah is lying on her bed reeking of the stuff and as drunk as that pig at Gorse Hall which ate fermenting apple pulp. Of course she attacked Elizabeth. She's the sort of woman who stores up grudges and then lets fly all at once.' She paused for a moment; it wasn't just Norah she was describing. 'Dismiss Elizabeth!' she went on resolutely. 'She's been with us since I was ten. No, it's Norah who must go and at once. I'll enquire for a new cook at the domestic employment agency tomorrow.'

Mama rose from the tea table in a surge of black crêpe skirts. 'All this commotion has given me a sick headache,' she said. 'Really Beatrix, you should be capable of such a small matter as managing the servants without bothering your father and I. I shall go to my room.'

Papa wavered to his feet as the door shut behind her. 'Now look what you've done!' he said bitterly to his daughter.

Beatrix retired to the nursery with a headache of her own. She collapsed into the rocking-chair and hoped she wasn't going to sink into one of her odious fits of low spirits, though really no one could blame her for doing so, living in this malevolent house. Now that was self-pity, one of the worst sins. She must not give way to that. A house of her own would be a tremendous comfort, somewhere in the clean northern air to which she could escape, like Bertram. It was as unattainable as the moon in her present state of poverty; she must stop dreaming of it. She would do better to consider more pressing matters or she would find herself having to do the cooking herself which, now she came to think of it, would be a very suitable revenge for her parent's unreasonable attitudes. Perhaps she should learn to cook, in case she ever did have her own establishment; learn to make pastry and whip up an omelette. Then Mama would really think she had gone mad.

She got up, took Peter out of his hutch and put him on the table, to the consternation of the mice who crowded to the back of their cage. 'Now Peter, it's time to practise your tricks. We'll start with jumping over this little cane.'

Peter, a naturally lazy rabbit, settled more firmly on his haunches.

'Come, come, exert yourself. We all have to do what we can in whatever situation we find ourselves.' She tapped his flank with the cane.

Peter jumped reluctantly forwards and backwards and then thumped angrily with his back legs to indicate that was his limit. Beatrix remembered her conversation with Elizabeth on the subject of energy. She put down the cane and stared out of the window, where she could see the autumn leaves beginning to curl and die. How melancholy it would be to reach that stage in life, the sere and yellow leaf, without any achievements at all, not even a house of her own. She too must exert herself. There must be more and better ways of making money that just painting greeting cards. With elbows on the windowsill and head cupped in hands she considered ways and means. Peter, marooned on the table, went to sleep again.

# CHAPTER EIGHT

Ordinary people proved to have more foresight than the Government. Boer commandos launched their attack in the October of 1899, with the loss to the British of Kimberley and Ladysmith and over a thousand men. It was February, a full step into the new century, before British forces under Lord Roberts began the process of pushing them back.

Mr Potter found the war news a welcome stimulant. He had mounted a map of South Africa on the study wall and every morning at breakfast he consulted *The Times*, reading through despatches from the war correspondents. His daughter was required to move the coloured pins on the map according to his directions. He had *The Times* spread across the damask cloth one morning in late February when Elizabeth came in with coffee and the post.

'That fellow Kipling, writing from Simonstown,' he remarked, 'says the Boers have surprising notions of geography. They think the world is flat and England a day's trek from Cape Town but they run circles round English troops on their home ground. Oh, thank you, Elizabeth.' He took the letter, the address an illegible scrawl, from the silver salver. 'I know that writing, it's Canon Rawnsley.'

There was a letter for Beatrix too. Thick, and the postmark was Wandsworth.

Elizabeth went for more toast and when she came back found that Mr Potter had got no further than the first line of his letter.

'If it weren't impossible, I'd say his writing's got even worse,' he said. 'It's going to take me most of the day to decipher this.' He looked quite pleased at the prospect, as though faced with a particularly interesting triple acrostic.

'What are you corresponding about?' Beatrix asked. Breakfast was a comparatively relaxed and talkative meal, in her opinion the best of the day. Mama took hers in her room.

Mr Potter looked embarrassed, a small boy caught stealing apples, and got up to help himself to another *oeuf en gratin* from the side table. 'These eggs are very good, I must say that Mrs Pearson does us well these days. Can I offer you one, Beatrix?' Beatrix, eating pressed beef, shook her head.

Mr Potter sat down and re-established his napkin across his front. 'I wanted to know what he thought about the Darwinian theory. It's something I can't take to myself, man descended from a jabbering, scratching monkey, and as far as I can see if we all thought that way it would lead to general anarchy.'

'And what did he reply?' Beatrix was amused.

'Pshaw. Romantic nonsense, that's what I'd call it. He said that the search for knowledge would always go on and quoted Tennyson, not even Wordsworth! I can only remember the first two lines: "Let knowledge grow from more to more,/But more of reverence in us dwell". All very well for Tennyson, but not much use to the greengrocer round the corner. He wants something to look forward to, like heaven's pearly gates. Wrote and told the Canon so. I'll take this in the study and see what the answer is. There's nothing in the paper today anyway.' He pushed back the heavy dining-chair and left the room in a brisk and purposeful fashion.

'All our greengrocer round the corner thinks of is getting rid of bad apples to unsuspecting customers and that's not going to get him to heaven's pearly gates,' Beatrix said to Elizabeth, who had made up the sluggish fire and was waiting to clear. 'Papa does enjoy a good theological tussle, though I think the Canon is more than a match for him. Tell me, how is the new under-housemaid settling down?'

Since the abrupt departure of Norah, sent back to her brother in Yorkshire in disgrace with £20 in her pocket from Mr Potter, Elizabeth had been promoted. 'There isn't a female equivalent for butler,' Beatrix had told her, 'so it'll have to be head-housemaid. According to Mrs Beeton, that means you can put your feet up and let the rest of the staff do the work!' Another housemaid, Betty Anderton from the Borders, had been engaged, as well as Mrs Pearson for the cooking, and now, with Lily having left to be married, an under-housemaid called Violet. It had meant an increase in Elizabeth's wages.

'She seems quite happy, Miss Bea,' Elizabeth said now. 'She's made friends with the housemaid from No. 8 and goes out with her on her half-days.'

'Good. I'm sure she'll come to like this burrow very much.' Beatrix, her mind certainly not on Violet, was sorting out illustrated letters, rabbits predominating, from the thick envelope she'd received in the post.

'Those are some of your picture letters to the Moore children,' Elizabeth said. 'Don't they want to keep them?'

'Well, if it's anybody's, it's your fault, Elizabeth. You said to me some time ago that these letters were like little books and I've been thinking about it since. I wrote and asked Mrs Moore if the children still had the letters, and if so, would they lend them to me for a time. Here they are and a great surprise too. I would have thought they had been used as candle spills long ago; I wouldn't have been in the least offended. Which shall I choose?'

Laid on the cloth, between the apple marmalade, the butter shells and the muffin dish, was a letter with drawings of a circus horse and a performing bull, another with dogs balancing balls on their noses, a third with mice up to no good in a larder and several letters with Peter Rabbit in his best jacket. Elizabeth looked at them carefully.

'It wouldn't be right not to start with Peter, Miss Bea,' she said. She was smiling involuntarily at the cheerful sketches but then straightened her face as a head-housemaid should. 'Yes, start with Peter; he'll be as much a favourite with young children as he is with me.' She began clearing up in an efficient fashion that declared war on sentiment.

'I'll have to copy it all out again.' Beatrix picked up a Peter Rabbit letter, the one where Peter lost his clothes. 'It'll be no use offering a book to the card people; I wonder who might be interested in publishing it?'

Mr Potter came in at that point, still with the Canon's letter in his hand.

'I am most distressed, Beatrix, I fear the Canon's pretty wife is very ill. He doesn't actually say what is the trouble, just that she's weak and in pain and there's to be an operation in the spring.'

'Let me see it, Papa.' His daughter stood up and took the letter to the window to get the best of the muted daylight filtering through the net curtains. After a minute a slight gurgle escaped her, but she looked perfectly serious when she turned round.

'It says,' she told Mr Potter, ' "Edith wants to paint and we are thinking of Oberammergau in the spring." '

'That certainly relieves my mind. I remember now, one of her watercolours was hung in the Academy last year.' Mr Potter went back to his study.

'It relieves my mind too,' said Beatrix, suddenly cheerful, 'or at least it gives me an idea.' Elizabeth looked at her questioningly, but she didn't elaborate.

The last two weeks of February were warm. March came in like a lamb and by the second week the first of the daffodils, the wild golden lenten lily, were generously scattered over the grass in Crosthwaite Vicarage garden. Hardwicke Rawnsley stood on the terrace above the sloping bank, admiring the picture they made under the blue sky and fat white clouds and composing a poem in their honour.

'Do come in to breakfast, Hardy. Your eggs are getting hard.' Edith, in the negligée with the swansdown on the cuffs, had opened the French window.

The poem floated away in the direction of Borrowdale, a bright bauble disappearing over the lake. Never mind, perhaps it would reach heaven as a prayer of thanksgiving for spring.

'Coming, dear,' he said.

Edith was pouring his coffee as he sat down at the oval table in the large, white-panelled room that overlooked the front drive. 'You've dozens of letters,' she said. 'Why not leave them until after breakfast? Annie Stones will be in this morning.'

'My new amanuensis.' He bowed his head, studying the twenty or so letters piled beside his napkin. 'For what we are about to receive, may the Lord make us truly thankful,' he said. That would cover the letters and Annie Stones as well as his eggs. Edith brought his coffee round the table and he looked up.

'Just allow me to open one or two, my dear, to stimulate the appetite,' he pleaded, sitting down and buttering a piece of toast.

He knew as well as she did that he would open them all before the end of the meal. Edith tried every morning to prevent her snowy cloth and delicate china being submerged beneath scraps of paper that acted like magnets to butter, marmalade, milk, preserved ginger and honey. It meant a clean tablecloth almost every day. He felt very guilty about it but he could never resist the challenge of an unopened letter.

The boiled eggs *were* a little hard, but with the addition of a lump of butter they were perfectly palatable. His hand strayed towards his post.

'What are your plans today, Hardy?' Edith was peeling an apple with a silver fruit knife, the rosy peel flowing in a graceful, unbroken twist onto her plate.

'I must go and see Herbert Maryon at the Industrial Arts workshop to see how they are getting on with the brass tablet for the Duke of Westminster's memorial,' he told her, and for a moment was again overcome with sorrow for the loss of his old friend. He was surprised to find, when the spring sunshine had restored him, that he had the first envelope in his hand already slit with the butter knife.

It was an appeal, after some compliments about his 'delightful account of Keswick in the *Standard*', for recommendations of cheap boarding houses which provided good food and clean beds. Well, that would be something for little Annie to start on, though perhaps, on second thoughts, he ought to reply to it himself to soften the refusal. The second letter made him laugh.

'D'you remember, Edith, the woman who wanted to come and live with us a year or so ago? Well, she's trying again. Just listen to this. "The Lake hills constantly call me, my love for them fuelled by your inspiring descriptions of the countryside around Keswick. If I could be taken *sub rosa* as a paying guest," – that's the phrase I recognise but I think she's used a different name – "you would find I am well-read and can arrange flowers with great delicacy. I am not strong, being subject to faintness and nervous debility, but I give no trouble and will be content with my books and Nature." I wonder what little Annie will make of that?'

'It's what I make of it that disturbs me, Hardy.' Edith dipped her fingers in a shallow fingerbowl and wiped them delicately on her napkin. 'Your constant eulogies about the Lake District are going to bring a stream of unsuitable people to live here who will end up by turning it into the surburbia that is their spiritual home. Are there no interesting letters?'

'There's one from Mrs Rylands confirming the driving tour we are to take together in May, and suggesting we go to Oberammergau by way of Zurich, Landech and Fuessen. Oh, and a pleasant surprise, a letter from Beatrix Potter with a sketch enclosed.'

Hardwicke passed the sketch to Edith, noting it was of a small rabbit in bed being dosed by a motherly rabbit figure, and settled down to read the letter with close attention.

*Dear Canon Rawnsley,*
*Some time ago you kindly offered your assistance, should*
*I need it, in the pursuit of a publisher for any of my work.*

*I have put together a little book for young children, 'The Tale of Peter Rabbit and Mr McGregor's Garden,' based on a letter I wrote to a young child a few years ago, and am wondering where to send it with a view to publication.*

*I enclose the text of the book, also a copy of the coloured frontispiece. Other illustrations are in black and white. It may not prove to be to any publisher's taste, but as it seems to please young children it should be worth pushing it a bit.*

*I would appreciate your advice.*
*Yours very sincerely,*
*H. B. Potter*

'But this is a quite delightful painting, rather in the style of Walter Crane,' Edith suddenly exclaimed, her face animated and flushed. 'I had no idea that your little Beatrix was a real artist; I thought she just dabbled in watercolours to pass the time. What does she want you to do?'

'How d'you know she wants me to do anything?' her husband enquired.

'Because everyone who writes to you wants you to do something, and the vexing thing is you usually do it,' Edith said impatiently.

'She's written a children's book and wants me to help her find a publisher.'

'Well, if all the pictures are as good as this, the expression, the fine detail, you simply must help her get it published.'

Hardwicke forebore to mention that Edith had changed sides. 'I don't think my publisher does any children's books,' he said doubtfully.

'You'll have an idea, Hardy, you always do. You must! I'll tell you something I haven't mentioned before. Last year, when we visited the Potters at Lingholm, I learned how difficult your Beatrix finds life with her extraordinary mother. You and Beatrix were somewhere in the grounds looking for fungi and I was sitting with Mrs Potter on that long terrace that overlooks the lake whilst little Noel played with a kitten. She was doing her usual impersonation of the Queen, black dress and white lace cap, and she said to me, her eyes on her hands and apropos of absolutely nothing, "What a handsome man your husband is." I agreed, and she went on, "Of course Beatrix is very susceptible to almost all men, but particularly to those who are handsome. I keep her with

72

me as much as I can because of this – men do so hate being pursued by plain women – but your husband is so saintly he probably won't even notice and I'm sure you will understand." I hadn't the slightest idea what to say to this monstrous accusation. Poor Beatrix is not in the least plain and so shy she would no more think of running after a man than she would think of flying. I was so furious that when Noel pulled the kitten's tail I smacked him.'

'Why didn't you tell me at the time?'

Edith looked a little confused. 'I suppose there were complicated reasons. For one, Beatrix would not have thanked me for making you pity her. A woman hates to be pitied.'

Harwicke looked at her with appreciation, full of loving amusement. She had wondered if he might have looked at Beatrix with new eyes, softening towards her as he did towards all unhappy creatures. He might have too.

'I can guess the other reason, my love,' he said. 'You have no need to worry. You are right in one thing though, I hadn't realised all she has to contend with. She will have my very best endeavours to get her book published.'

It was almost the end of March, with cold winds snapping the stems of the cultivated daffodils in Bolton Gardens, so their heads hung like flags at half-mast, when Elizabeth received a letter. She hadn't known the handwriting, but the Liverpool postmark made her open it quickly.

Dorothy was very ill, her husband said, and asking for Elizabeth.

Miss Beatrix was most concerned when Elizabeth took her the letter. 'You must send a telegram to say you are coming and leave as soon as you can. Papa can look up the train times for you in his *Bradshaw*,' she said. 'We'll manage here; Betty Anderton can do most of your work and I'll do the rest.'

For a moment Elizabeth had a funny feeling. Was going up a bit in the world going to mean that she was no longer irreplaceable?

Miss Bea seemed to catch her thought. 'We shall be most relieved to see you back, but don't hurry. Do all you can for your sister.' To Elizabeth's intense surprise, Miss Beatrix took her hand and pressed it before pushing her off upstairs to pack.

The best train was early the following morning which meant she was still there to see Fred that evening. He was already in the kitchen reading his paper when she came down from finishing the dining-room. The others had gone out.

'What would you like, Fred? A rarebit suit you?' She'd tell him in a bit, when they'd eased into their usual companionship. He seemed stiff, somehow.

'Champion, Lizzie. Cup o'tea would go down a treat, too.'

She bustled about, making toast and grating cheese and giving him a glance now and then. He seemed intent on his paper.

'It sez here,' he said suddenly, 'that British troops in South Africa are "slaking their brutal instincts in furious excesses on shrieking women and desolated homesteads." '

'Who says so?' Elizabeth was pouring boiling water from the kettle into the teapot.

'*Reynold's Weekly* is reporting what 'er Majesty's Opposition is speechifying about.'

'That's not true,' she said indignantly. '*The Times* says the British Army found it impossible to leave the Boer wives and children defenceless in their homesteads at the mercy of their Kaffir servants. That's why they took them into camps.'

'So you don't think the army is "the uneducated hireling of a callous aristocracy which has sold itself to the Hebrew financiers"?'

'Course not. The Boers wanted everything for themselves and they should learn to share. They're not so bad, though. There was a tale in *The Times* about a small company of riflemen being captured by a Boer commando. They were just turned loose again, though without rifles or trousers. Better that than an unknown grave in the vastness of the veldt.' She was quoting *The Times* and she wished she hadn't mentioned graves.

'Fred . . .' she began, handing him his tea and as delicious a Welsh rarebit as human hands could devise, 'my sister . . .'

He didn't hear. 'I'm glad you feel like that about it, Lizzie, because I've joined up as a volunteer.'

She sat down, because her knees would no longer hold her, and took off her cap. 'Oh Fred! What d'you mean by going and doing a thing like that? What are the police force thinking of to let you?' She could feel the tears at the back of her throat and swallowed angrily.

'As for the police force, we've got dispensation if we want to join up. As to why, that's another thing. I want to see more of the world and the money's not so bad. It won't be forever, Lizzie. I'll write, promise, and they say it'll be over in eighteen months. It's not as though I can get any further in the force; they don't promote uneducated bumpkins like me to anything over sergeant. Say you understand, Lizzie. I want us to part friends.'

Friends! Elizabeth swallowed again. She understood all right and half of it was her own fault. If she'd agreed to live with him in Hampstead this would never have happened, but as it was he felt trapped, with a wife, two sisters and a mistress, and wanted to get out. He was sitting slumped in his chair, as handsome as ever but looking slightly sullen, ready to justify his actions from here to kingdom come. There was nothing for it; to preserve her self-respect she'd have to be Noble. She didn't want to be Noble, she wanted to lie on the floor and drum with her heels and moan through clenched teeth. She poured herself a cup of tea.

'Yes, of course I understand, Fred,' she said. 'Only wish I could come with you. It's a pity they don't take head-housemaids, all ready with brush and dustpan to clear up after the army's finished making a mess. We'd show you how to do it properly.'

Fred sat up and his eyes began to sparkle. 'You are a one, Lizzie. There's no one like you. When I come back I'll have a bit of the ready and we'll go off together round the world. How would that be?'

Something to think about during the long days and grey nights that stretched ahead. 'Grand, Fred. I'll have me sola topee and me elephant gun ready packed for when I next see you.'

Fred finished his rarebit and drained his cup. 'Come and sit on my knee on the rocking-chair!'

So Elizabeth never did tell him about Dorothy.

# CHAPTER NINE

—— • ——

Queen Victoria died at Osborne on 22nd January 1901. The arrangements necessary to bring her body reverently and ceremonially to London and then on to Windsor had already been planned, in all their fine detail, by the Queen herself. She had decided that the draped coffin should be borne on a gun carriage drawn by six white Flemish horses, first from Osborne House to Trinity Pier at Cowes for embarkation, then by train to London where there would be a service in St Paul's Cathedral. After that, the funeral procession would move on to Paddington and entrain to Windsor for a final service in St George's Chapel. The interment, naturally, would be in the Frogmore Mausoleum. She had even arranged the processional placing, deciding that the Prince of Wales should walk with his cousin the Kaiser on his right.

What the late Queen had not taken into consideration was the stamina of the various clergy who would be required to follow the cortège on this long journey. Hardwicke Rawnsley, sitting next to Dr Diggle in St George's Chapel, where the coffin was overdue owing to a slight miscalculation, was becoming a little anxious about his colleague. It behoved him to do something for him for reasons of pure humanity, setting aside the fact that the man had been named as the next Bishop of Carlisle. He fished about in his tail-coat pocket, knocking his hat off his knee in the process, and found what he was looking for at last.

'Could I offer you a butterscotch?' he whispered in the Doctor's ear. He usually carried them for children, but the man was quite pale and drawn behind that bushy beard and he'd always understood that sugar had a reviving effect.

The sweetmeat was accepted without demur and its annihilation begun forthwith. Dr Diggle relaxed and looked more human.

'You've shaved my life,' he said out of the corner of his mouth, his cheek bulging. 'I've been following thish coffin for two daysh and not one deshent meal have I had in all that time!'

'Not much longer now,' Hardwicke said encouragingly. The poor fellow was really very low. 'And though the occasion is undoubtedly sad, it is a happy thought, is it not, that the Queen is shortly to join her beloved Albert?' He didn't think originality was appropriate to the situation in which they found themselves.

They bemoaned the passing of the Victorian era and worried about the approaching Edwardian age together, but still the cortège did not arrive. Dr Diggle moved on to plain gossip.

'Rawnsley, isn't it? Yes, I thought so. Crosthwaite, near Keswick. I know you have a soft spot for Borrowdale, you write about it often enough. You might like to know that some of the Derwentwater shore is coming up for sale shortly. It's quite a pleasant spot and if it's sold in building lots I might be interested in one of them. A holiday villa, you know. M'wife would like it. Bramblehow I think it's called, something like that. You'll know it, of course.'

Hardwicke saw his future Bishop through a red mist of rage. He felt like Jehu and wanted to drive a chariot furiously round and round the walls of St George's Chapel. If not even the Church saw the need to protect natural beauty, what a task he and the National Trust had ahead of them! The lovely Brandelhow oak woods, pale green in spring and gold in autumn, carpeted with emerald mosses, holding calm airs even as waves crashed on the shore and upper branches creaked in the wind. He could smell the earthy scent of them after rain, when sunlight dappled the mosses, even through the mothballs of the chapel. He'd saved them once from the axe of the railway navvy; now it was all to do again. He turned to Dr Diggle, intending to find out more, only to be hushed with an urgent hand on his sleeve. The congregation was stirring and rising. Hardwicke implored heaven for help and with a great effort of will brought his mind back to the business in hand. He kept it there until his late sovereign was on her way to join her consort.

By then, of course, Dr Diggle had lost his horns and tail and was merely an anxious elderly gentleman in need of a lavatory. Fortunately Windsor station catered for his requirements. Hardwicke saw him into a fly at Paddington and meditated, an obstacle in the path of would-be passengers, on his next move.

Ordinarily in this sort of crisis he would have gone straight to the National Trust office and begun organising an appeal to enable the Trust to buy Brandelhow woods: confirmation of the sale first, then arrangements for speeches, articles, interviews with influential people, bishops, Members of Parliament. He felt a surge of energy lift him up on his toes at the thought. Today, though, the office would be shut; not even the faithful Harriet Yorke would have thought it suitable to work at a time of national mourning. He would have to stay over and do that tomorrow instead of catching the night train north as he'd planned. Which left him with some unexpected free time. He'd telegraph Edith and then go and see Beatrix Potter with his latest idea for getting her *Peter Rabbit* published.

No. 2, like the other houses in Bolton Gardens, had all the blinds down in the front windows and looked like a fortress under siege. Hardwicke, who never allowed mere appearances to deter him, pulled strongly on the door bell. The door was opened by a fresh-faced maid whom he'd not seen on his previous visits. She informed him, in an accent that brought a vivid picture of the Border hills, that the Mistress was not receiving callers today.

'No, of course she isn't,' he said, marching firmly into the hall so the maid had to fall back or be run over. 'This is no day for visitors and I am not one of them. I'm Canon Rawnsley, a friend of the family, come to see Miss Beatrix.' He looked more closely at the maid and saw she was red-eyed, as though she had been crying. Surely the death of the Queen would not have touched her so deeply? 'What's your name, my dear?'

'Betty Anderton, sir.'

'Run along Betty and tell Miss Beatrix. I'll wait here.'

He wondered, pacing up and down the hall between the unbrella stand and the castor-oil plant, if he was perhaps being a little forceful. Edith was always telling him he shouldn't consider other people's houses as his own, walking in without knocking, as he always did in Keswick where no doors were locked, and then banging the door behind him and giving a shout so everyone knew at once who had arrived. It saved such a lot of valuable time. No, of course he was right to come. What was it Kipling had said in that poem? 'If you can fill the unforgiving minute,/ With sixty second's worth of distance run.' But there was no feeling of welcome here. Over the years he'd had much experience as to whether houses were welcoming or not and this one felt secretive, deeply secretive. And there was something else as well. By heaven, yes, that was it. Like St George's Chapel, it smelt of mothballs and death.

Betty came down looking, if possible, more mournful than before. 'I'll take you up, sir,' she said.

The stairs took their usual toll and Hardwicke had dropped back by the time they reached the fourth floor. It puzzled him to see Betty hesitate quite perceptibly before opening the door of the old nursery but he found the reason when he got within earshot. Someone was weeping. Betty announced him over the sound of a nose being vigorously blown.

Beatrix came forward to meet him. She was wearing a severe costume with a wide leather belt and was pale and tight-lipped, her hair in wisps, but it was Elizabeth, sitting at the table still in her brown morning uniform and looking at him woefully behind her handkerchief, who had been crying.

Hardwicke didn't believe in beating about the bush. 'Whatever is the trouble?' he asked.

'Peter Rabbit died this morning,' Beatrix said. 'Poor Elizabeth feels it dreadfully because she looked after him a lot of the time and he was very fond of her. I'm afraid it was old age, he was nine years old. He didn't want to go out to his hutch last night. He kicked and bit when I tried to take him, which he never did because he had beautiful manners. So I let him stay here in his box and when I came in this morning he was dead.'

'The worst of it is,' Elizabeth snuffled, 'that now the mice feel they've won. They've been waiting to take over as Lords of the Nursery and now they have.' She stared at the cage where three mice were certainly showing signs of high excitement, running round in circles and ringing the little bell above the swing so there was a perpetual chime from that corner of the room.

Hardwicke saw a large tear trickle past Elizabeth's little *retroussé* nose. Her spirits were certainly at a very low ebb, but dealing with death was part of his life. He applied himself to finding healing words for the bereaved.

'No wonder you are suffering from some distress of mind,' he said, addressing his audience impartially as Betty was still hovering by the door. 'But if ever there was a rabbit who had a satisfying and creative life, then it was Peter. Without him, a sweet-natured animal who would act as a model without complaint for hours together, who provided inspiration for what I believe is going to be a famous book, all your lives would have been the poorer. Nature will not be gainsayed, his life-span had been run, but through the brush of a creative artist his memory will always remain green. Have arrangements been made for the burial?'

This practical question seemed to bring them all to themselves. Hardwicke had noticed before that practical matters were a help when comforting those in grief. Beatrix said yes, that had been attended to, Elizabeth gave her nose a final blow and got up to go, and Betty enquired if Miss Beatrix wanted anything.

'If it's not too much trouble,' said Hardwicke plaintively, 'a cup of tea would be much appreciated. I have had nothing since breakfast.'

He was relieved to find that the sympathetic flurry produced by this statement quite cleared the air.

When the maids had gone, Beatrix settled them both by the fire. 'Don't worry about the mice,' she said. 'I gave them hemp seed this morning by mistake because I was upset about Peter. They probably think they're Lords of the World, never mind the nursery.'

'It's a moot point as to whether animals can communicate, and if so what they say to each other.' Hardwicke was prepared to follow whatever leads presented themselves.

'Elizabeth is convinced that the most awful feuds go on in here, but I don't think Peter was involved,' Beatrix said, even more gruffly than usual. 'The reason he was such a good model was that he was too lazy to move once I had fixed him in a pose, he usually just went to sleep. As for my *Peter Rabbit* book becoming famous, that seems most unlikely. Have you heard from any publishers lately?'

'I am still hopeful of Warnes,' Hardwicke replied. 'They liked the general idea of the book but had reservations on details. A mention was made of children preferring rhymes to plain text.'

'Yes, I had gathered that. Also that they don't like the small size I have stipulated for the book and dislike the black and white illustrations. Mr Warne puts me in mind of *Pinafore*. "His bosom should heave and his heart should glow,/And his fist be ever ready for a knock-down blow." There don't seem to be grounds for agreement there.'

From the firm look of Beatrix's mouth, Hardwicke concluded that any concessions would have to come from Warnes. He repressed a sigh and wished the tea would arrive. The path of a go-between was never strewn with roses but this particular path had proved to lead through thorns from the first. Still, Edith had set him the task. The time had come to make his suggestion.

'With your agreement,' he said tentatively, 'I could perhaps turn your prose story into rhyme. I have had some practice in that direction.'

To his relief, Beatrix smiled her wide smile and her eyes crinkled with amusement. 'So I believe. *Punch* mentions it occasionally. Go ahead if it amuses you,' she said. 'As far as I am concerned, I have decided to publish the book myself. I'm even more determined to do so since this morning, because the book will be a memorial to poor old Peter, but at least that way I can produce it in the form I consider most suitable for children, the right size and the right price. I have taken the advice of a friend who knows about printers and approached Strangeways & Sons of Tower Street. I'm having the coloured frontispiece printed in the new three-colour process by Hentschel of Fleet Street. I can just about pay for the publication from what I've earned this year designing cards, so you could look on it as a form of investment.'

Well! So much for Beatrix being an object of pity. Still, admirable as it sounded, publishing one's own work never made any money – his own efforts in that direction had proved that – and money and independence were the object of this exercise. He'd have to continue to roll the stone up the hill.

'We'll both work on it, then,' he said largely. He could hear teacups rattling as a tray was carried up the stairs.

Elizabeth had to wait for the kettle to boil again for Mrs Potter's tea. She stood by the kitchen fire, watching steam trickle out of the spout. It reminded her of Fred, the way he used to smoke cigarettes. She'd had three letters from him since he'd gone to South Africa, all of them uninformative. Of course there was censorship, he couldn't say where he was or what was happening, but all he had said was that he was in good health and he liked the climate and the country, particularly the fruit-growing region round the Cape. He'd climbed Table Mountain too and said the wide horizons made him realise the smallness of England. He sent her his best love. Those letters had made her feel distinctly uneasy. Still, *The Times* said the war was all but over now.

She'd written back of course, to an anonymous Army number. She'd told him about Dorothy's death and how she'd had to stay in Liverpool for three weeks to sort out her effects, so the springcleaning at No. 2 had been two weeks late, though he wouldn't realise how extraordinary a break that was in the routine of the year. She hadn't told him how she felt at losing the last relation she had in the world, the Isle of Man lot not counting because she'd never met them, as she wasn't sure he'd understand. Fred understood you were sad or upset by the way you kissed, by the feel of your body under his fingers. Words to him were something to convey plain facts. Dorothy had always been a refuge in times of trouble who would admonish but at the same time protect. Now she was gone Elizabeth felt like a ship without a rudder; you couldn't count Fred, he was a rudderless ship himself at the moment. She saw the kettle was boiling over onto Norah's rag rug.

Mrs Potter was sitting in her chair by the desk as usual, but was not employed in writing notes; she was just sitting, staring at her hands in the half-light of waning day and drawn blinds. She looked desolate, though it took Elizabeth a moment to understand why. When she did, she felt sorry for her. Mrs Potter was grieving, of course, for the death of the Queen. Not, or probably not, because she had been extraordinarily fond of her, but because she had modelled her life on the life of her sovereign and now was left behind – all washed up as Fred would have said. Poor old geezer, as he also would have said, now what would she do?

'I'll draw the curtains, shall I Madam?' She didn't expect an answer and got none. Mrs Potter allowed her to put down the tray, light the gas and draw the green velvet curtains across the windows before she spoke.

'I hope that rabbit has been put on the rubbish dump by now,' she said in her hard, deep voice. 'If not, it will start to smell.'

Elizabeth's feelings did a quick about-turn. How could she have felt sorry for the old besom?

'I want to see Canon Rawnsley. Would you tell him?' Mrs Potter picked up the teapot dismissively.

Elizabeth shut the drawing-room door behind her with exaggerated care to prevent herself giving it a ferocious bang. She then stood with her back to it and directed a silent scream at the ceiling. Now she'd have to wait around until the Canon came downstairs, because climb nearly to the top of the house again to summon him she would not. Let them finish their conversation in peace. Funerals took it out of you, as she knew to her cost, and he needed his tea and a rest, and Miss Beatrix, even if she didn't realise it, needed his company, someone reliable to talk to, a prop like her Dorothy. It wasn't so much Peter Rabbit she was grieving for, she realised, though the Canon had set her right there, it was Dorothy. Like Mother used to say, the dead bring the dead. She sat down on the stairs and blew her nose again.

By the time she heard the Canon coming down she'd

82

recovered. She was going out tonight to the Tivoli with Mrs Pearson, who wanted to hear someone called Phoebe Mercer sing, supposed to be a splendid contralto. It was time she pulled herself together. She greeted the Canon cheerfully.

'Mrs Potter said she would appreciate it if you would have a word with her in the drawing-room, sir,' she compromised.

When she'd popped him in she didn't quite shut the door and stayed where she was. Really, she told herself, you should have given up listening at doors at your age. She still stayed where she was.

Courtesies over, the Canon opened the batting.

'Apart from the pleasure of your company, I am delighted to have the opportunity of seeing you today, Madam. I have a most important request to make.'

He's buttering her up, Elizabeth thought. He must be collecting again. She liked the Canon, but it wasn't difficult to follow his mind.

'I am starting an appeal on behalf of the National Trust for money to save a very beautiful stretch of Derwentwater shore from being sold as housing lots. Your daughter has promised to donate some of the profits from her little book when it is published. Can I hope that you too will contribute something to save this fragile countryside, which you must know well from your holidays at Lingholm?'

'No, Canon Rawnsley, you cannot hope that I will contribute.' Mrs Potter sounded peevish. 'In my opinion the countryside is greatly improved by the civilising effect of superior housing and well-kept gardens. Beatrix is a fool, but then she always was a fool, to throw her money away on grass and stones and mud that won't pay her any interest. It was about her book that I wished to speak to you. How are you getting on in your efforts to get it published?'

Elizabeth heard Tom clattering buckets down in the kitchen and shot downstairs to send him round the corner to bring the Canon a cab. The poor man was going to need every comfort he could get. When she got back he had just finished telling Mrs Potter of his unavailing efforts with all publishers but Warnes, who he felt might in the end take the book.

'Yes, yes,' said Mrs Potter impatiently. 'But that's not what I want at all. Publishing a book herself is quite acceptable, I can tell my friends about it and they might even be interested to take a copy. But actually going into trade, having dealings with a publisher and making money from what is nothing but a pastime, is quite disreputable and not to be countenanced. In her position Beatrix has no need of money. I want you to see to it that no publisher takes the book. She'll never make the effort to sell it herself, she's too lazy. Can I rely on you?'

The Canon had tipped his chair back, because Elizabeth heard the front legs hit the floor with a thwack as it came forward. 'But . . . but . . .' He was stuttering with rage. She heard him get up and walk towards the window.

'Mrs Potter,' he said at last, 'the most reputable people have written and sold books. Dickens, Carlyle, Stevenson, Ruskin, to name a few. You can't call any of them disreputable.'

Oh dear, thought Elizabeth. He's going to be caught out now. I hope Tom has got that cab.

'Personally I read very little except the Bible,' Mrs Potter replied in scathing tones, 'but by reputation I understand Dickens was nothing but a journalist, Carlyle one of these new socialists, Stevenson a failed lawyer and as for Ruskin . . .' She gave the name a peculiar emphasis, as though biting into a lemon. 'You must realise Sir John Millais and his wife were family friends. Lady Millais told me all about Ruskin. He is not a man I care to discuss.'

Properly rolled up, horse and foot, Elizabeth decided. He should have remembered that Lady Millais had been Ruskin's wife, his little Effie, before she ran away with Millais and got the marriage annulled as being unconsummated. Elizabeth giggled as she decided she'd heard enough and moved out of earshot. Effie had found satisfaction later. That much had been obvious when she came with Sir John to Dalguise House in Perthshire, where the Potters always used to take their summer holiday. Also in her later life Lady Millais had been anything but little. When Mr Potter had taken their photographs in the garden, with the day's salmon catch in the foreground, Lady Millais had fitted so snugly into the folding chair she had chosen that she had been unable to get up without bringing it with her. It had been Elizabeth who had had to perform the delicate extraction.

The Canon emerged from the drawing-room muttering to himself. Elizabeth caught the words 'that woman is impossible' as she brought him his coat. In spite of his well-valeted appearance, he looked downcast and forlorn.

'Never mind sir,' said Elizabeth, not specifying what he hadn't to mind. 'Tom has got a cab for you and it's a nice evening.'

The Canon looked at her sternly and then his mouth twitched, finally relaxing into a smile. 'It would seem,' he said, 'that the good Lord has seen to it that both of us should find a comforter on a day of many discomforts.'

# CHAPTER TEN

Printing of the first two hundred copies of *The Tale of Peter Rabbit* for private publication, at the cost of £11, went ahead without complication. The books were ready in time for Christmas. They were bound in a greyish-green board and on the front was a drawing of four rabbits with ribbons round their necks sitting between the title and the name of the author. The frontispiece was the only coloured illustration.

Several boxes of new books stored under the cages quite changed the atmosphere in the old nursery. There was a feeling of excitement in the air, as though the books brought with them the ideas and aspirations of a new century. It couldn't be contained; the house was like a stagnant pool stirred by the bubbling of a fresh spring. Beatrix went from one task to another with a prickly feeling of purpose and noticed in her mirror that her eyes were brighter and she had more colour. It wasn't just the book that had caused this, she decided, though it was a lovely little book and did Peter Rabbit more than justice, but also the unexpected interest and acclaim it brought.

'Oh, Elizabeth,' she said one morning, 'you'll be interested to hear that Dr Conan Doyle has bought a copy of *Peter Rabbit* for his children. He read it himself and because of his good opinion of the story and the words has commended it to his friends.'

'Oh Miss Bea!' Elizabeth was quite overcome by the thought of praise from such a great man; her favourite book was *The Speckled Band*. 'Now your name will be made.'

Beatrix laughed. 'I'm not so sure about that,' she replied, 'but I'm running out of copies. We'll need a reprint.'

Family reaction was, not unexpectedly, cautious. Bertram was home for Christmas and, though more cheerful than usual, he damned the drawings with faint praise.

'Jolly good show, old girl. They're really quite good, though old Mr McGregor looks a bit of a gargoyle. I like the text though. Father rabbit having an accident in Mr McGregor's garden and being put in a pie is a masterly piece of sinister understatement.'

Mr Potter, on being presented with a copy one morning, had looked at it as if he had been given something for which he had no possible use, like a lady's parasol.

'Just a memento, Papa,' Beatrix had said encouragingly. 'You might even come to be quite proud of it in time.'

'You know I like your drawings, Beatrix,' he replied. 'Haven't I always said so? But I didn't realise they might lead to something *commercial*.'

'Don't worry, Papa.' Beatrix had been amused. 'I can assure you that there will be a loss, not a profit, from this particular venture.'

Mrs Potter was neither asked for, nor gave, her opinion on the book.

A sounder commercial proposition arrived the following day in the form of a letter.

'That's Canon Rawnsley's writing, I'd know it anywhere,' Mr Potter said as he watched Beatrix slit open a thick envelope Elizabeth had just brought in.

Beatrix let her coffee go cold as she deciphered the scrawl. 'I sent a copy of *Peter Rabbit* to the Canon,' she said at last, 'and he has approached Frederick Warne again with the suggestion that the text should be turned into rhyme in his own inimitable fashion. The publisher seems to have shown renewed interest. His letter is enclosed.'

'Is Rawnsley going to see him about it for you?' her father asked.

'The Canon is unable to be in London at the moment, being engaged in the organisation of bonfires to celebrate King Edward's coronation, and suggests I make an appointment to see the publisher myself. He also suggests I take a member of the family with me for support. In case I once more get rejected, I suppose, and feel faint.'

To Beatrix's dismay her father took her seriously. 'A very sensible suggestion on the Canon's part,' he said, extracting his table-napkin from its anchorage round his waistcoat button and dabbing his mouth and chin. 'Let me know when you've made the appointment and I'll come with you. A legal mind is what you require for negotiating any agreement you may reach with Warnes.' He departed for his study, leaving behind a stunned silence.

'A legal mind?' Bertram said incredulously. 'To the best of my knowledge, Barrister-at-Law though he calls himself, he has never accepted a brief in his life. I don't believe he even remembers the first principles. Will you take him?'

'I've no option,' Beatrix said. 'Mama's right, I have no sense. I should never have read that bit aloud. For the first time in my life I would prefer to brave a lion's den on my own, a remarkable admission for a nervous person like myself, but now Papa will have to come. I think I must mention to Warnes that I shall be bringing him.'

'Has the Canon sent you his versification of *Peter*?' Bertram asked.

Beatrix shook the envelope and a small hand-made booklet fell out, bound with a black ribbon. She began to read it, then started to laugh.

'Oh no,' she said. 'He's made poor Peter into a moral tale, which is most provoking. Listen to this verse! "And rabbits, like children, who run very quick/After eating too largely are sure to feel sick . . ." '

'He's left out the bit about the pie,' said Bertram, reading over Beatrix's shoulder.

'This again is what comes of not thinking. I should have realised that with the success of his *Moral Rhymes for the Young* it was inevitable Peter would be made a *bad example*. Do you think Warnes will like it?'

'Cripes, I should hope not. Look at this bit. "Peter the naughty, I grieve to relate,/To the garden of McGregor went straight." It doesn't even scan. I could set it to music though. How about singing it to "Hold your hand out, you naughty boy"?'

Beatrix's indignation dissolved into mirth as she joined with Bertram in trying to sing the Canon's rhymes to the music-hall tune. They were suddenly nursery companions once more, a united front.

'It'll be all right, Bea,' Bertram said. 'Not even Warnes would use something like that. Tell you what, though, it's cheered me up and I'll tell you a secret on the strength of it. I'm thinking of buying a farm, somewhere on the Tweed near the Eildon Hills. I'm giving up painting. Having this gillie tagging along behind me quite takes away any pleasure I have in capturing a view, and besides, it's getting me nowhere. Now a farm would be different, it has a future.'

'What gillie tagging along behind you?' Beatrix was astonished.

'Didn't you know? No, I suppose Papa would consider it his duty to keep such sordid matters from his womenfolk. He engaged a man to keep an eye on my drinking, to dissuade me, forcibly if necessary, from entering such dens of iniquity as inns or beer houses when I go to Scotland to paint. He is a shambling youth who carries the easel and I maintain the fiction that he's a gillie for the look of the thing and call him William to annoy him as his name is Alfred. If I have a farm he'll have to spread the muck and serve him right.'

'Papa did that! That's infamous, Bertram.'

'It's not as bad as having my allowance stopped and having to live at home all the time, which was the alternative. I've got to get away for good, I can't stand them both laying down the law as to what I should and should not do, then looking at me with that "this hurts us more than it does you" expression. I shall be a farmer, I've made up my mind.'

'At least they can't say that's trade, not if you call yourself a gentleman farmer. When you consider that we all live on the money Grandfather Potter and Grandfather Leech made in the cotton trade, it's rather rich that the Aged Ps should have this aversion to anything with the faintest whiff of commerce about it. To their way of thinking, trade is a dirty business fit only for the lower classes; the English middle class should only invest, wearing kid gloves of course. You'll be all right. Being a gentleman farmer is a back way into the landed gentry class, quite acceptable.'

'It's not like you to sound so bitter, Bea.' Bertram was surprised.

'Isn't it? Then consider this. They'll let you go, and I'll be glad for you. But what about me? If I ever get away, it'll be a miracle.'

Beatrix wrote to the firm of Frederick Warne to secure an appointment. She mentioned that she would be bringing her father with her and they were not to worry if he should seem a little difficult. Elderly gentlemen, she told them, were often provoking. A date was agreed.

The office in Bedford Street, Covent Garden, was not impressive in the grey afternoon light of a December day, though Beatrix didn't think it deserved the disparaging sniff her father gave when Beckett had driven off with instructions to return in half an hour.

'Are you sure you want to go through with this, Beatrix? It looks rather shabby and down-at-heel.'

The expression on his face was a mixture of outrage and apprehension. It reminded her of the time she had taken him for a row on Windermere in a very small boat and he had been obliged to outride the swell from one of the lake's launches. She suppressed a bubble of mirth and wished she wasn't always subject to a fit of giggles at moments of importance in her life.

'Come along, Papa,' she said.

The representative of the firm who greeted them seemed very gentlemanly; even Papa couldn't object to the well-cut suit, the impeccable silk tie with gold tie-pin and the small carnation worn in his lapel. Beatrix, who had been impatient at the time, was suddenly grateful to Elizabeth for fussing around her before they left, making sure her hat was straight, her gloves a pair and her petticoat well out of sight. He was fairly young too, about her own age, with shy brown eyes and a very gentle smile under a rather bushy moustache. The desire to giggle, she found, had faded.

This paragon of good tailoring introduced himself as Norman Warne, the youngest of the three sons of Frederick Warne, now retired. He seated his visitors in his office and expressed his admiration for *The Tale of Peter Rabbit* and his opinion that, with some alterations, the firm would be interested in publishing the book. He then fell silent and started fiddling with the pen sitting on the blotter on the table before him. Beatrix realised he was as nervous as herself and felt like giggling again. At this rate they'd never get down to brass tacks and would still be sitting here when the office closed.

'What are your terms?' her father demanded. He hadn't removed his hat, though perhaps that wasn't the custom when discussing business matters, and was sitting bolt upright beside her on the opposite side of the table to Mr Warne. He looked quite terrifyingly aggressive, his side-whiskers, more white than grey now, giving him the appearance of an indignant white-ruffed guinea-pig.

Beatrix saw Mr Warne blink in apprehension and felt obliged to speak herself, though earlier she had quite decided to leave it to her father.

'I would like you to tell us what alterations you want made,' she said quietly, feeling if she didn't treat him carefully, as she would a nervous young squirrel or mouse, he would flee the room.

'We understand that Hentschel of Fleet Street have the blocks for the coloured frontispiece, which is an excellent start,' Mr Warne began, then took a deep breath, perhaps to steady his nerves. 'The firm, that is my brothers and our artists and father, feel that all the illustrations should be in colour.'

' "And so do his sisters and his cousins and his aunts," ' Beatrix murmured to herself, then realised Mr Warne had heard her and blushed deeply.

'Beatrix!' Her father was astounded. 'Apologise to Mr Warne at once.'

'No, no – don't apologise,' Mr Warne exclaimed, evidently horrified at the idea. 'Our family is a bit like that. I'm glad you like *Pinafore*. So do I.'

Beatrix pulled herself together. Really, this was becoming a shambles. 'I've explained before that a good many of my subjects are drab in colour, rabbit-brown and green. Also that I don't want the book to cost more than one shilling, or just over, so that small children can afford to buy it. Coloured illustrations throughout would make it too expensive,' she told him.

'Don't know what you're worrying about,' her father growled. 'As long as the parents can buy it, what's the difference?'

'I think I can see what Miss Potter means,' Mr Warne replied courageously. 'A book you choose yourself is always more important than one that is chosen for you.' He turned to Beatrix. 'We may be able to get over the extra cost, especially if we cut the number of pictures down to thirty-two and sell enough copies. And I rather think we'll sell enough copies if you agree to colour the pictures. You could put in points of colour in contrast to the browns, like the robin's breast and the carrots.' He smiled his gentle smile at Beatrix.

Beatrix looked back at him with a solemn face. 'There's still the question of the text.'

'Well, I'm afraid I must be firm about this. Canon Rawnsley's rhymes simply will not do. I have this feeling, I don't know where I get it from, that moral precepts are not popular with children. We – all the sisters and the cousins and the aunts . . .' He smiled again at Beatrix who this time, in her relief at the demise of the rhymes, smiled back, '. . . would prefer the original text. I like the bit where the sparrows implore Peter to exert himself.'

'Nothing wrong with moral precepts. Children need them

drilled into their silly heads,' her father growled. 'Parents are too soft with them these days. My opinion is that the Canon is right.'

'I think, sir, that your daughter's book makes the point without labouring it. A very pleasant change, if I may say so, from books like *Struwwelpeter*. There is one thing, Miss Potter, that I'd like to mention.'

'What is that?' asked Beatrix. He wanted a larger book. She wasn't going to stand for that, she was determined.

Mr Warne looked disconcerted by her sharp tone. 'I hesitate a little to ask you, in case I am wide of the mark, but would I be right in thinking your picture of Peter by the locked door in the garden wall is a parody of Anna Lea Merritt's *Love Locked Out*? The one where a naked boy, presumably Cupid, is leaning against a door in much the same attitude as Peter?'

Beatrix was astonished. 'I never thought anyone would see that,' she said. 'It was just a private joke between myself and Peter Rabbit. After all, he is without clothes too.'

'D'you mean to say, Beatrix, that you copied that shameless nude in the Royal Academy? Well, all I can say is, you'd better not tell your mother! On second thoughts you'd better take it out altogether; other people might see the connection.'

Papa now had the fidgets, as he always did when anything even faintly immoral was discussed.

'Oh no, you mustn't do that,' said Mr Warne quickly, then looked apprehensive in case he'd been too adamant. 'What I mean is, all the rabbit drawings are perfect, though some of the figures . . . I think we're going too fast. Would it be agreeable to you if we did some costings, and when we've worked out a price for the book that includes the cost of coloured illustrations and some royalties for Miss Potter, we'll write to you.'

Beatrix felt greatly relieved. The difficulties of controlling her father and this nervous young man were getting too much for her; a headache was beginning to pound behind her left eye.

'Yes, that will be best. Come along, Papa.'

Bertram, packing cheerfully to return to Scotland despite the threat of Alfred alias William hanging over him, was encouraging.

'It'll take a bit, Bea, but I'm sure you'll work it all out with Warnes as you want it. I'd help if I could, but I must get back. Tell you what, you come and stay with me in the spring. May perhaps? Papa and Mama won't want to come, it's not their idea

92

of a spring holiday, and you could help me find a farm. How would that be, eh?'

Beatrix, disappointed that Bertram was leaving again so soon and thinking he was stretching it a bit to say he 'had' to get back, agreed that this was a good plan. But it would be herself and not Bertram who would have the task of persuading their parents that the Border Country in spring was not for them, as well as cajoling them into giving her leave of absence for a week or two. It all depended, probably, on whether Warnes, in the person of Mr Norman Warne, was able to come up with a satisfactory contract and she could feel she was getting somewhere. She had an idea for another little book already.

# CHAPTER ELEVEN

——— • ———

Kelso Station was well outside the town. It stood on the side of a wooded hill with a good view of the rose-red ruins of Kelso Priory and of the magnificent bridge across the Tweed built by James Rennie. Below the bridge, breasting the current, a swan was patrolling an area of reeds where his mate was sitting on her nest.

In the peaceful station yard there were several horse-drawn conveyances of different kinds waiting for the passengers from the Edinburgh train, among them a battered trap under a tree. Its driver was slumped over the reins studying the strong hind-quarters of his piebald mare who was taking a nap whilst she had the opportunity. He lifted his head as the passengers started to emerge.

Bertram Potter was one of the first at the top of the steps, a case in each hand. Beatrix trailed after him, tired to the bone by the long journey.

'There's Patrick,' Bertram said to her, pointing with his chin towards the trap. 'He acts as the Douglases' man of all work and his bark's worse than his bite so give him a chance. Come on Bea, look happy, you've got two weeks holiday in front of you.'

'If I'm not sent for . . .' Beatrix said dubiously, clutching a portmanteau in one hand and preventing her plain straw hat from slipping off her head with the other. 'Where's your paragon of virtue?'

'Follow me.' Bertram strode across the yard, busy now as passengers sorted themselves out, with Beatrix puffing in his wake like a tug-boat pursuing a steam yacht across a crowded harbour. At least that was the simile that came to her mind.

Patrick was well lapped in sacking and tweed, but a bright, assessing eye was apparent under the uncertain brim of his aged hat. 'Yon train took its time,' he greeted them. 'Thirty minutes late.' He rolled his rs alarmingly. 'Dinna hang around. Hup wi' ye.'

Beatrix looked at him doubtfully. He seemed to slur his words a little as well as roll his rs. But it was still early in the day –

it might be old age or bad teeth or both. She mounted as instructed.

The luggage and passengers loaded, Patrick clucked like an old hen and the piebald woke up and followed the last of the foot passengers out into Station Road. Here she turned confidently towards the town, but Bertram tapped Patrick's arm and shook his head when the old man raised an enquiring eyebrow. The piebald, puzzled, changed direction and laboured up the rest of the hill. At the top was a wide view of a green plateau bounded to the east by the Cheviots.

It was a bright May day. Summer sun flickered over the thick cream of may blossom, brought a sheen to the young gold of oak leaves and sent knots of excited lambs leaping over the ditches.

'Mint sauce,' said Beatrix, to take them down a peg or two. She removed her hat and forgot the long night journey.

'Mint sauce,' said Patrick, 'is a sin agin good meat. Eckford kirk wad show you what to do with folk who put mint sauce on lamb collops.'

Beatrix looked enquiringly at Bertram.

'Oh, there's a sort of bridle hung outside the church, they call it a "jougs", which was once used as a punishment by the Kirk Sessions for people who broke the sabbath. I'll take you up to see it, it's not far, though what it's got to do with mint sauce only Patrick knows. There's lots of other places within an easy drive you'll enjoy, it's fine country. But first there's a farm for you to see. It's coming up for sale in the autumn. Not too much land, but a good house.'

'Grand place for Mr Bertram; just above Ale Water,' said the irrepressible Patrick.

'I'll be glad to look at it,' Beatrix said. 'It's what I came for after all.' It was beginning to dawn on her that Patrick must be Bertram's drinking companion.

Patrick gave a distinct hiccup. 'Aye, mebbe yer right and mebbe yer wrong, about that and other things,' he said. 'Those who live will learn.'

'Patrick, watch your driving instead of talking in riddles.' Bertram had gone pink and pompous.

'So we can mak a kirk o' a mill out o' that,' Patrick returned, then shut his mouth like a gin trap.

'Oh, there are the Eildon Hills,' Beatrix said. Bertram's pleasure at the prospect of showing off the Border Country had not been lost on her. This was where he felt at home, perhaps had done so for years, and she'd been too absorbed in her own miserable affairs to realise it. She should be ashamed of herself.

'Such comical little humps,' she went on, 'but they do make good landmarks and they remind me of our old nurse. Do you remember, Bertram, how she used to talk about the Queen of Elfland who lived in the Eildon Hills and "True Thomas" and "Jamie the Poeter" who wrote "Kilmeny"? "When the ingle glowed with an eiry leme./Late, late in the gloaming Kilmeny came hame." I feel a bit like Kilmeny myself, though it's not fairyland I've escaped from. How far is Kalemouth?'

'We'll start down into Teviotdale soon. After that we'll be there in no time.'

Beatrix wasn't in any hurry to arrive, she was still in a state of astonishment at having been allowed to leave Bolton Gardens. If it hadn't been for Bertram's insistence that she should return with him to Scotland after their Easter fortnight in Sidmouth, she would never have made the effort, it was really too exhausting. Just as she had supposed, Mama had had the greatest aversion to the idea of losing her invaluable daughter for a whole two weeks. It was amusing how invaluable she became whenever she tried to take off. Papa, though, had for once been on the side of his daughter. He had shown unexpected interest in *Peter Rabbit* and agreed with Bertram that in Scotland Beatrix would have peace and quiet in which to redraw the illustrations returned by Warnes for more work. Mama had been promised a visit to the new resort of Worthing for a few days, so they could consider whether it suited for next year. Just this once, Papa had said, he would take over Beatrix's job of looking after the luggage.

Beatrix, let out on bail as she put it to herself, was sceptical about this change of heart, more inclined to think that her father had decided it would be less expensive for his daughter to keep Bertram company than hiring the 'gillie' again, but she did indeed mean to draw. Life was much less drab since *Peter Rabbit* had made his appearance in book form and she intended to persuade that well-tailored young man at Warnes not only to accept her drawings, but to like them as well. As to how things would be when she returned to No. 2, or even whether she would be allowed to stay her time out, she could only repeat Patrick's words: who lives may learn.

'Twa letters for you at the house,' Patrick told her, having endured all the silence he could. 'Lunnon postmark.'

'Good,' said Beatrix enigmatically, to Patrick's evident

disappointment. He peeked at her under his hat and shook the reins on the piebald's back. The mare responded enthusiastically, breaking into a raking trot as the road twisted down through hanging woods towards Kale Water and the River Teviot.

'Hey, watch the corners Patrick, you'll have us out.' Bertram was alarmed.

Beatrix, hanging on with white knuckles, was reminded of a similarly wild ride in Wales, behind a harum-scarum little iron-grey mare with long fetlocks and red eyes. On that occasion they had landed in a ditch. They fared better this time, the piebald eventually deciding enough was enough, bringing down her speed by using her back legs as brakes in a quite individual manner. Beatrix wondered if she'd once been in a circus. They arrived at the bottom of the hill in decorous style, to jog over a bridge and turn left by the side of Kale Water.

'The horse'd be better doing the driving and you between the shafts,' Beatrix said witheringly to Patrick, who was hiding under his hat.

The farmhouse they were approaching could only have been found in the Borders. It was built of the same rose-red stone as Kelso Abbey and single-storeyed, though to get the best of both worlds there were attic bedrooms under the eaves. Behind it was a small barn and cowsheds, to the side the peat-brown Kale Water and all around were soft green pastures. Beatrix suddenly experienced a wave of shyness at the thought of new faces. She fought against it; how silly, she had thought she had grown out of this.

'Bear up, old lady,' said Bertram, looking concerned. 'You're tired, that's what it is. Rest is the ticket, and we'll leave Ashieburn until tomorrow.' Bertram, it was clear, was making a great concession.

By the following day Beatrix was beginning to relax. To her surprise, Mr and Mrs Douglas had made her welcome in the sort of manner that indicated anything to do with their lodger was bound to be good, even an unmarried sister of indeterminate age and a nervous disposition. 'Two arteests,' they'd said, smiling all over their broad, high-coloured Border faces. 'That's guid.' She was so used to Bertram being in disgrace at home that she had unthinkingly expected the same condition to hold true elsewhere. Instead, he seemed to be well respected. That was the first surprise and why it should be a surprise she couldn't imagine; after all, she liked Bertram herself. The second came the next day, which started with the inspection of Ashieburn Farm, which was being temporarily managed by a factor.

The farmhouse, large, double-fronted and square with five bedrooms, was more impressive than the land, which only ran to thirty acres. Good acres though, on a south-west slope above Ale Water with a far view of the Eildons. Having been through the house, nice enough, though too big, Beatrix was just settling down to give the farm itself a thorough going-over – the quality of the soil, the stock, the buildings – when she found herself being hustled, there was no other word for it, back to the trap.

'We're having lunch at the Cross Keys Inn in Ancrum,' Bertram said, taking his half-hunter out of his waistcoat pocket, 'and we're late.'

'Late for what?' asked Beatrix, settling her skirts resentfully. She had been enjoying what she was doing, with an exciting idea growing at the back of her mind that some day she might live in this pleasant countryside with Bertram and have a hand in the farm management. 'They'll not mind what time we arrive if I know anything about such places.' That was another thing, being taken to a public house without a by-your-leave.

'You'll see,' said Bertram, urging the piebald to unaccustomed speeds over the short distance to Ancrum.

The village consisted of a long line of brownstone houses with the Cross Keys in the middle, facing the village green. The piebald and trap were easily disposed of by giving them into the charge of a small boy whom Beatrix thought should have been at school. Then she had to face going into a place where alcoholic liquor was sold. This was so definitely not what Papa had had in mind that she hesitated.

'Come on, Bea. I need a refreshment. Anyway, you've been into enough hotels in all conscience and there's no real difference. You can have ginger beer.'

They went into the bar parlour, its crackling fire welcome after the chilly breeze. Beatrix settled herself in the window seat with a view of the green and saw the bar was nothing more than a discreet window with a sliding shutter through to the taproom. She still felt uneasy.

Bertram ordered ale for himself and ginger beer for Beatrix through the window and then closed the shutter. 'Someone will bring them,' he said.

Beatrix wondered why.

The girl who brought in the drinks was large-boned, tall,

broad-faced and brown-eyed, with a shy smile and a cloud of soft fair hair.

'This is Mary Scott, Bea.' Bertram was grinning in what Beatrix thought was an extraordinary manner, almost foolish. 'I've known her now for two years, ever since I boarded with her aunt in Birnam, and she has at last agreed to marry me.'

Elizabeth had taken advantage of the family's absence to give the larder and back kitchen at No. 2 an extra good clean. Spring-cleaning this year had stopped at the kitchen itself, time having run out. She had managed to catch Tom, who was mostly down at the Bolton Mews these days with Mr Beckett, and had set him whitewashing the walls. She had then got the copper going for extra hot water for Mrs Pearson, up to her elbows in suds washing the best china in the butler's pantry with her round face pink and moist. After that she had started to turn out the little-used cupboards in the back kitchen. Betty Anderton had gone home to see her brother, wounded in South Africa, or she as the youngest would have been given this thankless job.

Cap put aside and swathed in Norah's old sacking apron, she was scrubbing out the deep cupboard under the stone sink, surrounded by objects resembling ancient flotsam retrieved from hidden depths, when she heard the knocking on the area door.

'Can you answer it, Elizabeth? I'm too soapy!' Mrs Pearson called.

Elizabeth blew a cobweb off her nose and rolled her eyes. She felt more like a blackamoor than a head-housemaid. Even so she backed resignedly out of the cupboard. Mrs Pearson was all right, even if she did look like a bun loaf. She didn't drink and she had a sunny temper, but she was as easy to move as St Paul's when she set her mind against it.

Drying her hands as she passed the roller towel, Elizabeth noted Tom had finished the passage and disappeared, probably back to the stables. She discarded the apron and tidied her skirts, but was aware that her hair was all anyhow as she opened the door. She hoped it wasn't the Fish, she rather liked the Fish.

She thought it was a stranger for a moment, then saw it was Fred's sister Dottie. When she looked at Dottie all thoughts of her own appearance left her. Dottie had her handkerchief out, her hat on one side and eyes that were pink like an angora rabbit.

'He's dead,' Elizabeth said. 'Fred's been killed in battle.'

'It's worse,' said Dottie.

'How can it be worse?' said Elizabeth. 'Oh, don't stand there, come on in.' She took Dottie's arm, dragged her over the threshold and sat her in the rocking-chair. 'Now, out with it, what's he done, a murder?'

'No,' Dottie said, her mouth quivering, 'he's gone and found a black girl and he's going to settle in South Africa. Here, he sent a letter for you but he wanted me to bring it.'

Elizabeth snatched the crumpled letter from Dottie's damp hand and took it over to the window.

Holding Fred's letter seemed to bring him to life; she could see him standing in front of her, smiling his sunny smile and telling her to keep her hair on. She held the paper up to read it:

*My dearest,*
*You are not going to like this and I have no doubt it will send you into one of your tantrums, but here it is.*

*South Africa is a fine country, especially round the Cape where they really understand fruit-growing. I like it here and when I think what I have to come home to, a shrewish wife who won't let me go and a mistress who won't come and live with me, there isn't really a choice. They'll let me take my discharge here and I'm stopping. Also I have met a girl. She is what they call 'Cape Coloured' which means half-caste and her father needs help on his fruit farm and will take me on. She's an only child.*

*Dottie will bring you this letter and both she and Gertie will have a lot to say about what I'm doing, so you can all three get together and blacken my character to your hearts' content. When you've finished though, try to look at it from my point of view.*

*I'll always remember you; part of my heart is yours. You'll be all right, you still have your Miss Bea and your pride in your work and your sense of fun. I'd be glad if you could keep in touch with Dottie and Gertie too, just to see they're all right. They've got the house and all the money there was to spare – I saw to that before I left in case I was killed – but they might do something daft without good advice.*

*So now all that remains for me to say, dear Lizzie, is that you must keep your chin up and not think too badly of*
*Your Fred*

'Badly! What I think of him would fill a book. That girl will be lovely with a figure like an hourglass, and he'll marry her regardless of his wife at home and when he's tired of her he can grow fruit and have a fine old time. I know him.'

Elizabeth dragged her fingers through her hair, stamped her heels on the stone flags of the kitchen floor and crumpled the letter in her hand. Then she caught sight of Dottie's face, anticipatory under all the woe, wanting her to make a great scene, a drama she could relate to Gertie when she got home.

Elizabeth had only met the sisters once before, when Fred took her out to Hampstead for Sunday tea. Gertie was thin and Dottie was not so much fat as square and they both had sparse, fairish hair, dull skin and hungry eyes stuck in their faces like raisins in a dough cake. She'd soon found out what they were hungry for: life of any sort, second-hand if need be. Scandal and gossip kept them alive and Fred had been right when he'd said they would be glad to have him and Elizabeth live with them. That would have been real life actually in their house. Elizabeth pulled herself up and forced her stiff face muscles into what she hoped was a normal expression.

'What did he say to you?' she demanded.

' 'E said we'd got to be good girls and not do anything daft and to listen to you,' Dottie said bitterly. ' 'E said 'e might come back and see us in a year or two, when he'd got things to 'is liking, an' not to worry about him in the meantime. Worry! It's not 'im I'm going to worry about, it's us. Gertie's took to 'er bed.'

Elizabeth wanted to scream with rage. Not content with deserting her, Fred had lumbered her with his sisters, vulnerable, inadequate, liable to do themselves a mischief.

'I'll put the kettle on for a cup of tea,' she said. There was no sound from the butler's pantry. Mrs Pearson was listening to what was going on. Well, why not? Tell the world that Fred was gone. 'We could all do with one to buck us up.'

When Dottie had departed, bucked up with Best Darjeeling and placated by Elizabeth's promise to come to tea on Sunday, a stimulated Mrs Pearson returned to the china, while Elizabeth threw back the flotsam into the under-sink cupboard and looked round for something on which to vent her wrath.

The dirty old carpet in the butler's pantry came to mind. She'd never got round to it and scrubbing up the pile would just about suit her mood. She whipped it out from under the feet of the protesting Mrs Pearson, threw it out into the back yard and followed with a bucket of warm water laced with ammonia and green soft soap.

For a while she scrubbed blindly, the ammonia fumes at least an excuse for the flow of tears. After a time she sat back on her heels to blow her nose and mop her streaming eyes. The warm May sun on her back was soothing. She gave a final sniff and looked without interest at the carpet to see if she was making any impression. What she saw made her gasp. The carpet, from being dingy and grey and fit for nothing but an intervention between stone flags and tired feet, was coming up with the glow and scintillation of the Orient. Emerging from the dirt was a royal blue ground with an intricate pattern in colours of gold and purple, pale blue and duck-egg green. It was beautiful.

'Well, I never,' said Mrs Pearson, whose excuse for coming out was that she'd finished the china and wanted a breath of air. 'Who'd have thought it? It's a Persian carpet you've got there, ducks, wot I've bin spilling dirty water on and dear knows wot else. Waluable that.'

The jewelled colours, soft in the sunshine, the silky pile just beginning to dry, seemed to have appeared like magic, her own creation. Elizabeth found herself suddenly comforted and remembering something Fred had once quoted about a thing of beauty being a joy for ever. She set to work again with the scrubbing brush.

Beatrix was allowed her full two weeks and she arrived back in London with a portfolio of coloured drawings for *Peter Rabbit* and, in spite of everything, a feeling of well-being. In the course of several encounters she had come to like Mary, who continued to call her Miss Potter against all persuasion. Bertram's choice, Beatrix had finally decided, was a motherly soul who would look after him with unswerving loyalty. The great problem, of course, was how to keep it all from Papa and Mama. Mary was the daughter of an inn-keeper and had once worked in a Hawick woollen mill. To hope that their parents would countenance such a marriage was, Bertram had said, as much good as wishing on the moon. Beatrix had promised to make no mention of Mary and to dissuade them from taking an interest in Ashieburn Farm, though they would have to hear about it in time. The idle dream, Beatrix told herself severely, that she might one day live in the Borders had been just that, an idle dream.

London, though, was not too unwelcome. She had

exchanged several letters with Norman Warne during her time in Scotland on aspects of *Peter Rabbit*, and as well as doing more drawings she had taken a photograph of Mrs Douglas to provide a model for a more amicable Mrs McGregor. She had already arranged to visit Warnes' office and she had made some progress with a new little book, all about a tailor who lived in Gloucester.

A cab dropped her off in Bolton Gardens late in the evening, a May evening of bird song and balmy airs. She was smiling when Elizabeth opened the door, but one look at the maid's distressed face was enough to bring her back to earth.

'It's Mama, isn't it?' she said.

'Oh Miss Bea, I'm so glad to see you. She's really bad this time. I think it's influenza and I've sent for the doctor. She has a dreadful fever.'

As Beatrix hurried upstairs to see her mother, she told herself to remember to write to Mr Warne tomorrow and tell him she couldn't keep the appointment.

# CHAPTER TWELVE

—— • ——

The breakfast room at Crosthwaite Vicarage was not its usual cheerful self. An October gale, sending dark clouds speeding across the sky, was the cause. The gas-sconces on the wall were flickering in the draughts and the chimney was quite frankly smoking.

The pervading gloom was affecting those who breakfasted. Hardwicke Rawnsley, wearing morning dress with a white gardenia in his buttonhole and occasionally patting his grey top hat on an adjacent plush-covered chair, looked at the passing weather as he ate his porridge. His wife, at the other end of the oval table and still in a morning wrap, silently ate crumbs of toast with a preoccupied expression.

'Even a mouse couldn't survive on the amount of breakfast you've eaten,' Hardwicke said at last. 'Do have a little more or you'll never get through the day.'

Edith ignored the plea. 'Hardy, there's a small matter I know you will have attended to, but I must ask. Have you thought of the Princess's bodily needs?' She was sure he had forgotten.

'Well, there's a meal arranged at the Lodore Hotel after the ceremony, if that's what you mean.'

'No of course it isn't. To put it plainly she must be offered a bathroom and lavatory somewhere in the town. You don't mean to tell me you haven't thought of it!' The silver coffee pot tilted dangerously.

'My dear, do take care. Do you really think it necessary?' Hardwicke's eggcup, ornamented like a Fabergé Easter egg, was resisting all his attempts to unhook it in the middle so he could actually eat the breakfast egg that waited in its silver nest. He tried to use his egg-spoon as a lever.

'Necessary! Think of the programme.'

Why, Edith wondered, did the male sex close their eyes to the fact that women were subject to the same laws of nature as men? Then, with some horror, she saw Hardwicke's efforts with the delicate spoon. 'Oh, you'll never do it like that, do stop.' She

104

rose with her usual grace and went round to undo the hook with the tip of an opal fingernail. 'I don't know why you have such trouble.' Hardwicke blew her a kiss as she returned to her end of the table.

'Now, consider carefully,' Edith continued, 'She's spent the night with the Lowthers, so there's a drive of over twenty miles from the Hall to Keswick. Then she's to visit the lacemakers at Ruskin Cottage and the students at the Keswick School of Industrial Arts before being presented to the Mayor and Town Council. All that is only a prelude to the drive to Brandelhow and the opening of the Woods to the public. Princess Louise may be Royalty, but she's no fairy spirit, above earthly needs.'

'No my love, indeed she isn't.' Hardwicke suddenly chuckled, no doubt picturing the not inconsiderable proportions of Queen Victoria's third daughter. He scooped out the last of his egg, got up, dabbing his chin, and went to the door.

'Annie,' he called, his voice deepening to a roar, 'Come here.'

Annie Stones appeared from the study. She was a model secretary in her dress, severe navy serge and white shirt, but spoilt the picture by having merry blue eyes and soft brown hair from which hairpins dropped like gentle rain. Now she looked at Hardwicke enquiringly.

'WC for the Princess, with facilities for her to wash and a mirror.' He thought for a second, his head bent. 'And lots of flowers, though not so many she can't turn round.'

Annie nodded and went away.

'Annie's a Fabian,' said Edith, finishing her coffee. 'You don't think she'll send the Princess down the back yard at Ruskin Cottage?'

'No, no. She'll get Herbert Maryon at the Keswick School of Industrial Arts to arrange something. I think the two of them will make a match of it one of these days.'

'That's a pity,' said Edith, who was putting hot water in the coffee cups to prevent the Sèvres china being marked in the interval before they were removed. 'You'll miss her. She's a good secretary and her brother is a good curate. Where is he this morning?'

'I sent him back to Skiddaw Cottage for breakfast. He's been up since 5 o'clock and down at Brandelhow organising teams of men to hold down the guy ropes of the marquee. He says it should be all right, but if this wind gets under the canvas, the whole thing might blow up and take off.' He looked anxiously out of the window as smoke billowed yet again from the fireplace. 'I've been looking forward to this since the old Queen's funeral last year and now see what happens! I'd better go down to Brandelhow myself shortly.'

'Well, leave the gardenia behind and don't be too long.' Edith knew it was useless to urge him to change his clothes before he went, she'd known him help dig an unfinished grave whilst wearing surplice and bands. 'You've got to be back to greet the Princess when she arrives. She's doing this as a personal favour to you, remember.'

'*And* I want to ask her to take over as President of the National Trust, now Westminster's gone,' Harwicke said absently. He looked out of the window again as rain rattled against the panes. 'At least she's getting a typical Lakeland welcome. Now, Edith, there's something you could do for me this afternoon if you will. I've invited Beatrix Potter to the opening and it would be a kindness if you would seek her out and make her feel at home. She's so shy it's almost an illness, but she does know you. I've persuaded her to come over from Sawrey – the family are still at Lakeside – to see what the Trust is doing, and I want her to enjoy it.'

'Hardy, I know you too well. You're not bringing her all this way just to see Princess Louise cut a ribbon. What devious plan have you got for poor Beatrix?' Edith was sure that sometimes he'd no idea he'd got a plan, until it all worked out.

Hardwicke, ever restless, had started pacing the end of the breakfast room with his hands clasped behind his back. He looked at Edith out of the corner of an eye as he turned at the wall. 'You read too much into too little. I just thought it would be a pleasant day out, away from her difficult parents. Though, come to think of it, Beatrix will inherit a lot of money from those same parents one day.'

'Which you think she might just leave to the Trust with suitable persuasion. There's someone at the door.'

The thunderous knocking could hardly be missed. The housekeeper showed in a wet, draggled man in oilskins.

'I'm sorry, Reverend,' he said to Hardwicke, 'but she's been and gone. A blurry great sough of wind took her up just like a balloon and she came down a shattered wreck. Mr Maryon sed I should tell you.'

Hardwicke looked at him for a moment and then started to

laugh, not a chuckle but a great bellow. 'There, you see George. Man proposes, God disposes,' he said. 'Often to man's betterment. Was anyone hurt?'

'Nowt to write home about,' George reassured him.

'Well, we'll see what we shall see, but it's my prediction that the gale will now depart, having received the tent as a sacrifice, and the skies will clear.'

'Could see if I could get another tent in the time, smaller like,' George offered.

'No. Fate has taken a hand and it doesn't do to argue. We'll accept the verdict that we should not have a marquee.'

'It seems to me,' said Edith, after George had gone, 'that you have got faith and superstition profoundly mixed over this affair.'

'But my dear, they have been since the early Christians. Surely you knew that?'

Edith was unable to think of a reply. She decided for the umpteenth time that she would never, if they both lived to be a hundred, understand her husband.

The gale had blown itself away to the south by the late morning, leaving behind ragged lengths of grey cloud with blue linings. Wedges of sunlight touched the tops of the fells, bracken on the lower slopes seemed alive with amber flame, deep blue shadows filled the ghylls and combes. Beside the shore of Derwentwater a growing number of people collected on the small area of tilted pasture above Brandelhow Woods and the lake, including Miss Potter and her maid.

Beatrix had decided to bring Elizabeth as the dear girl seemed a little *triste* these days. She seemed to be enjoying the spectacle. Beatrix too was pleasantly amused. First there was the disappearance of the marquee and the description of its passing by a local farmer. 'Went up just like one of they new airships, mum, and came down like a burst paper bag,' he'd said. Then there were the pathetic survivors, the little red dais and the few forlorn chairs. Added to this, the people who were gathering on this wet fellside wore clothes that were ridiculous in this setting. Long, tight hobble-skirts seemed to have come in from somewhere, she hadn't noticed their arrival until now, worn with cartwheel hats ornamented with complete birds' wings or huge buckles. One woman, relentlessly hobbled, slithered helplessly past her on the wet grass, falling to earth with a bone-shaking thump, her dislodged hat landing gently on a cowpat. The men were also having trouble staying on their feet as smooth-soled patent leather shoes were the correct wear with morning dress.

'Really Miss Bea, you shouldn't laugh.' Elizabeth seemed to admire these dreadful fashions and had rescued the badly treated hat and wiped it carefully with grass, but its owner didn't seem anxious to wear it again.

'They have no appreciation of the fitness of things, that's what makes it so funny,' Beatrix said, viewing her own flat brogues and ample tweed skirt with complacency. 'Farmhands in a drawing-room would produce the alternative effect.'

She looked away from the crowds at the more satisfactory autumn colours, from the dusky grape shades of the heather on far Skiddaw to the gold of the oaks on Walla Crag across the water. She noted how the blue and gold of the surroundings reflected in the lake below her, washing out from the small, rocky bays. Could she, she wondered, get just that effect in some of the backgrounds to her little pictures? It would be an interesting problem. That sort of colouring would be perfect for the squirrel book she'd mentioned to Norman. He seemed to want another Lake District book, not the nursery rhymes she'd had in mind, though he had promised to look at *The Tailor of Gloucester* when her privately printed edition came out next month. In the meantime *Peter Rabbit* would be on the bookstalls within a fortnight. One of the wedges of sunlight hovered over the waiting crowd and she was suddenly glad that she'd defied the enemy and come today, though she'd have to pay for it later. Oh, good heavens, there was Edith Rawnsley.

Edith's progress towards her was serene and steady, people giving way before her implacable smile. She was wearing a long, fitted pelisse in dark-blue cloth over a blue and white walking dress and had in tow a dumpy sweet-faced woman with fine eyes and an indefinable air of distinction. She was introduced as Miss Octavia Hill, and though her clothes were as practical and understated as Beatrix's own, her hat anchored with veiling tied under her chin, Beatrix at once felt gauche, inadequate and uneasy. What do you say to someone who has received praise from Queen Victoria for her work in housing the London poor, who is a friend of Florence Nightingale and who has helped to found the National Trust? There was some scandal to do with Ruskin, she remembered, but then everything to do with that man was a scandal.

It transpired, after the introduction, that Edith had a

problem. 'Hardwicke forgot to tell me if he wanted his poem distributed before or after the opening,' she complained. 'I shall have to ask Mr Stones, he may know.'

'What poem?' asked Miss Hill.

Edith's delicate pearl complexion turned a faint pink. 'He wrote it a few days ago, of course, with no idea of what the weather might do.'

'Have you got a copy with you?' asked Miss Hill, who seemed to have a persevering nature.

'A considerable number,' said Edith feelingly as she withdrew printed sheets from what Beatrix now saw to be an overladen reticule. She handed a copy to each of the ladies. 'You'll see what I mean.'

Beatrix read the poem with a mounting bubble of internal mirth; really she was having a delightfully funny day. Miss Hill read it with little exclamations of pleasure and finished first.

'This is a wonderful commemoration of a wonderful day,' she said. 'These lines – "And here may mortals, weary of the strife/Of inconsiderate cities, hope to come/And learn the fair tranquillities of earth" – are perfect. They totally express the peaceful spirit of this place.'

Beatrix and Edith looked at each other involuntarily and then looked away, trying not to gaze at the battered remains of the marquee bundled behind a group of trees.

'If you'll excuse me,' said Edith hastily, and set off down the hill.

'I don't know where my niece and her friend have gone, nor my sister Miranda,' Miss Hill said, looking round. 'We're all staying with the Marshalls on Derwent Island, so delightful to live on an island, probably they are standing with them.'

Beatrix thought herself that living on an island was something of an affectation these days, not to say inconvenient in times of storm and tempest. Reminded of her own companion she looked round for Elizabeth and saw her near the gate, where there was a bustle as several carriages discharged their occupants. HRH Princess Louise, Duchess of Argyll, had arrived.

The Princess was accompanied by a lady-in-waiting and an equerry. She wore black and white, understandably still in half-mourning for her brother, and her beautiful hat, in whorls of black and white satin, reminded Beatrix irresistibly of a peppermint humbug.

The Olympian group was swept down towards the red dais,

Hardwicke Rawnsley briefly glimpsed trotting after the Lord Lieutenant. The equerry was swearing softly as he passed Beatrix and he stopped further down to wipe his shoe on the grass.

Princess Louise stood on the dais surrounded not only by the smartly dressed members of the county families but also by dozens of local people who had come to see Royalty in the flesh, but who would never, if things had gone as planned, have been allowed within the marquee. Beatrix thought it splendid. After all, the National Trust was opening this lakeside land to everyone, not just the hobble-skirted brigade.

Opened it was, in a high cultivated voice that carried well and spoke with sincerity. Then it was time to plant the four commemorative oaks. Beatrix reflected that Royalty, with all the practice they got, must be expert tree planters.

'So there it is,' said a voice beside her. 'The first National Trust property in the Lake District and surely the first of many.'

Beatrix started slightly as she had successfully forgotten Miss Hill.

'Yes,' she said politely, 'it is a good thing to do, to protect the land from housing developments and railways and all the other ills that men wish upon it.'

'But surely,' said Miss Hill, sounding slightly puzzled, 'what we are really doing is not so much protecting the land as giving it as an open space for the general public to enjoy. Contact with the beauty of the natural world is an essential factor in the happiness of the people.'

Beatrix began to feel a little warm, in spite of the cool breeze that had followed the gale. 'It's a question of point of view,' she replied. 'People are all very well, but though this land is beautiful it's by no means natural; it's man-made and needs management. You can't just leave it alone, it must be grazed, trees must be felled from time to time and replanting must be done.' She was thinking of the farm above Ale Water, now almost in her brother's hands.

'Oh surely not,' said Miss Hill in an infuriatingly comfortable tone of voice. 'Grazing animals make such a mess and trees should be left as they are. I don't think felling should be done on National Trust land. In any case, who would do it? Our policy is to have small committees to look after each property and we really don't have money to employ foresters.'

'Let me tell you now,' Beatrix said, forgetting entirely to whom she was speaking, 'that if those are the sort of woolly ideas current in the National Trust, then land it owns will not be the heritage of natural beauty the Princess was talking about, it will be a damned disgrace to the nation. I wish you good afternoon.' She marched off, brushing past Edith Rawnsley who had been standing transfixed beside them.

Beatrix had nearly reached the gate when Elizabeth caught up with her.

'Oh Miss Bea, do stop a minute. Your hat's crooked and your hair needs pinning up at the back.'

'Never mind that,' Beatrix said, giving her felt hat a severe downward tug. 'We're going back to Sawrey. Now.'

'I thought you were to be introduced to the Princess,' Elizabeth reproached her.

'The Princess can manage very well without meeting me,' Beatrix said grimly. The day was no longer amusing.

As they were moving down the long line of carriages looking for their own, Beatrix gave a little nod. 'Yes,' she said, 'I've quite decided. I shall buy a small farm somewhere in the Lake District as soon as it is humanly possible. Then I shall show the National Trust how land should be managed.' The day might have its importance after all.

'. . . so you see I was quite right not to allow another tent to be found. Everyone there was able to see and hear the Princess and the behaviour of the crowd was impeccable.' Hardwicke Rawnsley found the conjugal couch the most restful place to discuss the day's events. 'I should never have countenanced a marquee in the first place. My only complaint is that Octavia got in first in asking the Princess to take over the office of President, I should like to have done that myself. Octavia is . . . well, never mind, Princess Louise has accepted and it's the greater good that matters.' He took a satisfied sip of his hot milk decorated with flakes of nutmeg, supposed to ensure a good night's sleep, and then admired his wife's beribboned nightcap against the frilled pillow. It made her look like a rather pretty snowy owl. He wondered if she was tired after the day's events, which had left him seething with energy. 'How did you get on with the poems?'

Edith put down her book and took off her spectacles. 'Not as well as I would have liked. I went to find Mr Stones to enlist his assistance in distributing them and discovered him among the trees with his arms round Mildred Maryon. I didn't see him being much help in those circumstances and left him to it.'

'You were your usual tactful self,' Hardwicke said soothingly. 'It looks as though we'll have a double wedding with a brother and sister from each family.' He drank a little more milk and then had another question. 'Did you find Beatrix Potter? I never saw her.'

'She went early and with good reason,' Edith said. 'She may have been shy when you last saw her, but not today.'

'You sound portentous, my love. Whatever happened?'

'She gave Octavia Hill a piece of her mind, and swore as well. It was quite astonishing.'

'You amaze me,' said Hardwicke placidly. 'I wonder if those two ladies have more in common than they realise. What was it all about?'

'Oh, land management, whatever that may mean, but that's not all. Earlier in the afternoon when I first saw her, Beatrix had an unmistakable look on her face, a sort of softening like chocolate left in the sun; it looks the same but the consistency is different. If someone had persuaded her not to wear that awful hat she'd have looked quite pretty. She's in love, Hardy, there's no mistaking it, though I'm sure she doesn't know it herself. That's what gave her the confidence to speak her mind to Octavia, who took it very seriously and you'll hear more about it in good time. But who with, and what it will bring, I have no idea.'

Hardwicke finished his milk. 'Cupid *has* been busy,' he said and put the glass on the night cabinet with a small thump. 'I can guess who with and I know just what it will bring. Trouble for poor Beatrix.'

# CHAPTER THIRTEEN

In May of the following year, Beatrix was back in the Lake District staying at Mrs McTavish's boarding house in Portinscale, Portinscale House no less. The day after her arrival she sat patiently on a horsehair sofa in the tidy parlour, reflecting that 1903 seemed to be a year when she was destined to be constantly on the move, a reluctant comet.

There had been the visit to Gwaynynog in February, a mistake as it had been cold and Uncle Fred too mean to allow much more than damp wood and coal dust on the fires. Then, after that, the short period she'd set aside to get on with some drawings – very necessary as she now seemed to be juggling with three books at once – was cut short by cousin Ethel's demand that she should go to Melford Hall to keep her company. Of course this was the one family visit she was allowed, even encouraged, to make on her own and she had been despatched, as it were, by return. Being Lady Hyde-Parker had accustomed Ethel to getting her own way on all occasions. The family Easter fortnight holiday had been spent at Folkestone, a complete waste of time as far as drawing was concerned, though the weather had been good. And now, when she had counted on a couple of clear weeks for consultations with Norman Warne on the proofs of *The Tale of Squirrel Nutkin* and the new drawings for *The Tailor of Gloucester*, Bertram had demanded that she should meet him in Portinscale. So here she was, together with a cageful of mice, as she must have something to show Norman when she got back, waiting to know what Bertram wanted. It was unfortunate that Mrs McTavish did not like mice, whilst her tabby cat took a great interest in them.

'Oh, there you are, old girl!' Bertram, standing at the door of the parlour with his deerstalker in his hand, spoke as though he had been looking for her high and low, whereas she was sure he had been reading the morning paper. She rose from her prickly perch – really horsehair stuffing was an invention of the devil – and followed Bertram out of the front door into the soft drizzle of rain that had begun at breakfast. She hoped the mice would get through the morning safely, perched as they were on top of the wardrobe, and hoped also that the time had come for Bertram to unburden himself. Last night they'd both been too tired after their journeys and at breakfast Mrs McTavish's attentions had been tiresomely vigilant.

At first there was no sign of confidences. Beatrix remembered gloomily that Bertram had always needed to wind himself up to a point of resolution, sometimes taking days to do it. As they strolled along through woods in which the tide of bluebells was threatening to overwhelm the path, Bertram chatted about Ashieburn Farm, his to call his own since February, and his plans for the farming year now begun. Beatrix noted a snakeshead fritillary beside a young wild cherry and thought her feet were beginning to feel damp.

'How is Mary Scott?' she asked.

Bertram, the rain darkening the shoulders of his green Norfolk jacket, looked straught ahead, swinging his stick as though he would like to hit away the question like a cricket ball. Then he splashed through a puddle, swore as mud flew onto his knickerbockers and immediately apologised. Beatrix laughed and this seemed to break the tension.

'That's partly what I wanted to talk to you about, old girl. We got married last November, don't you know, and she's up at the farm getting on like a house on fire.'

'Married, without telling me! Bertram, you couldn't have.'

'Well, I could you know. Better that way so there was no unpleasantness at the London end. We didn't even tell Mary's mother until it was all over. We were married in a registry office in Edinburgh and her sister Lizzie and her friend were the witnesses. Mary wore a lovely hat.'

For a moment Beatrix felt on the verge of tears, but managed to laugh instead and reach up and kiss Bertram on the check. 'Every happiness to you both,' she said.

Bertram looked startled. Affectionate gestures were rare in their family. 'That's not really why I wanted to meet you here,' he said.

'Well it should have been. Marriage is important.'

'No, there's something else and I didn't want to ask in front of Mary. I'm cleaned out with buying the farm and we need stock. Neighbours have been good with runts when their pigs have had large litters and given us one or two motherless lambs she's bringing up on the bottle, but we need a few sound sheep and cows. Wondered if you could help, with *Peter Rabbit* doing so well, as I hear. Just until my allowance is due.'

There, she should have known! Ever since she could remember Beatrix had schooled herself never to expect her hopes to be realised, only this time she hadn't seen what might go wrong. *Peter Rabbit* had surprised them all, not least Warnes, by being well into his fourth printing only seven months after publication. Her royalties had begun to look promising and for most of last winter, when she'd seen that neither her mother nor her father were in favour of her producing more books and were going to put every obstacle they could find in her way, she had comforted herself with thoughts of buying her own farm at the Lakes.

'How much do you need?' she asked Bertram.

'About £100 would get me going.'

Just about all she had saved. It was funny really to be asked for a loan, when all her life she had never had more than twopence to rub together. It was rather a shock, she found. Money was power and choice – her independence or Bertram's new life. Of course he might never manage to make a go of things even if she helped him; he'd not had much practice, poor Bertram. On the other hand she was bound to get her independence in God's good time, whenever that might be. She plodded on under the dripping trees with Bertram remaining mercifully silent.

The path brought them out of the woods under the hump of Little Cat Bells, and a kissing-gate set in iron palings led them down to the lake and the jetty. Beatrix clumped solidly in her walking boots along the wooden boards and stood looking south down the lake towards Grange-in-Borrowdale and Castle Crag. Even in such sad weather the view had great charm. The high fells stretched into the distance in shades of grey and pearl, withdrawn behind their veils of mist. A cormorant perched on a dripping branch as though carved in ebony.

'It's no use having a farm without stock,' Beatrix said at last, as cheerfully as she could manage. Her old Scottish nurse had always impressed on her that the Lord loveth a cheerful giver. 'I'll let you have the money but I want something in return.'

'What's that?' Bertram looked nervous.

'See if you can improve my owl for *Squirrel Nutkin*. He's called Old Brown and I keep getting him cross-eyed. You can draw owls better than I can.'

'Is that all? I'll do that as soon as we get back.'

'No, it's not quite all. I only got permission to come and meet you here because I said it would be an ideal opportunity to find a house for the summer. Lingholm is not on the market this year and so far nothing else has turned up. I would be greatly relieved if you would beard the agent in his den for me, that poky little hole near the George, and allow me to get on with making drawings of mice, that is if Mrs McTavish's cat has left me any to draw.'

'I am a thoughtless idiot,' Bertram said, banging the heel of his hand theatrically against his forehead. 'It never occurred to me that you would be busy. Somehow one thinks that children's books don't take long to do. Perhaps I should write one myself when I get the farm straight.'

'It'll be enough for the moment if you just get Old Brown straight,' said Beatrix drily. 'Then the mice and I will go home on Friday.'

She abandoned the end of the jetty after a last look at the hills and Bertram tucked his arm through hers as they started back to Portinscale. 'At least you can get some work done when you get home.'

'You'd think so, wouldn't you?' Beatrix said. 'And so I would if someone could persuade Mama and Papa that I shan't go blind with doing such close work; they have convinced themselves that I shall and are determined to prevent it. Also, if someone would tell all my relations that I don't require to be out of London at the moment. They are convinced I do and won't take "no" for an answer. I have to go down to Gloucester next week to see Caroline.'

Paddington Station was busy and porters were difficult to catch. Shafts of morning sunlight dazzled the eyes of hurrying passengers, motes of dust wriggling upwards in the beams like tadpoles caught in a tank. Elizabeth had lost Miss Bea and the Stroud train went in three minutes. She stood still, the two covered baskets clasped to her chest, then saw Miss Bea ahead with a porter. It was as she took a new grip on the baskets and started to run after her that she thought she saw Fred.

He was talking to a ginger-whiskered porter in charge of a trolley piled high with boxes of baby chickens. He was clean-shaven and wearing a strange wide-brimmed hat, but if it wasn't Fred it was his double.

Her feet continued running but her brain was in a whirl and

116

her grasp on the baskets loosened so one fell on the platform. The lid burst open and a small brown furry animal hopped out, looked dazedly round, then rapidly climbed up the cliff of cardboard boxes on the trolley and disappeared into a cavity. Elizabeth stopped with a despairing cry.

'Which is it, the rabbit or the squirrel?' called Miss Bea, craning to see over the heads of a small flock of schoolgirls shepherded by a nun.

'It's Nutkin Miss Bea and, oh heavens, there's the guard's whistle!'

'We'll have to catch the train, the porter has put the mice in with the luggage. Come on, Nutkin will fend for himself. Give me the rabbit before you drop her as well – and bring Nutkin's basket.'

Elizabeth's arm was grasped and she was propelled towards a carriage door held open for them by a resigned-looking porter. In the distance the guard's whistle sounded frantic and the locomotive's wheels were starting to turn. They stumbled into the first-class compartment, empty except for their luggage and the mice in their cage. Miss Bea fumbled in her pocket and handed Elizabeth a shilling to give to the porter, now cantering alongside with his hand through the open window.

As Elizabeth pressed the shilling into the waiting palm the train slid past the cheeping trolley-load and she saw the ginger-whiskered porter holding poor Nutkin by the scruff of his neck and watching the carriage windows. She shrieked, loud enough to be heard over the engine's valedictory whistle, waving both arms to catch his attention. He saw her, leapt forward to catch up with the now swiftly moving carriage and thrust Nutkin at her through the window.

''Ere y'are Miss. Nearly kep' 'im fer me dinner!'

Over his head she saw Fred or his double blow her a kiss.

Her knees gave way and she collapsed on a seat clutching Nutkin and feeling quite demented.

'Well, that's a blessing,' said Miss Bea. 'I don't know which it would have been worse to lose, the rabbit or the squirrel: I'm still using them both. What a kind man.'

'Reminded me of a fox,' Elizabeth muttered. Miss Bea didn't hear her.

'Now,' she went on, 'put Nutkin in his basket before you strangle him and then, though I'm not sure I should be the one to mention it, you might like to tidy yourself up. Your hat's on crooked and your hair is coming down!'

Caroline Hutton was in wild good looks after the windy drive from the station to Harescombe Grange in spring sunshine. She was delighted to see Beatrix, her brown eyes shining with pleasure and excitement, but not too pleased about the animals. None of them were at their best after the train journey and she looked at them with dismay. 'Couldn't you have left them in London?'

Beatrix was unpacking, having put the cages on the window-sill to provide their occupants with sunshine and fresh air. 'Who would look after them when I have Elizabeth with me? Mrs Pearson's legs won't take her beyond the first floor and our new little tweeny maid has been educated to think that wild animals are "nasty" and wants to take a poker to them.'

'What about the aged Ps?'

Beatrix gave up her struggle to undo the drawstring of her shoe bag and plumped down on the bed beside Caroline.

'You're always trying to make my parents sound normal, like your own. Not that Mr Hutton is quite normal, I'm sure you won't mind me remarking his innumerable eccentricities, but he's kind and so is Mrs Hutton. Mine are not. I'm sorry to have to say this, but you must understand that they have cultivated the art of selfishness to such a point that it is impossible to ask them to do anything. It would cause such dreadful rubs I daren't risk it.'

'You're right about Papa,' said Caroline. 'His latest idea is to buy an automobile, of all crazy things. They're only a passing fashion. He did think about a Stanley Steamer, until we passed one on fire the other day. Now he is fixed on a Crossley, even though everyone tells him the brakes don't work in wet weather and you have to surprise it into gear. Mama says she won't set foot in it.'

'Perhaps I'll get one some day,' Beatrix said. 'Think how wonderful it would be to reach the top of a steep hill in the Lakes without having the horses on one's mind.'

'The Lakes! Sometimes you seem to think of nothing else. How about your books? I would have thought they would be your first concern at the moment.'

'They must be whilst I'm here, or at least *The Tailor* must. I have to redraw most of the illustrations that Norman's using from my privately printed edition. I'm afraid I did them in rather a hurry, wanting to get on. Norman has shown me where I've skimped on things.'

'So you'll need to go into Gloucester for the backgrounds and

118

you've brought the mice models with you. What about the cross-legged tailor? Parton's little boy you used as a model last time is bigger now. Anyway he saw the privately printed *Tailor* and doesn't altogether fancy sharing the book with mice; says they give him the cold shudders.'

'Then it's just as well that Norman says that illustration will do. The figure's got his back to the reader and the light is on his work so the poor drawing doesn't matter.'

'I can hear Norman Warne's strictures in your every sentence. The dear man seems very opinionated about the work of a gifted author and artist intent on making her fortune!'

'Oh, but Caroline, he really is a good editor. I did my best to get him to leave in some of the rhymes he's cutting out of this new edition of the *Tailor*. We had quite an argument, but he was adamant and now it's done I can see he was right.'

'You lost the battle and instead of stumping off in high dudgeon you remain to praise the victor! Really Beatrix, you surprise me. That's not your style at all.' Caroline had her eyebrows raised and a quizzical look on her classical features. 'I'm beginning to wonder just what your feelings are towards this young man. And what his intentions are towards yourself.'

Beatrix felt her face grow warm and got up and went over to the window. Of course Caroline didn't mean it; she was being deliberately provoking, making fun of her, but she did wish she wouldn't do it. It was worse than her previous leaning towards metaphysics.

'Gammon, Caroline. Gammon and spinach. You only do it to annoy because you know it teases.'

'What does he look like, this Norman of yours?'

'He's not mine! Rather good-looking really. He's not too tall, his ears are very neat and he has nice brown eyes, well apart, and a pale complexion. Plenty of hair, but not too long and he's always beautifully turned-out.' Beatrix tickled the little lady rabbit under her chin and took her out of the cage. 'He's very gentle too, and likes animals.' When she turned round she found Caroline looking at her extremely thoughtfully.

'Have you met his family?' she said at last.

'I don't know what that's got to do with it, but yes, I have. Norman lives with his mother and sister Millie in a tall house in Bedford Square, round the corner from the office, and they happened to walk past one day when he was seeing me into the carriage. His two brothers are married and live away.'

'What are the mother and the sister like?'

'Really Caroline, you're as bad as your father for cross-examining a person. Millie is a spinster a little older than me and very pleasant. Norman is his mother's favourite, there's no doubt of that. You could tell from the way she looked at him.'

'You know what you've done, dear cousin Beatrix?' Caroline looked quite dismayed. 'You've found a young man who, like you, has made himself a doormat for his family and is indispensable. He'll be the fulcrum around which that house revolves. Millie will consult him before making any kind of decision and, being recently widowed, his mother will rely on him to manage all her affairs. The two married brothers will expect him to be the one who stays late at the office in times of crisis. Any idea of his getting married and leaving them will provoke a battle royal. They'll use every dirty trick they know.'

'Caroline, you're romancing. They were very kind and there's no question of his getting married. You've made the whole thing up in your own head. He is good to them all, of course he is, but you're creating a storm in nothing so large as a teacup; a doll's eggcup say.'

'I bet there was a storm in that Bedford Square household after they'd seen you,' Caroline said darkly. 'Thunder and lightning and a strong wind howling in the chimney. And as if that wasn't enough, there's your own situation to be considered. How do the Aged Ps take your visits to the office?'

'Badly,' said Beatrix before she could stop herself. She stroked the lady rabbit's ears so hard she whiffled her whiskers and sneezed. 'Apart from reiterating at every opportunity that I will ruin my eyes and go blind before I'm forty if I continue with these delicate illustrations, they have now decided it's *indecorous* for me to visit my publishers without a chaperone! It wasn't so bad when it was Elizabeth who went with me; she stayed in the carriage and talked to Beckett. Lately they've decided Elizabeth should not be taken away from her duties and it has to be Papa. When applied to, it's a wonderful thing how busy he is and unable to be of help. So now I mostly have to write letters, which can lead to misunderstandings.'

'There, you see. Your Aged Ps are going to fight as well! Oh, Beatrix! How are we going to get you out of this coil?'

# CHAPTER FOURTEEN

In the last weeks of the winter of 1904, Beatrix was hard at work finishing off *Two Bad Mice* and starting *Benjamin Bunny*, both scheduled for publication in the autumn. *The Tale of Squirrel Nutkin* and *The Tailor of Gloucester*, published the previous year, were doing well and she found work brought satisfaction and quite a high degree of pleasure.

It also brought problems. The letter she had received from Norman Warne that morning was a case in point. In it he had confirmed that afternoon's appointment and gone on to say that his mother would be pleased if Beatrix could find the time to take tea with her when they were finished with business. This was a dreadful worry as she really felt she should go. It would be very rude to refuse when almost on the doorstep but she did wish she need not. It would mean insisting on attending the appointment on her own; she couldn't arrive at a tea party with Papa, it would be much too vexing for everyone.

After lunch Beatrix went down into the kitchen at No. 2 Bolton Gardens to find Elizabeth, still in her morning uniform, peering out of the area door and watching passing feet on the pavement above. Dead leaves were scurrying in, blown by a cold north wind.

'Are you waiting for someone, Elizabeth?' she asked. Elizabeth shook her head slowly, as though in a dream. 'Then why don't you shut the door?' Beatrix suggested. 'It's not too warm today.'

Elizabeth jumped like a March hare, then shut the door with a bang.

Beatrix blinked in surprise, but she was in a hurry. 'I may be out for afternoon tea, Elizabeth. I've just received a letter from Mr Warne. He says his mother would be pleased if I could find the time to take tea with her, though goodness knows why, after my appointment at Warnes' office.'

For a moment Elizabeth seemed bewildered, then her face cleared.

'Of course Miss Bea, I'll manage. I'm sorry, I'm not quite myself this afternoon.'

Well, Beatrix thought, that makes two of us. The necessity of taking tea with Norman's almost unknown relations was making her feet cold and her head hot. She had turned to go when a stentorian voice from the hall made her clutch the stair-rail.

'Beatrix, come up here at once,' her mother was demanding. 'I want you in the study.'

They were both in there when Beatrix presented herself at the door, Papa at his desk with his eyes on anything but her, Mama sitting in an upright chair staring at her hands folded in her lap.

'Your Aunt Clara is not at all well,' her mother said abruptly. 'She has just sent a note to say she is confined to bed. I must visit her at once and will need the carriage this afternoon. Your father will come with me.'

Could matters be going to arrange themselves so that she could carry out her plans without difficulty? No, of course they couldn't. Beatrix almost nodded in self-congratulation as she was immediately proved right.

'You will come as well,' her mother concluded.

'But Mama, I have a business appointment. I can't just break it to visit Aunt Clara, fond of her though I am. I will send my affectionate regards through you and go tomorrow to see her.' Beatrix knew this was a useless effort, but it had to be made.

'Business indeed! Drawings for children's books are not *business*! Write the man a letter if you must, but I can't see why he doesn't just get on with what you've given him. Next thing, you'll be meeting his family socially, and that I will not tolerate. You've given him ideas above his station, going down there so often. He might do better if you didn't keep bothering him. A tradesman is what he is, printing is his trade. Tell him to do it.'

'No, I must go.' Beatrix realised her hands were clenched together behind her back, as though she were a naughty girl being reprimanded. She unclenched them and allowed them to fall to her sides. 'It won't matter that Papa can't come; it's quite usual for ladies to visit business offices on their own these days.'

'It may be for *some* people,' said her mother darkly, 'but not for this family. There is no way I could allow you to go without your father.' She turned her head sideways, towards her husband. 'Tell her so, Rupert.'

Her father looked unhappy and fretted in his chair. 'Perhaps she could go alone just this once. It appears a perfectly respectable place.'

Mrs Potter untucked her chin from her jabot and shook her head at him, making her jowls wobble. 'You are sadly mistaken, Rupert, to think that appearances have anything to do with it. A room of fine furniture and a suit of good clothes can conceal much depravity. No, you must come with us, Beatrix. You've just time to write a note with your instructions to Mr Warne before Beckett brings the carriage.'

The thought of the Warne offices being depraved made Beatrix want to giggle. All the clerks were ancient and fussed over her in a fatherly manner, one of them so exactly like the White Rabbit she was always expecting him to exclaim 'The Duchess, the Duchess! Oh, my dear paws. Oh my fur and whiskers.' Did Mama expect the Duchess to appear and say 'off with her head'?

'No, Mama. I am going to keep this appointment,' Beatrix heard her own voice say, remarkably calmly, though the quiver of amusement was just discernible. 'I shall go in a hansom cab.' Now that was bold indeed and calculated to stir things up even more.

'Indeed you will not, my girl. Rupert, tell her this instant that she can do no such thing.' Her mother's voice was beginning to rise and Papa pushed himself to his feet in alarm.

'Beatrix, how can you be so defiant?' he asked, pink with distress and his hands trembling on the desk. 'I've never known you like this before and look what you're doing to your mother.' Mrs Potter was breathing very fast and shallow, each breath drawn in on a low moan. They both watched her for a moment in silence. Then Beatrix turned and walked out of the room.

Outside, she nearly fell over Elizabeth who had undoubtedly been listening at the door. Beatrix wondered if she made a habit of it.

'Oh Miss Bea. What a turn-up! Whilst you change your dress and that, I'll run round to the mews and get you a cab.' She was off downstairs before Beatrix had time to say that she hadn't intended to change, but on second thoughts it might be as well, she'd got paint on this skirt.

Putting on her new blouse from Bourne and Hollingsworth, Beatrix wondered if her parents would physically try to prevent her leaving the house; lock her in her room with nothing but bread and water perhaps. Oh rubbish, she told herself with a giggle. She was thirty-seven years old and could have been a grandmother if she'd married young. Bread and water indeed!

She was still laughing as she came down from her room carrying her portfolio, and perhaps it was this that prevented her father from saying anything as she passed him. There was no sign of Mama.

Elizabeth had a cab waiting for her out of sight of the house and hurried her over. She doesn't want me to have time to change my mind, Beatrix thought, her heart hammering.

The hansom looked very precarious. 'D'you know, Elizabeth,' she puffed breathlessly as she mounted the step, 'I've never before gone totally against my parents' wishes.'

Elizabeth's reply was almost inaudible in the clatter of horses' hooves, but Beatrix's inner ear relayed the words as the cab set off for Bedford Street. 'Not before time, Miss Bea,' she'd been told. 'Not before time.'

Beatrix was still feeling pleased with herself when she reached Warnes' office. Looking in the little mirror in the waiting-room, she saw that for once her colour was good and her hat on straight. Norman came in with a flurry of apologies for keeping her waiting and every possible enquiry after her health and comfort as he always did. She cut him a little short; it already seemed a long time since breakfast. He made no remark on the absence of her father and neither did she.

First he had to show her the record of sales. Beatrix didn't see the need, there was so much to discuss, but realised it gave him pleasure to detail how well the books were doing. She calculated that if she hadn't helped Bertram, a farm at the Lakes would now have been within her reach, *Peter Rabbit* being mainly responsible. At least she'd bought that field near Hill Top last summer, when they'd gone over to Sawrey for the day from Fawe Park.

'What a dreadful amount of Peter,' she said.

Norman laughed. He had a most infectious laugh and Beatrix joined in. 'Not many of our authors would have phrased it like that,' he said. 'How are you getting on with the next rabbit book?'

'The backgrounds are not too bad, the plant pots and wheelbarrows and even the wall round Fawe Park kitchen garden that I sketched last summer, though getting the different colours right has taken time. They fit in very well. I've brought the ones that are ready.'

Beatrix untied her portfolio and they went over the

drawings, Norman making comments and suggestions from time to time. Then he caught sight of a mouse drawing.

'You haven't started *Two Bad Mice* already?'

'Yes, that's Hunca Munca. She was rescued from the cook at Harescombe Grange where my cousin lives. Poor Hunca Munca was caught under the cheese dish because she'd carelessly left her tail hanging outside and I saved her from death by meat hatchet. She's getting quite tame but I'm having difficulty drawing her. She will retreat to the darkest corner of her box to make her nest; what I really need is for one side to be glass.'

'I could make you a mouse-box like that if you like.' Norman suddenly looked eager, like a brown-eyed spaniel who has been promised a walk.

'Oh, could you? That would make things so much simpler,' Beatrix said. It was so seldom anyone offered to do anything for her that she felt almost tearful with gratitude. 'Then I can put Tom Thumb in with her and they can set up house together.'

'Tom Thumb and Hunca Munca. That was Fielding, wasn't it?'

'Well, I've just borrowed the names.'

'Not only a talented artist and writer,' Norman said, 'but a student of English literature too.' He sat on the other side of his desk, staring at her intently. She thought suddenly that she rather liked his nose. Then he smiled. 'We are fortunate to have you on our list.'

Beatrix found herself smiling back with a modest declaimer, but in one corner of her mind she agreed. The way her sales were going up was enough to give cause for unbounded gratification to the Warne family, sisters and cousins and aunts included.

'So you've got the two mice to draw and what you want now is a doll's house to put them in.' Norman was turning over the drawings and somehow his right hand brushed against Beatrix's left hand. It left a tingling feeling, something like stroking a rabbit's coat. 'I'm making a doll's house for Winifred's birthday, that's Fruing's eldest daughter. You could have a look at it today, if you are able to accept Mother's invitation.'

Beatrix didn't answer for a moment. She could turn back now from a final disregard of Mama's express wish that she should not meet the Warne family socially. She could make her excuses and leave behind misunderstandings and every kind of upset in order to remain a dutiful daughter. It put a person in a very difficult position.

'Your mother is most kind and I accept with pleasure.'

'That's settled then. I'll take you round myself. Now, let's have a look at this idea of yours for a Peter Rabbit board game.'

Mrs Warne's drawing-room was stiflingly hot and Beatrix had been edged into a low chair near the fire. Mrs Warne sat opposite on a small sofa that gave her height advantage over Beatrix. She wore a rather formal day dress of lilac silk in a princess style with a tie-back skirt. It made Beatrix, in her fine-checked tweed costume with a plain skirt, feel altogether frumpish.

Two little girls in white broiderie anglaise dresses with long sleeves and little capes sat on small cushions by their grandmother as though posing for a photograph. Norman's sister Millie and his sister-in-law Mary, his brother Fruing's wife, shared a Chester-field with a spaniel who looked like Spot. Afternoon tea had been placed on two low tables and a mahogany dumb waiter, adding to the difficulties of a room in which it was dangerous to move. The gentlemen's relish sandwiches were curling like wilting petals and the Victoria sponge looked tired.

Beatrix had expected Norman to join the tea party, but he had delivered her into Millie's hands and departed, saying something about doing some work on the doll's house and seeing her before she left.

'He never takes tea with us,' Millie had said in some kind of apology for him, but Beatrix wondered if his presence had been barred.

Mrs Warne was speaking. She had a sweet round face, blue eyes and a lot of fluffy white hair. 'I expect you find us a little overwhelming, Miss Potter, but you mustn't mind us; we're all one big happy family really, aren't we my little poppets?' Her grand-daughters nodded automatically without taking their eyes off Beatrix. Mrs Warne's voice matched her face.

Beatrix smiled and wished she could remove her jacket. The two little girls had stared at her solemnly since she arrived, as though expecting her to perform for them in some way. They both had rather large features and it made her quite nervous.

'Do have another cup of tea, Miss Potter,' Mrs Fruing said. She was large too, taking up more than her share of the couch and wearing a tight-fitting dress and a fashionable wavy-brimmed hat trimmed with feathers. It gave her the look of a colonial soldier and she had a voice to match, sharp and peremptory.

Beatrix declined politely. Her first cup of tea had been the colour of mahogany and thick with cream. With that and the heat of the fire, she was feeling a little sick. She sat silent and wondered what she could say. The subject of the weather had been exhausted, as had the general health of the company and Mrs Warne's dislike of the modern tendency towards divided and, even worse, shorter skirts. She remembered Hunca Munca and launched into a little tale of how the mouse had tried to carry a doll as big as herself up to her nest. This was received, at least by Millie, with some interest and she was encouraged to tell them that Norman had offered to make a mouse-box with a glass side so she could draw the mice more easily.

Mrs Warne pursed her lips. 'Norman gets tired easily,' she said. 'I hope it won't be too much for him. I would have thought your job, as an artist, is to provide the finished illustrations unaided.' Her voice, for a moment, lost its sweet tones.

The eldest child, Winifred, spoke for the first time. 'He'll be too busy with my doll's house,' she objected. Her younger sister Eveline put her thumb in her mouth.

'I'm hoping you'll let me draw your doll's house to go in the book with the mice,' Beatrix said, smiling at Winifred.

Winifred made no comment, continuing to stare.

'I'm not sure,' said Mrs Fruing, 'that she likes the idea of mice running around among all the dolls' things. It's not something she's accustomed to.' Nor, to judge by her cold tones, did Mrs Fruing like the idea either. Beatrix felt a big effort had been made to omit the word '*smelly*'. She wondered whether to try to explain that the mice would not actually be put into the doll's house. It seemed too difficult. She was grappling with the extraordinary idea that while her parents considered Norman a mere tradesman, Norman's mother considered Beatrix a mere itinerant artist and had invited her to tea to tell her so. It was altogether rather shabby.

'Are you fond of children?' Mrs Warne now asked.

'Why yes, of course,' Beatrix replied, 'though my acquaintance with them is limited to my cousins and the children of my old governess.'

'You must make friends with Winifred and Eveline,' Mrs Warne said. 'Large families ensure a happy marriage; we are expecting an addition ourselves.' She looked coyly in the direction of Mrs Fruing. 'But Norman tells us you are not very strong and prefer the country to London,' she went on. 'Now did he say you wished you could live in Scotland or was it the seaside you liked?' There was a suggestion of waterproofs and wooden spades in her voice.

'I find the Lake District suits me very well,' Beatrix replied. 'London often seems stuffy.' And she can make what she likes of that, she told herself. Mrs Warne's talk of large families was beginning to make her more nervous than the stares of the little girls.

'There's plenty of air in Surbiton,' Mrs Fruing said with asperity. 'I've never been to the Lake District, but I understand life there is rather primitive and the drains not above suspicion. Of course, living there, you wouldn't need to keep up with the changes in fashion.' Her eyes seemed to be on Beatrix's hat.

'Of course!' Mrs Warne's face took on a look of concern. 'It must be your age, Miss Potter. You'll be about the same as Millie, thirty-seven isn't it Millie? She's getting all sorts of silly ideas too. Not that she wants to leave London, but there are other things.' She shook her head at her daughter in mock reproof. 'Norman,' she went on, 'has always remained sensible, but of course he's younger. He likes London and prefers to go abroad for his holidays.'

Millie, who had been engaged in stroking the dog's ears and not apparently listening to the conversation, looked at the dog closely and sat up.

'Mama, I think I had better take Fancy out for a short walk; she's got a dry nose and is panting a lot, she may be too hot. Perhaps Miss Potter might like to come with me?' Millie stood up, a lean figure in a drab skirt and a blouse worn with a masculine tie and over her shoulders a draped paisley shawl in an ineffective clutch at a Pre-Raphaelite effect. To Beatrix she looked an angel of mercy.

'I should very much like to accompany you and Fancy,' she said quickly before there could be any objections. Mrs Fruing shut her mouth with an almost audible snap and unless a person knew Mrs Warne's sweet nature they might have thought she looked sulky.

Millie had put on an old black mantle and a black toque that tipped over her eyes as she fought to turn the key in the gate of Bedford Square Gardens. 'I always mean to bring some oil, it's so stiff, then I forget,' she said. 'I must ask Norman to do it for us, he doesn't forget things.' She smiled at Beatrix, a kind smile in an unremarkable face, but she had her brother's eyes.

128

The weather was pleasant for February and the late afternoon with the dusk falling had a hint of spring. Fancy gambolled clumsily, as spaniels do, scoring the earth with her claws and tearing up a small clump of snowdrops already almost in flower. Millie dropped on her knees regardless of her skirt, pulled off her gloves and replanted the bulbs. 'I can't bear flowers to suffer,' she told Beatrix, hauling herself to her feet with the aid of a sturdy laurel bush. 'What I would really like most in the world is a small garden of my own and, do you know, I don't think I would keep a dog.'

'What I would like most would be a small farm in the Lake District,' Beatrix told her. She liked Millie very much and she was the first person to whom she had confided this wish.

'That would be too ambitious for me, but you have to have something to work towards, don't you.'

Beatrix understood her perfectly. A person looking after her parents needed a goal over and above the everyday duties.

'Of course you have your books, so very clever,' Millie went on, without a trace of envy in her admiration. 'But even then – somewhere of your own. Yes, I can see that. I like reading of course, such a solace. At one time I had thought of keeping a bookshop after . . . but not now I think.' They paced in silence for a few yards, hardly able to see the garden in the deepening twilight.

'Mother's right about one thing, though,' Millie said suddenly in an apparent *non sequitur*. 'Norman does like London more than the countryside.'

Beatrix could think of no appropriate reply.

'Well,' Millie went on brightly. 'I should think that Fancy has more than emptied her little can by now and we can go back.' She whistled, just like a boy, to bring the animal out of the bushes.

They retraced their steps, again having trouble with the key, but once across the road Millie led the way round the side of the house. 'We'll go in the back way, I've got my feet too muddy for the front.'

The back door led into a flagged passage. Millie removed her shoes on a piece of sacking and pointed to a flight of steps leading to a cellar from which came an energetic sound of hammering.

'Why don't you go down and see how Norman's getting on whilst I find my slippers and wipe Fancy's paws? Millie said, still brightly. She trotted away before Beatrix had time to reply.

The steps were well lit with a gas jet and Beatrix went hesitantly down. The hammering stopped before she reached the bottom and Norman was standing there in his shirtsleeves, waving a small hammer in triumph.

'Oh, good. You've come to look at the doll's house.' His smile was like the beam of a lighthouse. 'There it is. What d'you think of it? Will it do?' Like a little boy amazed at his own cleverness, Beatrix thought fleetingly.

A two-storeyed red brick villa with small balconies for the first-floor windows stood on the battens of wood in the middle of the cellar. Norman had been nailing on the chimney.

'Look, the front opens and I've even got some stairs.'

'Why yes.' Beatrix understood that type of house perfectly. Everything had a place and with everything in its place there would be nowhere to live comfortably. It would be perfect for the *Two Bad Mice*, just right for wickedness. 'But I can't sketch it now. There's no time and anyway it's rather dark in here.' The cellar was both gloomy and damp and not a good place in which to work at all, Beatrix thought.

'Never mind, it will be in Surbiton soon, after Winifred's birthday, and you could go down there to draw it. Take your mother and stay to lunch; Mrs Fruing would be delighted.'

Beatrix was horrified. 'I couldn't take my mother, she wouldn't want to go, she hardly goes anywhere these days. And she takes dislikes to people, she might . . .' She looked at Norman in despair. How could she make him understand? The long day and the difficulties she'd had to face suddenly went to her legs and she wished there was somewhere to sit.

Millie came down the stone steps. 'There now, I knew you'd like the house and want to put it in your book, but you must come now as Mary and the girls are going; you too Norman. Norman, are you all right?'

Beatrix had been looking at Millie and turned to see Norman leaning rather heavily against the doll's house, his face whiter than usual.

'Yes, of course I'm all right. I tried to turn the house towards the light, that's all, and found it rather heavy. I must be tired. Go on up, I'll come in a minute.'

Beatrix followed Millie up the stairs, feeling surprised. The doll's house didn't look heavy. She'd thought it rather flimsy when she saw it first, but probably she was mistaken, being somewhat tired herself.

# CHAPTER FIFTEEN

*The Tale of Two Bad Mice* had been ready for Norman by the autumn and published as the now expected new Beatrix Potter book for Christmas. With all the business of the doll's house out of the way, for in the end she had made do with her brief inspection in the cellar and some photographs Norman had taken for her, Beatrix had got on with illustrating *The Tale of Mrs Tiggy-Winkle*, written four years before at Lingholm. This had gone well, the backgrounds from sketches she'd done in Newlands valley fitting in excellently. There still remained, though, the worry about Norman's health. He was always so very pale in spite of the warm and pleasant spring.

'Don't grunt so, Mrs Tiggy,' Beatrix said, looking up from her sketching as her train of thought was interrupted. 'That's not at all a proper way of expressing yourself. You've got into what little Miss Scott at Dunkeld used to call "a state of dishbill".' Mrs Tiggy, propped up against a pillow with her mutch cap over one eye and getting the fidgets, grunted again impatiently.

'Give me rabbits any time. Never mind, this is the last sitting. Just a touch-up that Norman suggested, and then the book is finished.'

Of course after that she had to do battle with *The Pie and the Patty Pan*. The backgrounds would be all right – she could use the houses in Sawrey, and the interiors, and some bits and pieces of her own such as her Edward VII Coronation teapot – but there was something wrong with the story. It had been hanging about ever since she'd written it in some desperation on that ill-advised holiday in Hastings two years ago. No one should ever attempt the seaside in November. *Jeremy Fisher* would have been preferable and frogs easier to draw than Pomeranians, but Norman thought children would not like frogs. The trouble was, Norman himself didn't like frogs and couldn't imagine anyone else doing so. Rabbits and mice he tolerated, but he preferred the traditional cats and dogs; hence Duchess with her bushy tail and Ribby with her apron. A townsman's point of view.

131

Beatrix was suddenly aware of being patronising. She mustn't forget that Norman had been a great help, particularly with *Two Bad Mice*. It really had been fun finding the right dolls, borrowing that policeman doll from a reluctant Winifred; and the miniature furniture and food he'd bought at Hamleys were just right. It was amazing how well the work went when it could be discussed with Norman. She could talk to him so easily and ideas seemed to flow between them. They had such comfortable conversations and when they couldn't meet, which happened too often as Mama got more and more demanding, his letters were a great support. He often put a hand on her shoulder when they were considering a drawing together and she didn't find it in the least distasteful.

Mrs Tiggy grunted again and then yawned. 'Sir John Millais wouldn't have given twopence for you as a model,' Beatrix said severely. 'You have no stamina. Come and sit on my knee and then I'll write a letter whilst you have a nap. I wish you were like Hunca Munca; I can never catch her asleep.' The little brown mouse, eyes bright and ears pricked at Beatrix's voice, looked up from her nest-building activities at the back of her box. 'It's no good building a nest,' Beatrix told her. 'Not now that Tom Thumb has gone.'

She wondered, for no reason she could think of, what it would be like to have a baby. No one had ever discussed the mysteries of *accouchements* in her presence, never mind the preliminaries that brought it about, and it would be impossible to ask. Hunca Munca had produced three babies without any difficulty, but then Tom Thumb had become jealous and that had been that. He'd even tried to eat one of them, not something likely to occur on the human level. Children were rather nice and seemed to like her all right – well the Moores did anyway. Actually looking after them might be different. There had been that mortifying occasion when she'd tried to help the Warnes' nanny and had put Winifred's knickers on back to front. The poor child hadn't been able to sit down and the nanny had been vexed but really all those buttons were most confusing. Mice wouldn't have that problem.

Mrs Tiggy's expected attempt to bite was frustrated by the duster used to move her. When she was settled Beatrix chewed the end of her pen and considered what to say to Cousin Caroline. Since the death of his wife Crompton Hutton's freakish fancies must have taken a turn for the worse, as on her last visit it had been obvious that the two sisters were having a difficult time with their papa. Something to take Caroline's mind off Harescombe Grange was needed. She began to write:

*Dear Caroline,*

*I would like you to be one of the first to know that I have bought a small tenanted farm in the Lake District. It became possible after I discovered that Aunt Clara had left me some money in her will, mildly astonishing as I never thought she had a fondness for me; she considered my taste in hats deplorable. With this legacy and my royalties I have been able to buy Hill Top Farm in Near Sawrey in Lancashire.*

*I have had an ambition to own property in the Lake District for some time, but had almost given up hope of ever achieving it. Then I received my legacy and shortly afterwards I had a letter from Sawrey. I had sent up some books for the children as there was an outbreak of scarlet fever in the village and Mrs Lord, who wrote to thank me, let drop among the exclamation marks that Hill Top Farm was for sale, tenanted of course. Our coachman Mr Beckett and his family always stayed there when we took Lakeside on Esthwaite Water for the summer, so I knew it well. I remembered the name of a Hawkshead solicitor, wrote to him with my instructions and, though it is taking an age for the details to be agreed, I have heard this week that all will soon be completed. This year, 1905, is an auspicious year. I have a place of my own.*

*I couldn't go to see it as that might have alerted the enemy, but there was no need. It sits just behind the Tower Bank Arms, which nicely conceals it from the village, and the farmyard and buildings are well sheltered by a small hill. It overlooks some of the most perfect countryside in the Lake District.*

*I know you think I have always been foolishly attached to the Lake counties and Sawrey in particular and I'm afraid my publisher feels the same, but just you both wait. When I've dealt with the state of the roof (Mrs Lord remarked on that particularly), and the lack of a water closet, the delights of Hill Top are unassailable.*

*I shall present this* fait accompli *to my parents as an investment. Looked upon in this light, there is every hope they may accept it without argument as it is something within their understanding. I am waiting for the right moment to bring it to their attention. My real plans for Hill Top will be unveiled in due course.*

*Mrs Tiggy-Winkle is snoring loudly on my knee and will soon wake to demand her bread and milk so I must venture into the kitchen regions to satisfy her appetite. 'Venture' is the appropriate word as life below stairs, though I'm seldom party to it, seems to have a measure of excitement sadly lacking in the higher echelons. One day I must tell you about the occasion when the cook got drunk!*

*I would much enjoy a letter from you when you have the time,*

> *Yours affectionately,*
> *Beatrix*

Mrs Tiggy having fulfilled Beatrix's prediction, she put her in her box and went down to the kitchen. She opened the door tentatively but today the maids were engaged in the innocuous task of cleaning the silver whilst Mrs Pearson washed cabbage in the scullery. Elizabeth had the bread and milk keeping warm on the hob. She also had a request.

'Would it be all right, Miss Beatrix, if I changed my afternoon off and went out today? Something awkward has happened and I have to go to Hampstead. I'll put out the tea things and Betty says she can manage.'

Mama would growl. She hated even such a minute change in her ordered life as a servant altering her afternoon off, but that was no reason to refuse Elizabeth. No need to ask why, either. No business of anyone but the person involved.

'Yes of course you can as long as Betty doesn't mind.' She saw the maids exchange glances as she took the bread and milk upstairs.

Whilst Mrs Tiggy made slobbering noises in her dish, Beatrix took Hunca Munca out of the mouse-box that Norman had made so meticulously. The little mouse liked to investigate the dark, mysterious regions under Beatrix's jacket lapels and collar and made first for the lapel, from which she emerged in a sneezing fit. Beatrix thought that she must give this old jacket a good brush or perhaps she should replace it, only it was so comfortable. By this time Hunca Munca had investigated the back of the collar and was climbing up Beatrix's rolled coil of hair to the top of her head. This was very bold but Beatrix didn't dare move quickly to lift her off in case of accidents. The next thing was that Hunca Munca leapt, like a squirrel, on to the chandelier above the table. Beatrix realised what had happened when it jingled and swung a little with the impact. Hunca Munca had not allowed for the swing and couldn't get a grip on the slippery glass surface. She scrabbled for a moment and then fell, hitting the table with a tiny squelching thud. Beatrix, taken by surprise and grabbing too late, was sure she had broken her neck.

For a moment, it seemed perhaps not. The mouse shuddered and then struggled up and made her way across the table to the steps up to her mouse-box, but before she regained her nest her legs failed her. She died in Beatrix's hand.

Beatrix, feeling shockingly sick, stared at the little corpse cradled in her fingers. The mice, lizards, rabbits, hedgehogs, bats and birds who had inhabited the old nursery from her extreme youth had all died in rotation and been summarily buried or, on occasion, had their flesh boiled off to expose the mysteries of their bone structure. Nature was cruel enough in all conscience and they probably lived longer in the nursery than in the wild. But if she hadn't been so careless, letting her get so close to the chandelier, poor Hunca Munca would still be alive. Haunted by the memory of bright eyes and sensitive ears attending to her every word, Beatrix wondered if she would ever come to forgive herself. 'I'd rather have broken my own neck,' she said aloud, and then decided she was indulging in histrionics.

It was a busy summer with work not helped by an interminable heat wave. London baked under an incandescent sky, and a paintbrush was slippery in the hand. There was also this visit to Wales in late July, standing like a crossroads in Beatrix's path with everything to be finished before she got there.

Mama was her usual self, requiring help with putting on her stays and needing embroidery silks matched without delay. Poor Papa for once tried to be helpful, but Beatrix found herself snapping even at him.

The day the blocks for *Mrs Tiggy-Winkle* were delivered for her scrutiny was hotter than ever. Beatrix looked at them and felt quite faint. Nearly every one was covered in spots, worse than measles. Norman must not know of her intense disappointment, but it was essential that something be done *immediately*.

She scribbled off a note to go back with the blocks asking

Norman to tell Hentschels – *firmly* – to rub the blocks down as much as they could. Norman was so sweet-natured there was no doubt he found it hard to be firm. She also advanced a theory that the heat had caused a chemical reaction with the etching fluid and suggested, to comfort them both, that the illustrations would look much better with the lighter blue that had been decided for the printing. That was the best she could do. She arranged for the blocks to be sent back to Bedford Street and went at last to her mother, who had been demanding her presence for the last half an hour to oversee the set of the sleeves in a new gown the dressmaker was fitting for her.

When a letter arrived from Norman two days later Beatrix expected it to contain news of the blocks, and perhaps the Peter Rabbit wallpaper with which little progress was being made. At first she could not make sense of what he had written. He felt they had much in common . . . do him the honour of accepting his . . . Then her brain cleared and she sat down slowly. Norman was asking her to marry him.

Now that was really civil of him. She felt a little breathless and her heart thumped uncontrollably. Then she realised she was smiling and her excitement was rising and bubbling like yeast in warm milk. She stood up and took deep breaths. What a wonderful prospect. She went over to the table to find pen and ink. But could she, dare she do it? She could, she would accept Norman's proposal. Could she persuade her parents to let her go?

Mama was in the hall when she came downstairs, sitting on one of the pair of chairs with an awkward nub carved into the back, so anyone leaning against them would receive a severe dig between their shoulder-blades. She was leaning forward, her head bent over her hands and still wearing her bonnet from her morning outing. Beatrix felt convinced she was there because some sixth sense had warned her that her daughter was contemplating action that would be detrimental to her comfort. She could probably actually see the letter from Norman in Beatrix's right-hand jacket pocket and her letter of acceptance in the other one. She felt a flush flood her face, as though she had been caught in some wrong-doing. Furious, she stumped through the hall without looking at Mama and heard the front door crash behind her.

The gong was sounding when she returned, so it was necessary to eat roast beef, rather tough, as naturally as she could manage. The boiled cabbage was the worst to swallow. Both

Mama and Papa made a remark now and then, but Mama kept pushing out her lips and occasionally shaking her head.

When the interminable meal was over she thought of excusing herself to write letters, and how many unnecessary letters she must have written just to get away, but Mama took a firm grip on her arm, pretending to need support as far as the drawing-room. Once there, she opened a direct attack.

'Beatrix, I'm very worried about you. You seem quite disturbed and it started with that letter from Warnes that arrived this morning. What was in it to affect you so?'

What could a person do except tell the truth and shame the devil? Perhaps it was for the best as no time was going to be a good time for this news.

'Norman Warne has asked me to marry him and I have accepted his proposal.'

Mama subsided on the sofa with a face of stone. Papa stood with his back to the empty fireplace as though to gain comfort from the ghosts of past fires.

'You can't accept a proposal without my consent,' he told her. 'There is no possibility I shall give it.'

'Papa I'm not under-age, I'm thirty-eight years old. There is no need for consent, I can marry whom and when I like.' Now she was on the defensive, which was not what she had intended. Her heart began to thump most unpleasantly.

'You are still our daughter.' Mama refused to meet Beatrix's eyes. 'The man's in trade and we will not allow you to demean yourself so.' She made it sound as though Norman was a grocer's assistant.

So they were going to continue with the same old argument. In addition any minute now Mama would look at her in that certain way and enquire if she were quite well, which by suggestion could bring on a severe sick headache. She told her heart to be quiet and waited a moment. She would try an attack as direct as their own.

'Mama – Papa, I realise you both feel it is the duty of a daughter to look after her parents as long as need be, and that neither of you is getting any younger and the time is coming when you won't be able to manage without me.' There, was that direct enough? Mama had flushed angrily at being called old and Papa was gobbling incoherently. 'I intend to get married, but I also intend to see you both properly cared for. Don't imagine I would shirk my duty. A housekeeper,' she went on, her voice annoyingly wobbly, 'a capable housekeeper would look after you perfectly well, no doubt better than myself. The house would continue to be comfortably run and you would hardly notice the difference.'

'A housekeeper!' Papa's outrage was almost funny. She might have been offering him a camel-keeper to pour his coffee.

Mama at last raised her head and looked at her daughter. 'You have most certainly taken leave of your senses but at least you can have the decency not to let the news get out. If you insist on this so-called engagement, it cannot go beyond the two families. You must promise there will be no announcement.'

So the underground war would continue, the subterfuges, the changes of mind, the prevention of meetings, every opportunity taken to drive a wedge between herself and Norman to prevent her leaving. Could she defy them further? A grey exhaustion clamped down on her body and mind.

'Very well Mama.'

The office in Bedford Street was not a romantic place for a meeting, Beatrix decided. Really the stares of the mahogany desk and the row of technical books in the glass-fronted cabinet were quite embarrassing. Nor was there going to be time for any lengthy making of plans. Norman had to catch a train to Manchester within the hour.

'Millie is so delighted we're to be married,' he said now, holding both her hands with his own and smiling his wide, warm smile that made her heart melt so pleasurably. 'She is impatient to welcome her new sister-in-law.'

Beatrix noticed he didn't mention his mother.

'You do understand, Norman, about my parents? They need time to get used to the idea of my leaving them. It's not a contingency they had ever considered.'

'Of course I do.' He was trying to sound convincing. 'Still, announcement or no announcement, you must have a ring.' He forced a thin gold signet ring off the little finger of his right hand and eased it onto the third finger of Beatrix's left hand. 'There, it fits. I shall think of you, when you are in Wales, wearing my ring.'

Beatrix spread her fingers, looking at the ring, that ancient symbol of unity, of completeness, and couldn't speak. Norman leant across and kissed her gently on the mouth, a sealing of their pact. She suddenly wanted to draw him towards her, to feel his arms round her. Her hands closed on his involuntarily, but there was a knock on the door.

'Yes?' said Norman, still holding her left hand.

A clerk came in, the one who reminded her of the White Rabbit, and gazed at the two of them, holding hands in working hours, in mild astonishment. Then he quietly gave it up.

'Your cab's waiting, sir.'

# CHAPTER SIXTEEN

Beatrix felt the Welsh dresser was doing it on purpose. It sat there in the hall, self-satisfied and bulging with knobs, plain as a pike-staff against the panelling, but somehow she was unable to get it down on paper.

She wasn't worrying about anything. Gwaynynog was serene enough, the house a complete muddle of dates and styles and stuffy with plush curtains, but redeemed by the elegant furniture bestowed on it by her Uncle Fred Burton. Outside, the apricots were over-ripe on the garden wall as no one had thought of preserving them, but the apples looked promising, as did the late summer landscape. Unfortunately Cousin Alice was busy elsewhere, hence the sketching.

There was one thing. Norman hadn't written for over a week. He'd probably been busy. Harold had been pleasant when she'd called to say goodbye to Norman and heard he was ill, but somehow she'd got the idea that Norman's elder brother was not a hard worker. He'd made a point of assuring her that Norman was only slightly indisposed and would soon be back in the office. He'd been most understanding about her disinclination to discuss the engagement, but there was no getting away from the fact that he looked the sort of person who would load his burdens onto others. Norman would have had a pile of work waiting for him.

At least the Welsh dresser wasn't decorated with the emblem of a cotton plant; Uncle Fred had confined this fancy to the brass fenders and those modern chairs. Not content with introducing Lancashire servants into a countryside where the local people scarcely spoke English, he also wanted to imbue a Welsh house with the spirit of Lancashire enterprise. But then all the Leeches were proud of their origins, even Mama.

Beatrix gave up the sketch, at least for the time being. The Welsh dresser must in no way be allowed to get the better of her, but some fresh air might help matters. She went out of the open front door, wandered through the rose-arboured garden and opened the gate into the straggling park.

The view across the Denbighshire countryside in the afternoon sunlight was most pleasant: in the foreground, summer woods and pastures and small stone-built farms, like those in the Lake Country; and in the background, a mountain. Rather lumpy, it was true, but making a fine composition which she really must paint, if only to give to Uncle Fred.

Norman would enjoy this peaceful country scene, or probably would. It was frightening to realise how little she really knew about him. What did he like for breakfast and which side of the bed did he like to sleep?

Beatrix took off her hat and fanned her face. It was really a very warm day.

She must learn, in time, all that and more. A happy marriage was what she aspired to and sacrifices might have to be made. Hill Top must remain a mere investment until Norman could be convinced that Lancashire Beyond the Sands was not wet, inhospitable and uncivilised but quite one of the best places in the world. She might even have to curtail her large correspondence with children, though she didn't wish to do so.

Crossing the park and nearing the house again, she became aware of another attractive composition, park walls and stately trees leading the eye to a farm gate with the building beyond. All it needed was a small rabbit in the foreground, perhaps wearing a blue pinny, to be quite perfect. Benjamin's wife – she would have him marry his cousin Flopsy. Then the offspring could be called 'The Flopsy Bunnies'.

She knew she was smiling when she went into the hall, a story about the soporific effects of eating lettuce occupying her mind. The maid Polly came bursting out of the door to the servants' quarters.

'Oh Miss Potter, theer's a telegram.' Her thin, freckled face was anxious. 'It come when you were out, Jimmie the Post biked oop. 'Ere,' she picked up the buff envelope from the hall table. 'See, it says "Miss Potter" clear as anything.' She looked at it as though at a miracle, a flying letter, before handing it over.

Beatrix ran a finger under the flap. Mama, Papa, sudden illness, carriage accident?

The pasted capitals shouted at her.

GRIEVE TO TELL YOU NORMAN DIED SUDDENLY TODAY, 25TH AUGUST. MY HEART GOES OUT TO YOU. LETTER FOLLOWING. MILLIE.

The room reeled and Beatrix found herself saying 'I won't faint, I won't faint' as Polly put a chair behind her knees and pushed her into it.

'Is it bad news, Miss Potter? Are you all right? Shall I get you something?' Polly's face loomed above her own and then disappeared.

It couldn't be true. How could Norman have died when only five minutes ago she was dedicating her life to him? She looked into a vortex and clung to the arms of the chair to prevent herself falling.

There was a pungent smell under her nose. 'Smelling salts,' said Polly smugly as Beatrix sat up, sneezed and felt for her handkerchief. 'Nothing like them. Mrs Burton always said so. She'd have known what to do. Olwen's bringing tea.'

More little maids, clucking in Welsh, and strong, sweet tea. This would never do, though the tea was reviving.

'A friend has died suddenly,' she murmured. 'The shock, that's all. I'm all right now.' She felt as though she was reciting lines in a play. It couldn't be real.

'You still look bad, Miss Potter.' Polly's eyes were round and scared and full of curiosity. 'The Master'll be home soon. I think you should go and lie down.' The three little maids, heads covered in wildly streamered caps, nodded in unison.

Beatrix found a violin accompaniment running in her head to a song about three little maids from school are we. That was *The Mikado*. What extraordinary things went through a person's mind when her life was turned over like an hourglass.

'Yes,' she heard herself saying, 'yes, I think I'll go to my room.' She took a firm grip of the telegram, *that* must not be left about, then she applied herself to the stairs.

She must have managed them, because then she was lying on her bed with the telegram in one hand and the smelling salts in another. The dizziness was receding. Shakespeare had replaced Gilbert with 'Sing willow, willow, willow/Her salt tears fell from her and soften'd the stones/Sing willow, willow, willow.' Outside she could hear a robin trying out his autumn song.

Uncle Fred must be told something. He would hear about the telegram, yes indeed, as soon as he got back. What could she say? Bad news, leave at once? There must be more than that; perhaps 'death of a friend' would be enough. Her throat suddenly constricted and the smelling salts came into use. It was as well she hadn't been allowed to announce her engagement. Too much sympathy would completely unman her. Or should it be un-woman? She got up. She must wash her face and prepare for anxious enquiries.

In the middle of the night she woke suddenly from a dream where Mrs Tiggy-Winkle had become her old Scotch nanny and was hurrying her along the path above Little Town towards the door in Cat Bells. 'Well anyway,' she heard herself say as she awoke, 'now I needn't go home. To do that would be the outside of enough.'

Waking up completely, she found that she had quite decided. She would not go back to Bolton Gardens. The news would have reached them but no mention would ever be made to her of Norman's death. Papa and especially Mama would be convinced that a benign deity was looking after them, disposing of anything that inconvenienced them, and the routine of the house would go on as though nothing had happened. In their view, nothing had. Tears rolled down her cheeks. She could not go back to *that* for a long time, whatever they said. Perhaps to Bertram, but Mary would be so solicitous. Exhausted sleep overcame her as she considered where to go.

Millie's letter, which arrived next morning, solved the problem. She had answered all the questions she thought Beatrix might possibly ask. Norman had died of pernicious anaemia, from which no one had suspected he suffered until at long last he'd been persuaded to go to a doctor. He'd relapsed into a coma and passed away peacefully without regaining consciousness; there had been no last messages. He was to be buried in Highgate Cemetery. Then, to her astonishment, Millie went on to invite Beatrix to stay in Bedford Square after the funeral – 'neither Mother nor myself will be going, just Fruing and Harold' – so that they might console each other. It was an extraordinary idea, such a departure from Beatrix's usual circumjacence that her pen was poised to refuse the invitation. Then she suddenly saw what a good idea it would be. The two of them would be able to talk about Norman to their heart's content, which she had never been able to do with anyone before. They could go together to look at the grave, she would not need to see Papa and Mama. She accepted, with grave formality. Her travelling companions, the rabbits and Mrs Tiggy-Winkle, would be surprised, but they'd have to put up with it.

There was still Uncle Fred to contend with. He was concerned that Beatrix should have been upset; naturally Polly had told him all about the telegram and its reception. He wanted to know, most of all, what the telegram had contained.

'It was just sad news, Uncle Fred,' Beatrix shouted. He became deafer with every year that passed, and more Lancashire. 'I shall have to go back to London pretty soon.'

'What's up, Lass?' he said. Sitting in an armchair you could hardly see him, such a little old man he'd become. 'I can see thee's bin shooken up.'

Beatrix was tempted but could see it would be better not to say. 'Nothing to worry about, but I *will* have to go.'

'You're having me on, that's what it is. You're just tired of bawling at my good ear,' said Uncle Fred, pulling himself up by his arms to a sitting position.

Beatrix was used to this sort of tease, she could see his eyes twinkling.

'I'll be back soon,' she told him. 'I'm going to write a story about rabbits in Gwaynynog garden.'

She posted a letter to Bolton Gardens that night.

Elizabeth was the first to read Beatrix's letter. She recognised the handwriting and steamed it open with the help of the kitchen kettle before the Master and Mistress came down to breakfast. Mrs Pearson nearly caught her but she got it into her apron pocket just in time. Somebody had to know what Miss Beatrix was up to.

'I've left my cap upstairs, Mrs Pearson, I won't be a minute.' It was crumpled into her pocket beside the letter.

To save her legs she only went as far as the drawing-room and stood by the window to decipher the close writing.

Miss Beatrix was sure her Papa and Mama had heard of Norman Warne's sudden death. In view of this unhappy news she would not be returning to Bolton Gardens this week as planned, but would let them know where she was and when she was coming back in the course of a week or two. She was their affectionate daughter.

Elizabeth subsided into a chair without realising what she was doing. She had never sat down in the drawing-room before in her life. Poor Miss Bea, what bad luck. She'd found herself a man at last, of sorts anyway, only to have him swept away by the grim reaper. Now she'd disappeared, but she'd be back after a time. Not in her nature to do otherwise. Elizabeth got up, suddenly realising where she was, and started putting on her cap with the aid of the mirror over the mantelpiece.

At least she knew what she was about now. She had full responsibility for running the house until Miss Bea felt able to return. She rather liked the responsibility bit.

She wondered, as she patted her cap into place, whether it might have been better if Fred had died in South Africa. Then she could have mourned him decently, like Miss Bea now, and got on with her life. With him still around, she'd not only got that on her mind but she was landed with his sisters. She'd never forget the day she'd been summoned to Hampstead and there they'd been, soft ha'porths both of them, laughing and crying over Fred's reappearance. He was still handsome but a bit pale and shabby and looked shifty when he saw her, as well he might.

Well, she had been short but had sat down for a cup of tea. She might have asked him where he'd been since she saw him on Paddington Station but she didn't – she was still not sure it had been him. Then he'd got rid of the girls to wash up and started. He'd been a fool over the Cape Coloured girl. She'd ditched him for one of her own kind, as he should have known she would. His only real love was Elizabeth, the thought of her had kept him going all the long months he'd been away. Didn't she still care for him?

'What have you been up to since she left you?' she'd asked.

'Nothing. I came back as soon as I could get a berth,' he had protested, but his eyes had moved away from her. 'Look, I've got the promise of a job in Liverpool. I can't stay here, my wife's still around and the girls are forever pawing at me. Come with me Lizzie, Liverpool's a fine place and we'll have a great time. You shouldn't be running after that Miss Bea of yours and cleaning up after other people. What d'you say?'

'How d'you know Liverpool's a fine place?' she'd asked.

He'd looked shiftier than ever and she'd realised what was missing. Her heart failed to miss a beat when he smiled, her blood no longer raced when he touched her hand. It had gone, all that lovely joy and excitement. She was her own woman again. She felt desolate.

'That's the port where we landed. Spent a bit of time looking round. Now come on, Lizzie, don't let me down.'

'I'm not coming with you, now or ever. It's all over Fred. Finished and done.'

He'd really got his dander up at that. 'You've got to come. I can't manage without a bit of help from your direction to give us a start. You must have a nice little nest egg by now, and Miss Bea

145

'ud give you a farewell present too. Now don't be silly, miss your last chance to get a man. There's not many as would have someone so long in the tooth.'

'I'm off,' she'd said, and made for the door. He'd grabbed her and hit her and she'd tripped and fallen heavily.

Gertie had been coming in from the kitchen. 'You've killed her,' she'd shrieked and blundered outside. Really, that Gertie could only be elevenpence in the shilling; she hadn't even been unconscious, only winded. Then Gertie'd brought in a policeman off the beat.

He'd followed her in, a big man with one of those expressionless faces. 'Oh,' he'd said, 'it's you, Fred. Learn this sort of thing in prison, did you?'

Then it had all come out: how Fred had been home for over a year, most of it spent in prison. He'd been caught on some fraud with railway goods, so it *had* been him at Paddington. He was only just out and still had to report to the local police station. He swore he'd been led astray by visions of quick money, that he'd never be so daft as to go wrong again, and Elizabeth, rubbing a bruised knee, didn't believe a word of it.

The local policeman said he wouldn't make a note of the disturbance for old times' sake. Elizabeth had left with him, glad of his size. He'd looked sideways at her but parted with a civil 'Good evening.'

Then she'd had Gertie's note this morning, same post as Miss Beatrix's letter. Fred had gone, taking what money there was in the house and the bit of silver from their mother's side of the family. What should they do? She'd have to go and sort them out. Lodgers probably. At least the girls could cook.

As soon as she arrived in Bedford Square, Beatrix learned that Mrs Warne was confined to her room, prostrate with grief.

'Perhaps I might visit her later,' she suggested. Guests, even in these unusual circumstances, had obligations.

'I wouldn't advise it,' Millie said bluntly. 'In fact I haven't told her you are here.' She drew a white shawl more tightly round the grey oyster satin blouse she wore with a dipping black georgette skirt. 'The truth of the matter is that Mother blames you for Norman's death. She has no reason to do so, it is just that you are conveniently outside the family and she needs to blame someone. Otherwise she might blame herself for not seeing that Norman was ill months ago and making him do something about it. Even then . . . with pernicious anaemia . . .' She dabbed her eyes with a large linen handkerchief. She looked the very picture of distracted grief, red-eyed and pale, but appeared to be quite practical at the same time.

'We could all blame ourselves in that way,' Beatrix acknowledged, taking off her hat with some relief; it was a muggy evening. 'But to blame me, just because he asked me to marry him. I don't see how she can!' She was surprised to feel quite indignant. She had thought she was beyond feeling anything at all.

'It won't last,' Millie assured her. 'She's quite a reasonable woman really but not at the moment. She says he didn't want you to feel he was a sick man, which you could have done if he'd started visiting doctors. That is quite absurd as Norman was a coward about seeing doctors. He said they did more harm than good. Oh dear . . .' The handkerchief was getting very damp.

They talked for a long time that night. It was a relief to Beatrix to find Millie so understanding. She quite appreciated how torn Beatrix had been between duty and love of Norman, though of course they didn't mention the word 'love'; she still wasn't sure what love meant and it was not a word to bandy about even in these circumstances.

'So,' she'd finished, 'I have to resign myself to going back to Bolton Gardens and to all the things I'd hoped to leave behind for ever.'

'Don't forget your little farm, dear,' said Millie. She'd been very interested to hear of the purchase of Hill Top. 'I remember you telling me once that your ambition was to own a small farm in the Lake District. It worried me at the time, but now you do and it could be quite the best thing for you. It could change your life, if you'd let it.' She looked as eager for this to happen as though it was her own life that might be changed.

'Could it?' This was a point of view that had not occurred to Beatrix. 'You mean I could become a farmer, like Bertram?'

'Why not go to look at it in a day or so? There's nothing to stop you at the moment and it might help to have something else to think about.'

'There are bound to be papers for me to sign still of course. It's a good idea.' She looked gratefully at Millie and her monumental self-abnegation suddenly struck her. 'You must at least come and stay with me at Hill Top when I've got it into shape.'

'Well dear, I think probably not. I'm like Norman, just a town mouse. I'd welcome seeds from your garden though. One day I will have a garden of my own.'

Alone in her room, in a strange bed, Beatrix found grief could no longer be kept at bay. There was only one small firm foothold in the morass of uncertainty she was facing. She owned a place of her own and she would go and look at it quite soon.

# CHAPTER SEVENTEEN

Hill Top did not look quite as Beatrix remembered it, rather smaller and not so well kept. The earth closet had already forced itself on her attention as she went up the garden path and when she saw a brown rat, big as a small cat, washing his whiskers and sunning himself on the rubbish heap, she began to wonder if owning a farm might not be an end in itself after all.

Mrs Cannon, homely and comely, certainly wasn't expecting a visit from the new landlord in the middle of a Monday morning, but, apart from deepening colour in her pink cheeks, she seemed prepared to take it in her stride. She wiped fingers veiled with soap-suds on her long white apron.

'Well Miss Potter, it's a pleasure to make your acquaintance. Would you be wanting to have a look round, like? Mr Cannon's in the barn.'

'I'll see the house first please, Mrs Cannon. I don't believe I ever came inside when the Becketts stayed here.'

'Certainly Ma'am, if that's your wish.' Mrs Cannon appeared mildly astonished that a landlord should want to inspect the farm at all, never mind the farmhouse. 'Well, this is the kitchen, where we live.' She opened the door wider, so it scraped a little on the flagged floor and Beatrix stepped over the door sill and entered Hill Top for the first time, feeling apprehensive.

She had an impression of a large, square room and heavy oak beams. A scrubbed kitchen table stood on the flags and a black range fitted snugly into the old fireplace. Even on a warm September day there was a fire. Of course, it was washing day. There were two enamel water buckets under the table, both full, both containing interesting and lively *daphnia*. That would be the drinking water. The stairs opposite the front door were good, oak and with shallow treads, and beyond them there was a passage through to the back door.

'What's in here?' she asked Mrs Cannon, indicating the closed door in the panelled partition to her right.

'That's the parlour, Miss Potter. We don't use it much.'

It smelt damp and there was a fan of green paper in the fireplace that looked as if it had been there through several winters. Dark green rep curtains, two hard chairs and two oak stools completed the furnishings.

Up the stairs, there was a pleasant half-landing with a window. What was needed here were crimson velvet curtains with a good grandfather clock against the wall. Then there were the bedrooms where the children slept (Ralph and Betsy, both at school today), and another with wonderful views and an uneven floor.

'We have to put bricks under the bottom feet of this bed,' said Mrs Cannon, 'or me and Mr Cannon would go trundling down on it and fetch up against the window.' She patted her piled fair hair in sudden embarrassment.

They both heard the scuttering of clawed feet on the ceiling above their heads. It was accompanied by a flurry of squeaks and a noise that sounded like something heavy being dragged across the floor.

Beatrix looked at Mrs Cannon, whose cheeks had gone very pink again.

'You've got rats in the house too,' Beatrix said. 'I saw one in the garden on the way in.'

'We complained to the agent,' Mrs Cannon looked quite desperate, 'but he said farms always had rats. We've done what we could, but they've got worse, not better. They just sit around as though they owned the place and they get on my nerves.'

'Oh they're not so bad,' said Beatrix tolerantly. 'But we can't have them getting so *very* bold.'

'You don't mind rats?' Mrs Cannon looked as though she didn't know what to make of such a statement.

'As pets they can be quite entertaining,' said Beatrix, feeling she must be fair to the memory of her white rat, Sammy, who had been completely irrepressible and sometimes affectionate.

Mrs Cannon stared at her. 'It doesn't make me laugh when they steal the very food off the table,' she said. 'Cats, that's what we need. More cats.'

If Mr Cannon was surprised to find his new landlord drinking tea in his kitchen, he didn't allow it to show. He scrubbed his clogs on the piece of sacking provided, took off his cap and gave Beatrix a sideways bob of the head by way of acknowledgement as Mrs Cannon, flustered, introduced him.

'You'll have finished with the solicitor then?' he asked.

He was a man of middling height and slightly built, but Beatrix could see why his Junoesque wife had taken to him. He was sturdy with dark, curly hair, and though his face was now as blank as a wiped slate, he looked as though he had a ready wit. He wasn't without his share of good looks either.

'Just about,' said Beatrix. 'There are only the formalities left.'

He stood still and silent, unsatisfied. She thought he had a strong resemblance to a wild thing, a rabbit or a squirrel, scenting danger and trying to identify it.

'I wanted to look at the farm, and the house, to see how it would fit in with my plans for the future,' she amplified.

'And what might those be, Miss Potter?'

He was nothing if not direct, like all northerners. Well, now for it.

'I'd like you to stay on as manager of Hill Top farm if that would suit you,' she said, 'but I shall be making a change.'

'And what might that be, Miss Potter?' his face looked as intelligent as one of his own turnips, which she found disconcertingly comical. Her heart was racing.

'I want to build on an extension for you and your family and keep the old house for myself.'

Mrs Cannon suddenly came to life. 'Proper plumbing in the new bit?' she said. 'And a back boiler?'

The benefits of modern plumbing for a family with small children were outside Beatrix's experience; she had expected Mrs Cannon to protest against being turned out of her home.

'If it's possible,' she said.

That seemed to settle matters. Perhaps Mr Cannon had thought she was going to make the farm into a park and put in deer and stone statues. He now seemed happy to show her round.

'Though you'll not be wanting to walk the boundaries yet awhile,' he said, looking pointedly at her light, buttoned shoes.

Beatrix thought he was putting a good face on circumstances, starting as he meant to go on. She agreed meekly that the buildings would be enough and mentioned that perhaps she might one day take to clogs. This produced a baffled silence and she suppressed a giggle.

The tall barn, with great boulders for quoin stones, the shippons with oak rafters like giant ribs, were more than enough. The yard alone, with its hens and ducks, the water barrel, the turnip cutter, everything in a balance of colour and texture asking to be sketched, to be painted, would have done. The ducks especially, with their comical waddle and their knowing air. Such material for her letters to her younger correspondents, such material for little books. She was conscious of a pleasant excitement.

Penned behind hurdles in one corner of the yard were several small grey sheep. She liked the look of them.

'Herdwicks,' Mr Cannon told her. 'They're sheep for t'high fells, live out all winter on the tops they will on a nibble of heather and a bite of marsh grass.'

'Why d'you keep them, if they're not a lowland sheep?'

'Mr Cannon looked sheepish himself, which made Beatrix hide a smile. 'I just likes them, they're lish little beasts. I'd a fancy to show them one day, but it takes a deal of time.'

An extraordinary idea took hold in the back of Beatrix's mind, but it was really impossibly foolish. She changed the subject.

'There was a mention in the deeds of a "share" in Moss Eccles Tarn going with the property. It seems a curious oversight, but though we've stayed here often, I've never been up to the tarn.'

'Bit of a step,' Mr Cannon warned. 'You'd best have a bite of dinner with us first.'

Well! She accepted with due gratitude.

The track up to the tarn was a delight all the way. First Market Street, where bread and pies were sold from the front room of a cottage and there was a grocers that might have come from a Kate Greenaway picture book. A joiner and undertaker completed the tally of services and the 'street' abruptly became Stoney Lane with Castle Farm on the left. The farmyard looked deserted but a door swung on a windless day. Then the village was left behind and the track wound up a hill. She didn't have to go very fast and could stop when her heart pounded. It was true there had been several sharp stares from under sun bonnets and a net curtain or two had moved in a mysterious way, but she wouldn't dream of complaining about *that*, she had scarcely hoped for such discreet interest. The countryside spread around her in sunny pastureland below the woods, with Claife Heights a promise in the distance.

It was extraordinary how much better she felt now that she had got out of London. It seemed unfair to Norman, it made her feel almost a traitor, to be happiest when she was away from everything that had made up his life. She considered the conversation during her recent meal with the Cannons. Mr Cannon was interested in moving into pigs, the price was going up, but as manager he deferred to the owner. What did she think? There might just have been a quirky lilt in his voice as he consulted her about breeds, but she'd enjoyed the discussion just the same. Norman would have thought she was being absurd.

Even the talk she'd had with his brother Harold before she left Bedford Square had resulted in the turn-around of Norman's wishes, for she'd persuaded Harold that her next book would be *The Tale of Jeremy Fisher*. Harold, she'd found, didn't have Norman's acumen nor his unexpectedly firm opinions. 'Putty,' she said aloud. 'Nothing but putty.' *Jeremy*, though, would be a success; that was positive. It would be a good idea to buy back her drawings for *A Frog He Would A-Fishing Go* that Nisters had taken about ten years ago. And the blocks. That would be one of the first things to do when she got back to London.

There, she'd said it. She came to a gate, put her arms over the top and rested her chin on them. She'd have to go back before too long, her conscience would not let her rest. This lovely country-side would wait. She could see the tarn now, a glinting, oval mirror lying in a dip of the hillside and sheltered by a crescent of trees. Beyond the trees the angular outline of the Langdale Pikes was pencilled against the grey and blue of the autumn day. She'd go, but not yet, not for a little while. This tarn, with bits of Esthwaite Water as well, would be the right background; more suitable by far than the old one of the River Tay, for Jeremy's story. She'd need some sketches to work on during the winter. She'd come up tomorrow and bring her camera too.

The views were even better on the way down. Over the grey slate roofs of Near Sawrey's cottages she could see Hill Top chimney stack and to the left the road going over the hill to Far Sawrey and the ferry. The colours in the stone and slate of the fellsides were repeated again and again in the walls of the houses and barns below her, so each was part of the other. She felt at home here, as though in this place she was truly herself.

'That's all very well,' she said, abandoning the view, 'but what about the rats?'

The next few days were busy. There was first the need to find a cat, and one that would be agreeable to Mrs Cannon's Tabitha at that. Tabitha's nature was not of the best. 'Thinks nothing of standing on the table and taking a clout at ye,' Mrs Cannon had said. When that was done Beatrix had to arrange for a builder, decide on the size and design of the extension to the farm, consult with Mrs Cannon to see if she was suited and make arrangements for minor changes in Hill Top itself. She had found lodgings at Belle Green with the Satterthwaites, the Sawrey blacksmith and his wife, so she could be near enough to keep an eye on the work.

Beatrix also found herself enlisted as extra help on the farm. There was no one to feed the hens when Mrs Cannon went marketing, so she stood in the yard casting corn, which reminded her vividly of her grandmother at Gorse Hall and the feeling of plunging one's hands into the grain bin, the hooting of the turkeys and the flutter of fantails' wings. A calf was taken ill one day and Mrs Cannon needed help giving it brandy through a horn. Then the butter scales had to be taken into Hawkshead police station to be tested. She nearly lost one of the weights when it rolled off the trap, and it was discovered they were out of register and needed altering. She was mildly astonished how fast the days went by.

Her last day coincided with Hawkshead Show.

'You'll be going, of course,' said her landlady.

Beatrix had been admiring the court cupboard built into the panelled wall in the hall and wondering how it would look if wrested from its carapace. She turned round to stare in surprise at Mrs Satterwaite, small and wren-like in contrast to her husband, poised in the kitchen doorway.

'I don't think so. I was going to pay a final visit to the solicitor,' she replied.

'Oh, they'll be shut. Everything shuts on Show Day. Best come along. Wear your strongest shoes.'

Life in Sawrey was going to require a new pair of boots.

It was a day of sunshine and showers and the Show Field, almost opposite Hawkshead Courthouse, was crowded. There were tents and penned animals and a ring being circumnavigated by ringed bulls led by men with metal goads and a beer tent whose sides bulged and retreated from mysterious pressures within. Beatrix wasn't at all sure this was a fit occasion for a nervous person like herself and took a firm grip of her umbrella, one of Norman's pressed on her by Millie.

The scent of crushed grass was calming and when Mr and Mrs Cannon, one each side of her, walked her round and introduced her to the Secretary of the Show and everyone else in sight – 'as was fit and proper', they said – she began to enjoy herself after all. Later Mrs Cannon shepherded her into the ladies tent, where straw hats of every shape and decoration were bent over jars of honey, sponge cakes and embroidered cushion covers. Mrs Cannon's face took on a deep wild-rose colour when they reached the butter. On Beatrix enquiring, she admitted to first prize.

'It's my mother's butter pattern too,' he said, pointing to the obese cow patted onto the golden sphere whose flavour had beguiled the judges. 'She would have been ever so pleased.'

'Hill Top butter,' Beatrix said. The words had a satisfactory ring to them.

Later still they went to find Mr Cannon, among his peers by the sheep pens.

'Na then, Miss Potter,' he said, 'ye want to talk to Mr Gregg here about them Herdwicks you liked. He's the man for 'em, he farms up Kentmere and runs Herdwicks on the fells.'

It appeared, though, that Mr Gregg, deeply bearded under a tweed cap, was to do the talking. He launched into a long story of how it had taken him three weeks, prodding snowdrifts with a stick day and night, to find and rescue five Herdwick ewes caught under frozen snow. 'All alive, not yan on 'em dead and nothing to eat. D'you kna how beggars kept alive?'

Beatrix, nearly defeated by the Westmorland dialect, said she did not. Mrs Cannon looked bored.

'Ate their own wool!' Mr Gregg was triumphant. 'Ate all wool off themselves, bar their tails, there was some left on their tails. I took out me flask, set them on the wall-top, an old broken wall, an' gave them a drink. Before I got me flask back, they were up and away down the fell.'

Beatrix thought this a questionable tale but it was apparently taken as gospel by those present. They were near a pen of well-horned Herdwick rams whose fleeces had been dyed a deep red. She asked why they had been subjected to this treatment.

'Why tups 'ave bin ruddled?' Mr Gregg tipped his cap forward, the better to scratch the back of his head. 'It's good for't fleece, makes 'em look fierce like, we've allus done it.'

'Don't you believe a word of it,' said Mrs Cannon into her ear. 'They ruddle 'em to hide any fault in the wool.'

Beatrix was getting tired of standing but felt the Cannons were expecting more of her than she had achieved.

'What points do the judges look for when they are judging a Herdwick . . . er . . . tup?'

'Now you're asking.' Mr Gregg beamed at her but there was a feeling of agitation coming from her other side.

'They need to have good teeth. Now there's no call to laugh' – he'd seen her smile – 'ah mean it. Teeth fall out, they can't get false 'uns and they can't eat, they get weak and they fall down on the job. Then they need good feet, strong legs that'll hold 'um up. They have to stand on their back legs half their lives, see, and they have to be good for it. Last, their testicles must be well developed and *even*. Oh, 'an they mustn't be sappy-arsed. D'you know what . . .'

'Another day, Jason. It's starting to rain and Miss Potter's ready for a cup of tea.' Mr Cannon looked startled, like a man prodded by his wife's umbrella.

Putting up her own umbrella gave Beatrix time to adjust her face. Dear Millie prophesied better than she knew, she thought, following Mrs Cannon across the churned grass, because if anything is calculated to alter a person's outlook on life, it's Mr Gregg on the subject of showing Herdwick rams. If she did go in for showing Herdwicks, though it still seemed an impossible idea, it had better be ewes.

Back in London, the whole escapade seemed like a dream. Beatrix had to look at her sketches of Esthwaite Water and Moss Eccles Tarn to assure herself she really had a place of her own, at least in the making, to which she could escape. There was the butter too, a pound of the prize-winning churning she had brought with her on the train wrapped in newspaper. Mrs Pearson had seemed less than enthusiastic when she presented it.

Mama and Papa, as she had anticipated, never mentioned Norman. Mama was petulant about the time it had taken to complete the purchase of Hill Top. 'You'd have done better to have bought shares, there would have been a dividend by now.'

Elizabeth had mentioned Norman, in the sense that she expressed her sympathy with Miss Beatrix on the sudden death of her publisher. She'd had tears in her eyes too, but Beatrix was not sure who the tears were for. Elizabeth suddenly looked her age, she must be about fifty years old, but had managed the running of the house in Beatrix's absence without a hitch.

It was a pity that Mama found a hair in the butter when it appeared at breakfast. It was all consigned to the dustbin.

# CHAPTER EIGHTEEN

Beatrix sighed as she took notepaper from a pigeon-hole in the cherrywood desk she had installed in her small library, once the parlour, at Hill Top. Even though it was four years since Norman had died, writing to his brother Harold made her realise her loss anew. If only Harold had been in the least like Norman she could have borne it better. On the contrary, he was argumentative, woolly-minded, a poor businessman who could never delegate. His letters were enough to drive a person quite mad. The best she could say for him was that he seemed to be a good father. Which reminded her his daughter Louie was due another picture letter, and her cousin Winifred who might get jealous if left out.

She looked out of the window at early daffodils nodding and bowing in the sharp March wind. Sharp was what she had better be with Harold if she was ever going to get their dealings on a businesslike basis.

*Dear Mr Warne*, she wrote, then paused with her pen in the air. It must be an indication of her feelings towards him that she never called him Harold, though she always addressed his brother Fruing by his Christian name. How odd that she'd only just noticed. She continued:

> *I would be obliged if you would let me know when I may expect another cheque. I understood there would be a settlement at the end of last year, Dec. 31st, 1908, and now we have run on to March 1909 with nothing to show for it. I am not complaining about the amount of money, which is what you always seem to think. All I ask for is a date. I am considering the purchase of the small farm beside Claife Woods which is shortly to come up for sale and it is essential I should be exact with the bank. I find your reluctance to send cheques as promised most worrying.*

Beatrix dipped her pen in the inkwell, shot excess ink over

157

the blotter in an arc of droplets and sighed again. It would not be so bad if it was only deferred cheques, but there were all the complaints about unanswered letters, the muddle that had been made about her copyright in America and now another one building up about the rabbit dolls. Harold really was a curiosity, but she'd better finish this if she was going to get into Hawkshead today.

> *There is small sign of spring here except for a brave show of daffodils, which have taken little harm from yesterday's snow. I trust Louie has recovered from her cold, though they can hang on at this time of year.*
> *I remain yrs sincerely,*
> *Beatrix Potter*

She felt better as soon as she had sealed the envelope. She wrapped herself in scarves and a thick coat with lifting spirits. It would be cold but there was a gleam of sun now and again and sunlit snow on the fells was not to be missed.

John Cannon was lifting the swill bucket into the trap as she arrived in the yard. She stepped up expertly (she was getting used to this vehicle), Mr Cannon unhooked the reins, swung himself into the driving seat, clicked his tongue at Molly and they were on their way.

Beatrix wedged her boot against the empty swill bucket to stop it rocking and enquired as to the market price of pigs.

She was given details of the latest prices and deals as they bowled past Esthwaite Water and she watched the play of sunlight on the grey ripples round the shore. Perhaps one day soon she could give up writing and illustrating one book after another. Farming gave her a deeper satisfaction and anyway she must be nearly written out. There had been five books centred on Hill Top and Sawrey now, *The Roly Poly Pudding, Tom Kitten*, then after the rats and cats, *Jemima Puddleduck* and *The Pie and the Patty Pan*. *Ginger and Pickles* was with Warnes now. Perhaps she'd saturated the market, which seemed to be the situation with the pigs, according to Mr Cannon. Pigs! One little pig went to market, one little pig stayed at home. They'd be pretty good to sketch, with their grinning faces. There was that black Berkshire they had at the moment, such a funny little particle . . .

'You're for the Heelis offices, you said?' enquired John Cannon.

Beatrix looked round to find they had come to a stop in the middle of the cobbled square in Hawkshead.

'There's the spot.' He pointed with his whip towards a low eighteenth-century building that formed part of the east side of the square and had a cart entrance at one side that must lead to a yard. 'You'll likely be shunted off on Appleby Billy.'

'Appleby Billy?' Beatrix said, preparing to descend.

'Willie Heelis fr'Appleby. He's partner to his cousin, Hawkshead Willie, and gets new clients; bin there shortest time.'

'How long would that be?' she asked, safely landed on the cobbles.

'Ten year,' said Mr Cannon, plainly thinking this no time at all. 'I'll be back in half an hour.' He clicked his tongue at Molly and the two of them set off towards the Red Lion where there might be refreshment as well as pigswill.

Beatrix brushed away a wisp of straw that her skirt had collected and settled her hat. She mildly regretted the absence of Elizabeth and her customary inspections for dipping petticoats, but Elizabeth was looking after them all in Bolton Gardens, Bertram included. Beatrix had been pleasantly astonished to find Bertram on the doorstep one morning, off the night train from Edinburgh and intent on what he called a 'proper' visit.

'You'd better push off, old girl, and have a holiday while you can,' he'd said. 'I can stand it for a couple of weeks.'

So here she was and would stay unless sent for, though 'holiday' was hardly an accurate description of her present flurry of activity. She wondered if Mary had been behind the idea.

A brass plate beside the door announced these to be the offices of W. H. Heelis, Solicitors. She stood outside for a moment, fighting a quite unexpected attack of shyness. She'd been getting on so well in the farming world. She remembered her triumphs and defeats outside the Director's office at Kew and seized the door knob, refusing to retreat ignominiously.

She was diverted by the surprisingly elegant interior. Instead of plastered walls and rafters, there was a Georgian feel to it. Fitted cupboards, panelled walls painted in cream and green, cast-iron fireplace with brass fittings. This must have been a prosperous little town a hundred years ago. The clerk at the desk by the door, looking as nervous as she felt, enquired her business.

She was conducted up an oak stairway which had a companion on the other side of the partition wall: one for clerks and one for clients. She pictured sporting dogs in high brown hats in search of gun licences ascending on this side, bespectacled field mice and the occasional vole scurrying down the other, repeating instructions in squeaky voices so they wouldn't forget them. She was smiling as she entered the office of Appleby Billy.

He seemed to rise from behind his desk for a long time as she came in. He looked about in his middle forties and had extremely blue eyes. Beatrix was offered a high-backed leather-seated chair and urged to take a cup of tea. She agreed, it might comfort her chilly bones which weren't being improved by the cold leather. This gave her a moment to look round the office as Mr Heelis spoke to the clerk.

On the walls were old prints lampooning blind Justice. The desk was a good one, leather-topped, and a mahogany bureau stuffed with law books stood against the inner wall. There were busy flames in a curious three-cornered fireplace and a golf-bag holding several clubs was half-hidden behind the door. She was smiling again as Mr Heelis turned to give her his attention. He smiled back, and Beatrix's first impression of a lean, aesthetic face was dispelled. Here was a pleasant, good-looking man. They discussed the possibility of his taking her on as a client.

'Though your firm dealt with my purchase of Hill Top,' she told him, 'my father's solicitor acted for me over the buying of Courier Farm and some small parcels of land. I have found their being in London a drawback to an understanding of the situation in this part of Lancashire, and Castle Farm is a bigger purchase, so it would be convenient if you could take it on.'

The tea arrived, brought not by a bespectacled vole but by a gangly youth who wobbled the liquid into the saucers. Beatrix immediately saw him as a young lizard just learning to walk on his hind legs. She wanted to giggle and wondered whatever had got into her.

Mr Heelis saw no difficulties. 'I will make enquiries and call for your instructions in due course,' he said.

So then she had to explain about the uncertainty of her movements. 'Sometimes I can get away from London if my parents are *well*,' she said, 'as now, but my father is subject to bouts of rheumatics which require my presence and my mother has a hearty aversion to my absence at any time. I shall be at Sawrey for another week if not summoned back and visiting again in August, if I'm spared, when we are at Broad Leys in Windermere.' Mr Heelis hooded his eyes and looked inscrutable. Beatrix thought he was trying not to laugh.

160

'Then we'll have to rely on the postal service,' was all he eventually said, and began to write busily on a small notepad.

Whilst getting into the trap, Mr Cannon being admirably on time though the pigswill inclined to slop, Beatrix had a feeling of *deja vu*. Thinking about it as Mr Cannon and Molly did a delicate *pas de deux* with a brewer's dray outside the Sun Inn, she found she had been reminded of how assiduously she and Norman had used the postal service.

The dray finished unloading and progress was possible again. Really, Hawkshead was such a sturdy little town, with its cobbled square and old houses with their upper storeys canti-levered out beyond the ground floor, she'd like to own a bit of it. Good gracious, what was she thinking of? This indiscriminate desire to buy property was something she'd have to watch.

The day had not fulfilled its promise and the sky was now uniformly leaden. Molly shied at a flurry of snowflakes as she trotted past Esthwaite Water.

Elizabeth simply could not understand it. There was no sign of Miss Beatrix, not even a letter, though Mrs Potter had written to summon her back to Bolton Gardens four days ago. That was after the Master and Mr Bertram had shouted at each other for over an hour and Mr Bertram, with a strong smell of whisky on his breath, had packed up and gone, saying that he, for one, found it more than flesh and blood could stand.

Elizabeth's imagination was running riot. As she toasted muffins and put them in the silver muffineer, she saw Miss Beatrix being lured away and taken for the white slave trade, like that Josephine Butler used to campaign about. Perhaps not. Arabs liked their slaves young and nubile, not like herself and Miss Bea. She'd wandered away into those great hills and broken her leg and died a lonely death among the heather. Though come to think of it, the hills round Sawrey weren't all that high and Miss Bea mostly kept to the flat on account of her heart. Well then, what? Miss Bea had never before failed to return when sent for. The most unlikely reason she could think of was a man. That would be a turn-up.

Not that she'd recommend taking up a with a man again. They'd both been disappointed, Mr Norman up and dying and Fred a pickle that had gone to the bad. They'd not hear of him again she was sure. Thanks to her, the girls were doing all right with two lady school-teachers as lodgers. She was doing all right too. With Miss Bea away she was taking more and more into her own hands. She managed the domestic staff now, well the under-housemaids anyway. She planned meals too, even if the planning was more like a discussion with Cook, and the yearly spring-cleaning was entirely hers to command. Miss Bea didn't have the interest, somehow, since she'd bought that farm in Sawrey. Elizabeth had been in it once, when they'd stayed at Lakeside. Pokey little place, and the draughts were something cruel.

She glanced at the kitchen clock on the wall. Nearly five, she'd better brew the tea, the tray was ready now.

Madam was crocheting with a crochet hook as thin as a needle and cotton as fine as cobwebs; the Master was reading *The Times*. A paragraph heading caught her eye as she placed the heavy silver tray on the table. 'Unseasonable weather: snow blocks northern roads'. So much for the white slave trade. Miss Bea was throwing snowballs at the sheep!

Beatrix returned to Bolton Gardens two days later, with the worst case of chilblains she'd ever had in her life. Elizabeth found her sitting in front of the nursery fire with her feet in a bowl of warm water and was horrified.

'Oh Miss Bea! However did you get them like that?'

'It was the snow, you see. It produced such very fine effects. I was out painting for five of the six days it lasted. Even with my good boots my feet were frozen, but it was worth it.'

Beatrix saw that Elizabeth, staring at the swollen red blotches on her ankles, was unconvinced. Impossible to tell her of the exhilaration she had experienced when she had understood that Sawrey was temporarily cut off, she was out of reach of everything. Or of the beauty of blue shadows on snow, reflected sunsets turning high fells the pale pink of a damask rose, Tarn Hows a sapphire in a setting of silver and gold. Looking back on it now, it seemed she had been perfectly intoxicated.

'Perhaps you could bring me the wintergreen lotion,' she suggested.


August often wraps northern hills in warm drizzle and clouds of midges. It was on such a day that Beatrix left her parents in a fine old grumble at Broad Leys, Windermere, and came across on the ferry to see how the workmen were doing at Castle Farm.

The drains were the trouble. Sewage had been backing up and there had been nothing for it but to open the main drain right across a field. Newton, a plumber from Ambleside who had been engaged for the work, was standing in the shorn hay-field surrounded by black, evil-smelling sullage and scratching his pink scalp when she arrived. He seemed pleased to have an audience.

'Na then Miss Potter, we've got some funny old work here! Done about eighty years sin, like as not?' He settled his cap again, looking something like Tweedledum preparing for a battle.

In Beatrix's experience, plumbers regularly threw scorn on any work but their own. She picked her way carefully to a point where she could see for herself what it was all about.

'He lost his level, coming up from the bottom, found he was too near the surface, so he let a step down. You can see it, there. So of course, stuff coming down the hill silted up against step and what d'you get, you get trouble.' Mr Newton sounded positively pleased.

'That's curious.' Beatrix had satisfied herself that Mr Newton had the facts of the case entirely correct. 'Dishonest, too. Whoever did it must have known what would happen.'

'Best remedy is a new main drain,' said Mr Newton hopefully. 'I can make you a price for digging it.'

Beatrix thought of her bank account, now improved, though only last week, by a cheque from Warnes and not to be used for drains. 'I think not. Instead, you could raise the sides of the sewer to give more headroom. It will silt up in time, but as it lasted eighty years in the first place, it should at least see me out.'

'That's about what Mr Heelis said when I told him what I suspected was the trouble,' said Mr Newton resignedly.

'Mr Heelis?'

'Aye, Appleby Billy. He's bin over a couple of times to see how I was doing. Speak of the devil . . .'

Beatrix turned to see a tall figure coming through the gate into the field.

His long legs enabled him to reach them in an economic number of strides, but he seemed in a silent mood and both Mr Newton and Beatrix received only a mute nod. A quizzically raised eyebrow was his response to Mr Newton's exposition on what had been discovered.

Beatrix found in herself a greater knowledge of the opposite sex than she knew she possessed. Appleby Billy was at a loss on what to say to her in front of Mr Newton, to whom he would doubtless speak quite differently.

'Can I return your former compliment and offer you some refreshment?' she asked him.

'That,' Mr Heelis replied, 'is an excellent thought.'

They walked together across the field and over the road to Hill Top, where Mrs Cannon provided a tray of tea and buttered scones just out of the oven. She put the tray in the library.

'How did you get here?' Beatrix asked Mr Heelis when they were seated, having seen no sign of horse or trap or even bicycle.

Mr Heelis looked positively guilty. 'On my motorbicycle,' he said. 'I have a Bradbury and I took the liberty of putting it in your farmyard. As you weren't here, I walked over to see how the drainage problem was going.'

'I must thank you for making sure all was well during my absence,' Beatrix said stiffly.

They both took refuge in a sip of tea.

'I have some final papers to give you regarding the farm,' Mr Heelis said after a long pause. 'Everything is in order and I hope you have found the work satisfactory.' He patted the pockets of his tweed suit ineffectively.

Beatrix noticed now that he had a gentle, pleasant voice with a slight drawl. 'Yes of course,' she said. 'Not many solicitors would have taken so much trouble with their clients' properties as yourself. I hope to be making more purchases soon.'

'Agricultural?' Mr Heelis looked like a pointer brought to attention.

'Very probably.'

'Then I may be able to give you advance notice of suitable spots coming on the market.'

'Thank you,' said Beatrix primly. She couldn't think why they were both so awkward.

'I've read all your little books,' said Mr Heelis suddenly.

'Good gracious, there was no call to do that.' Beatrix was startled. 'Did you like them?' she asked, after a pause.

'I liked what they told children,' he replied. 'There's a lot there on what life is all about. How to escape from difficult situations, the value of perseverance, the need to be tough in a world full of danger. You don't talk down to them or make moral points but it's all there.'

'Goodness,' Beatrix said, considerably shaken by the thought that such perception about her work could have been extended to what it told him about herself.

'There is one thing, though,' he went on. 'In *Jeremy Fisher* you have a trout taking a frog. Now that is not, I am sure, biologically correct. I do a certain amount of fishing and my experience is that it would have to be at least a pike to make off with something so large as a frog.'

Beatrix was irritated at such masculine didacticism. 'Surely I can stretch a point in a children's story. It was a very large trout.'

Mr Heelis did not agree. They had a spirited discussion at the end of which he gracefully conceded it was unlikely to affect children's perception of the underwater world.

By this time any awkwardness had inexplicably vanished and Mr Heelis took his leave very pleasantly. She learned he lived at Hawkshead Hall, owned by one of his multitudinous cousins.

'I shall have to go soon myself,' Beatrix told him. 'My parents don't really like Broad Leys which makes them feel very dull.'

'If you're going down to the ferry, I could take you in my side-car, it's quite comfortable.'

'Thank you,' said Beatrix, startled again, 'but I'm not quite ready to leave yet, I must have a word with Mr Cannon.'

After he'd gone, in a long rattle down the lane and an explosion like a cannon shot at the end of it, she was sorry she'd refused the lift. She giggled as she pictured herself untangling her legs from the confines of the wickerwork side-car in front of the carriages, carts and foot passengers waiting for the ferry. Tabitha Twitchett stalked in through the door at that moment and Beatrix picked her up and stroked her.

'With opportunity,' she told Tabitha, 'the world can be a very interesting place.'

# CHAPTER NINETEEN

Although it was a picturesque pigsty, stoutly built some time in the late eighteenth century, it was cramped quarters for sketching. Beatrix sat inside on a milking stool with her sketch book on her knee and talked gently to the sow, who was called Esmeralda. Esmeralda was not happy with this intrusion. She was like one of those housewives who prefer to keep themselves to themselves and sat in the corner, her back braced against the wall, her front legs stuck straight in front of her, wearing a puzzled expression. Beatrix wanted her to smile.

The reason for this sketching *in situ* was twofold. In the first place it was pouring with rain and Esmeralda did not go out in the rain; in the second place Beatrix wanted to finish *Pigling Bland*.

It had been held over for *Timmy Tiptoes*, published last year, and *The Tale of Mr Tod*, which was to come out this autumn, mainly because the other two went well and *Pigling Bland* didn't seem to come right. Now it really would have to be done because it had been advertised for publication in 1913, next year, and Mr Warne had taken orders in advance. Without previously notifying her of course.

Esmeralda snuffled and rose to her feet. Her expression was all at once just right and Beatrix bent over her drawing, trying to capture that gentle grin on paper. Suddenly there was a sharp tug on her right boot and she looked down. Esmeralda had hold of the laces and was chewing with every appearance of satisfaction, a lace end drooping from her mouth like a rat's tail.

When Beatrix disengaged and drew her feet under her long skirts, Esmeralda began to act for all the world like a terrier at a rabbit hole, snuffling under the skirts at one side, then skidding round the stool in case the boots had come out unbeknownst to her on the other. She nearly stood on her head in her efforts to locate these delectable morsels.

It was all too interrupting and Beatrix gave up and stood up, raising Esmeralda's excitement by several notches as the boots now appeared. Of course it took time to get herself and the stool and the sketching book through the narrow door of the sty, hindered by Esmeralda's efforts to nibble her boots at every turn. Once out she frankly ran, calling for Mr Cannon. The pig trotted behind, pregnancy slowing her down.

Mr Cannon appeared with a pitchfork but this did not worry Esmeralda. The last Beatrix saw of her she'd got into the sheep pen and was sitting looking at the farmer with a triumphant grin.

Beatrix abandoned pigs for the day. It was time she made her way over the hill to Far Sawrey and down to the ferry. She put on her new waterproof thinking ruefully that even William Heelis's side-car would be better than a wet walk. His visits were pretty frequent these days, and when he was unable to visit he wrote long letters about properties she'd bought – getting the deeds for those two cottages in the village had been troublesome – and properties he thought she should buy. He seemed to imagine she was made of money, but there was no doubt that he was more assiduous than the general run of solicitors. In fact she was beginning to wonder if he was actually, in the old-fashioned phrase, paying court to her. An extraordinary idea, though she didn't dislike it. But today he hadn't come. At least she didn't have a long walk both sides of the lake; this year they were staying at Lindeth Howe, just on the other side of the ferry.

The Windermere horse-ferry could take a four-horsed coach and a charabanc at one and the same time if pushed, but at 5 o'clock on a wet August day there were only a couple of farm carts and a minute donkey pulling a barrel organ waiting to get to Windermere. Beatrix folded her umbrella and placed herself with other foot passengers in the open-fronted shelter provided.

The engine started, the wire cable lifted, dripping, from the lake floor and the short but delightful journey began. The view today looked like a Japanese painting, all water and obscuring cloud pierced by strange peaks with swans floating in the foreground. They had reached the middle of the lake when Beatrix heard a noise she could only compare with the buzzing of millions of bluebottles against a background of a steam threshing engine. A large hydroplane appeared to come out of a cloud and swooped low over the boat before landing on the water in a bumpy fashion near Cockshot Point.

Both horses were startled and the donkey hee-hawed, legs braced and head thrown up, in a frenzy of terror. Hooves clattered and panic broke out among the sheep. For a few minutes there was turmoil.

'Experimental, that's what they say they are,' said a local auctioneer, watching the donkey's owner put an apron over its head to calm it down. 'I say they're damned dangerous. What would have happened to us if the Coniston Coach with its four horses was going over? They'd have jumped their traces and sunk the boat.'

There were murmurs of agreement.

'They're going to put a factory on Cockshot Point to build them in,' someone else contributed.

The bow grated on the gravel of Ferry Nab and bobbing umbrellas dispersed in the wake of the carts and the barrel organ. Beatrix paused to look north at the adjoining bay and the long curve of Cockshot Point and then stumped up the road highly exasperated. Whatever could anyone be thinking of, allowing a factory to be built on the shores of Windermere? And a factory whose products would buzz up and down the lake by day and by night, making a travesty of any kind of peace or safety. Something must be done and if the worst came to the worst she'd do it herself. But she'd need help. Her footsteps slowed as she thought about it. Of course, Canon Rawnsley and the National Trust. Her umbrella bobbed in triumph.

Tomorrow, she remembered, was Thursday and Grasmere Games. Papa had remarked only yesterday that the Games might be a diversion in what was proving to be a very dull August, with Beatrix over at Hill Top all the time and the weather so bad. She'd take him, it should be all right. Beckett could drive them in state and put the landaulette on the field. She understood that was the proper form. The Canon would be there; he was still, according to the *Westmorland Gazette*, undisputed High Panjandrum of the Games.

As the landaulette took its place on the side of the ring, in an amphitheatre of grass near the lake overlooked by the surrounding fells, Beatrix was visited by doubts. Papa looked distinctly unwell, quite yellow, and clouds were threatening the sun. Mama had set her face against the expedition – '*common* people in *such* crowds,' she'd said. Beatrix wouldn't have minded *that* in the least, but in fact Beckett had pointed out the Lowther carriages pretty near and, as he raised a discreet whip to a coachman acquaintance, the Lonsdales' coach almost next to them, black and yellow and waspish-looking. Altogether the upper crust. The Canon was present too, she could see him easily from the grandstand of the coach. He was beside the wrestling ring, distinctive with his folding chair and umbrella and his ringing shouts of encouragement. She left Papa with Beckett, both watching the parade of hounds.

The wrestling bout just starting, Beatrix discovered, catching glimpses through the press of spectators of long white drawers and black embroidered trunks, was for young amateurs. She wished for the ten thousandth time that she had a little more height.

'Git yer clogs off ready,' she heard the starter say. 'Nar then, off you go. Young lad's trying, hanging on.' This must be for the benefit of any tourists. 'Nar then, that's a dogfall, they both hit t'ground together.' Someone moved and Beatrix had a good view of a bowl of bright flowers embroidered in wool strained across the rear of the youngest wrestler.

There was a scent of damp earth, of humanity in the mass, of Herdwick tweed and excited terriers. There was a little man in exaggerated riding breeches taking bets on the outcome, people were jostling, there was enjoyment in the air. She suddenly felt quite at home.

'Why Beatrix, what brings you here?' enquired the Canon.

'Such a lovely day,' she told him, and then thought perhaps she sounded foolish. She considered the Canon; he looked a little less ebullient than usual.

'How is your wife?' she enquired.

There was a shadow across his face, a narrowing of his eyes as though forced to look at far horizons he did not wish to explore.

'She gets tired very easily, you see,' he said.

Beatrix did see. 'My father is the same,' she said. 'I must go back to him soon.'

'Where is he? Over there. We'll walk together and I'll leave my chair here for the moment. The fell race starts shortly.' The Canon was recovering, the programme at his fingertips.

As they strolled through the increasing crowd she told him about the hydroplanes and found, as she rather expected, that he already knew about them.

'The Trust can do little,' he said. 'The land is not for sale and the Trust can only protect by ownership. You and I, though, can do a lot. I've already written to *The Times*, the *Morning Post* and to *Punch*. We could canvas groups of people likely to object to the action these aircraft manufacturers are contemplating, *you* could approach farmers, and perhaps publishers. I had in mind to write to members of the Establishment who have consciences, there are a few even now, and persuade them to bring the matter up in the House.' The Canon was getting into his stride, his flat hat beginning to bounce a little on his head, and Beatrix was inspired by his enthusiasm.

'I could write to *Country Life*,' she said. 'I did so once before on the subject of owls and the letter was published, though I think they must have been short of copy. I'll canvas too, and send you the list of signatures to place where you think best.' They looked at each other with approval.

'So now perhaps you'll agree with the National Trust,' the Canon remarked, his eyes twinkling, 'that ownership is the only sure way of protecting land. All these little farms and cottages you're buying up to prevent them being put to unsuitable use, they should be willed to the Trust for their protection in perpetuity.'

'How did you know I was buying property?' asked Beatrix, annoyed at being caught out *in flagrante delicto* as it were. Having her motives revealed made her feel like a snail bereft of its shell.

The Canon twinkled more than ever whilst bowing graciously left and right to constant greetings. 'Our farming community,' he said, 'likes to keep abreast of the news. So what do you say?'

'I say you remind me of a Jesuit,' she told him. 'You never give up trying to convert me. I'll think about it.'

'Well, whilst you're thinking about it, you might let me have a subscription towards the purchase of Queen Adelaide Hill. We are trying, you see, to save at least a little of the Windermere shore from private ownership.'

'Very well,' she replied, 'but I can't manage it this minute as my publishers are being niggardly with royalties just now. I'll let you have something as soon as I am able.'

Papa was drooping a little, but he quite revived on seeing who was with her.

'Thought you'd forgotten us, Canon,' he said. 'Not seen you for a long time.'

'Forgotten! What an accusation from the man I made the first Life Member of the National Trust. Never forget a thing like that. I've come to sit with you for the fell race.' The Canon suited the action to the words, the carriage swaying a little under his weight.

The elderly gentlemen, the Canon expansive in clericals and

Papa in his morning coat and top hat, took up rather a lot of room. Beatrix stayed where she was. Beckett, on his box, had the best view of any of them.

The competitors for the fell race were being lined up and traffic was being stopped on the road to allow them to cross onto the fells. The bowler-hatted starter waved his pistol, shut his eyes and pulled the trigger. They were off, propelled by the roar of the crowd, a straggle of twenty or so young men with eager expressions that matched those of the hounds waiting for the hound trail to follow.

'They go up to and round Grey Crag,' the Canon was explaining, 'just under Alcock Tarn, and then turn. You can see it, there, almost in a direct line from Stone Arthur. It's the home stretch that's so dangerous, they run, they leap, they nearly fly over that rock-strewn course.' He looked as if he wished he too were leaping among bracken and boulders for nothing more than the joy of it. Beatrix remembered he had had a distinguished athletic career at Balliol.

She turned to look at Papa, to see if he was enjoying the race, and was seriously alarmed. He was lying back against the cushions, his eyes shut and his mouth open. His colour, too, was bad. She spoke to him, but he didn't respond.

The Canon took immediate action. 'A doctor,' he proclaimed to the world and scrambled out of the carriage to trot into the thick of the crowd, coming back pleased with his prize, a portly gentleman, just as Papa opened his eyes.

'Dr Morland,' he said to Beatrix as the doctor felt for Papa's pulse, 'very sound man.'

The 'very sound man' was of the opinion that Papa had suffered a mild seizure, not too worrying. Best get him home to his own physician.

Some weeks later Beatrix received a letter from the Canon enquiring as to her father's health and reminding her of her promise to subscribe towards the purchase of Queen Adelaide's Hill. At least that is what she thought it said after considerable study. She took it with her to answer at Hill Top. Sitting at her desk, she wrote:

> *Dear Canon Rawnsley,*
>     *My father is very much better now we have a nurse.*
> *She has done more for him than any doctor and got him to*

*follow a sensible regime. The difficulty is that she gets in my*
*mother's way, being somewhat dictatorial, but at least for*
*the moment I am able to stay here occasionally for a night.*

   *I shall be able to let you have a small subscription for*
*Adelaide as soon as I am paid for a ham, about £5. I am*
*sorry this had slipped my mind.*

Really, Beatrix thought, putting down her pen and staring
out of the window at the duck-egg green of the evening sky, it is a
ridiculous state of affairs when I have to wait to sell a ham before I
have any money. Warnes owe me royalties going back to January
last year. Harold Warne said in his last letter he was taking his
family to the seaside: I shall write to Fruing in his absence. She
finished her letter to Hardwicke Rawnsley and then addressed
Fruing Warne at length, so much so that she found herself
scribbling round the margins and the page finally resembling one
written by the Canon.

The following morning Beatrix tidied up generally and then went
down to the farmyard to look at the baby chickens. She had
incubated them herself over a low gas jet at Bolton Gardens and
brought them up on the train. She'd smuggled them in under the
seat so she didn't have to pay for carriage. They were doing well;
gas jets were better than lamps for incubation. Then she went into
the shippon. Mr Cannon had said it would be more convenient,
both for himself and the cows, if some of these new water bowls
that refilled automatically could be installed before the animals
came in for the winter and she wanted to see if it could be done. It
was her last chance as in four days she was to take Papa and Mama
back to Bolton Gardens, they weren't fit to travel on their own. It
might be some time before she was back.

   A door on the barn end led into the empty shippon, a double
row of stalls. She had just decided it would be a fairly expensive
plumbing job when William Heelis came in from the other end.

   'Mrs Cannon told me you'd be here,' he said. 'I came to tell
you that there's a good little hill farm coming on the market soon,
Penny Hill in Eskdale. It has its own heafed flock of Herdwicks
and built-in oak furniture including a long table.' William was
ruffled and flushed from his drive over from Hawkshead and
looked expectant, as though this was a momentous gift he had
found for her. He took off his tweed cap which, unusually,
matched his impeccably cut tweed suit.

172

'Ordinarily I'd be glad to look at it,' Beatrix said, 'but we return to London soon and anyway I may as well tell you I don't think my finances would be up to it.' She moved down the aisle to the cow stall in which he was standing, so there was only a waist-high division of large slates framed with wooden slats between them.

'Oh. Well I'd be glad to keep you informed about it, in case circumstances change. I had hoped to take you over there myself.' William's face had resumed its usual, sardonic mask. 'There's still some paperwork to finish over the cottages, I'll let you have what's left for signature as soon as may be.'

'It's making a lot of work for you, all these letters and the difficulty in arranging meetings when my circumstances are so uncertain,' Beatrix said. 'I do wish . . .' and stopped as William put his hands over her own, where they rested on the rough wooden slats.

'We could remedy that,' he said. 'I hadn't meant to mention it yet, but it would make our lives very much easier if we got married.'

For a moment she couldn't speak, then she burst out laughing. William looked disconcerted and hurt.

'Oh, I'm not laughing at you,' she said, 'I'm laughing at us both. Two middle-aged people contemplating romance in such unromantic surroundings. Yes, I quite agree with you. Our lives would be much less complicated if we got married.'

William vaulted over the slatted slates and kissed her soundly.

After that they went for a walk up to Moss Eccles tarn, oblivious at the time of the waving lace curtains and the light drizzle that was falling.

'Naturally I had meant to propose to you beside the romantic River Esk, when I took you to look at Penny Hill,' William explained. 'But perhaps a shippon is more to the point.'

'I wonder how we'll get on,' Beatrix said. 'Do we have enough in common?'

'We both love the countryside,' William said. 'Perhaps,' he added hopefully, 'I might teach you to play golf.'

Later, conscious that she smiled continually and that she had forgotten everything she meant to do before leaving, Beatrix wondered how Papa and Mama would take the news.

# CHAPTER TWENTY

There was no doubt that Miss Beatrix was very ill. Elizabeth, sitting beside the nursery fire at 2 o'clock in the morning in the company of a small, simmering pan of broth and Thomas the cat, felt lonely and frightened. She was fully dressed, down to her winter drawers, for who knew what might happen.

The reason for Miss Bea's illness was not hard to find. She had been brought so low by the Master and Mistress hammering at her morning, noon and night to break her engagement to Mr Heelis that she was an easy victim to influenza and bronchitis. Elizabeth was afraid this mixture was turning to pneumonia, and Miss Bea's heart wasn't up to the strain.

There was a sound from the bedroom and Elizabeth got up to listen. Yes, there she went again. Her high temperature was making her delirious and she was rambling, talking this time to – to old Peter Rabbit. Well, did you ever.

'See what you've done Peter, you've got us both into a pickle.' The monotonous gruff voice stopped for a difficult breath and a hand stroked the curve of the eiderdown as though it was the soft fur of a rabbit. Another rasping breath. 'You don't agree? My own fault. Make my own bed and lie on it.' She paused again and the hand stopped moving, as though to hear better. 'Or die on it,' she seemed to repeat. 'That's one way out. Box, Peter, back to box.'

Elizabeth moved forward. 'I'll put him in his box, Miss Bea. There now, he's settled.'

Miss Bea, her eyes shut and her face flushed, made no acknowledgement and turned restlessly. The doctor had said to keep her lying flat and still, but what could you do when she was struggling for breath like this? Elizabeth put more coal on the first fire in this room for she didn't know how long, using a coal glove so as not to make a noise, and adjusted the kettle so it steamed busily.

She was tiptoeing out when Miss Bea started again. 'It's all right for you Walter Bertram, you got your wish.' The harsh sound of her breathing seemed to fill the small room. 'And a wife to go with it,' she finished suddenly. It was a bitter accusation that brought on a fit of coughing.

Elizabeth was startled. Now that *was* telling the family secrets. No one had breathed a word of it to her and the Master and Mistress didn't know, of that she was certain.

Miss Bea had gone quiet but there was a sound on the stairs and she felt the hairs rising on the back of her neck. Ghosts? She'd always suspected there were some about. Or an intruder, with a knife? She forced herself to peer over the stairwell. It looked like a ghost. No. It was the Mistress in her old grey woollen wrapper. She hadn't climbed these stairs for many years; she'd interviewed the doctor in the drawing-room and appeared to dismiss his worries. 'Beatrix is as strong as a horse,' she'd said. Whatever had brought her up here in the small hours of the morning?'

The Mistress looked up and saw her. 'Oh Elizabeth! I didn't know you were sitting up with Miss Beatrix.' She was making heavy weather of it, breathing nearly as bad as Miss Bea.

'Well Madam,' Elizabeth whispered, 'she was that poorly, but she's quiet now. Come into the nursery so as not to wake her.' There now, she'd never told the Mistress what to do before. She'd be for it.

Surprisingly, it appeared not. Mrs Potter did as she was told, sinking into the little armchair with a sigh and holding her hands out to the fire. Thomas blinked at her sleepily.

'Why not have a little of this broth, Madam, if you're cold? Miss Bea is never going to take it as she is now.' Elizabeth handed over a cup of the good, strong chicken broth and was again surprised as Mrs Potter accepted it, hardly appearing to know what she was doing. She looked rather as if she had been sleep-walking.

'It *is* a daughter's duty to look after her parents,' Mrs Potter said, almost as if Elizabeth wasn't there and she was persuading herself she was right.

'Yes Madam, but she can't do that if she dies,' Elizabeth heard herself saying. 'The doctor said her heart was in a poor way.' She perched herself on the edge of a straight-backed chair, the first time she'd sat down when the Mistress was in the room.

Mrs Potter took a sip of the broth and sat silently, her head bowed over her hands which were clasped round the cup. Then she looked up at Elizabeth. 'You're making too much of things,' she said, 'you always did. But we'd better have a nurse, as from tomorrow. You can't do your work and sit up all night, and whether it's needed or not, I can see you intend to do so.'

'Yes, Madam,' said Elizabeth, shocked to discover that Madam had some powers of observation after all.

'She's much better in the country,' Mrs Potter mused. 'Or at the seaside. Perhaps we should not have come to London, it never served in the end. Mr Potter didn't stir himself so we were never accepted.'

So that's why, years ago now, Madam had spent her afternoons leaving cards over half of London, according to Mr Beckett, to be rewarded by only one or two 'At Homes' and a few, very few cards to put on her own silver salver in the hall. She'd wanted to be accepted by London society. It was difficult not to feel sorry for the old besom.

Miss Beatrix started to talk again and the Mistress put down her empty cup, rose and rustled through to the bedroom.

'Well, there's one thing,' Miss Bea said, her voice quite audible, 'at least I got a place of my own.' She coughed, weakly. Elizabeth went over to rearrange her pillow and see if she would take a sip of lemon barley water. When she looked up, Mrs Potter had gone.

It was a long night, spent listening to Miss Bea's ragged breathing and the small ghostly wind that occasionally rattled the casements like someone trying to get in. At the end of it Elizabeth had come to a decision. She was going to write to Mr Bertram, she knew where Miss Bea kept her address book, and say he was needed here. Then, when he came, she'd tell him what he had to do. She'd always been able to manage Mr Bertram.

By the time Bertram arrived the nurse had gone and Beatrix was allowed to get up for a few hours each day. Her chest was quite clear but her heart still pounded at the least exertion and she hadn't yet attempted the stairs. She was worried by the accumulation of letters and was looking through the pile, distressed that she was too shaky to put pen to paper yet, when Bertram came into the nursery. She was so pleased to see him that, to her surprise, weak tears spilled down her cheeks.

'Now then old girl, there's no need to cry. Elizabeth tells me you're coming on famously now and will soon be your old self.' He kissed her cheek, gave her a hug and stood back to look at her. 'You do look a bit rough still,' he acknowledged. 'We'll have to see what we can do for you.'

'The most useful thing you could do at the moment,' Beatrix said, blowing her nose, 'is to write some letters for me. I'll tell you what to say and sign them. Just a few, the most urgent.'

'Well I really ought to go and see the Mater . . . Oh all right, I'll do them now before giving them both the glad news that their prodigal is here.'

They disposed of three letters companionably. Then Bertram, looking anxiously at his sister, told her that was enough for today, he'd act as her secretary again tomorrow. He rose from his chair and hovered, there was no other word for it.

'Mary all right? All well at Ashieburn?' Beatrix asked.

'Everything's going swimmingly, the Borders are the place to live you know. It's not that, it's you old girl. This marriage you're thinking about. You said something in one of your letters.'

Beatrix swallowed hard, she really *mustn't* cry again. 'They won't have it. It's just as it was when I wanted to marry Norman. They wouldn't have a daughter marry beneath her. On and on, all winter, until I felt like going mad. What they really want is to keep their housekeeper and nurse; Papa is not well. I can't see getting away unless they agree to it and they won't give in.'

'Oh yes they will. I'm going to have something to say to them.'

Beatrix was startled. 'Whatever could you say to change their minds?'

'Just you wait and see. Mind you, you'll have to come down to the drawing-room, say for 5 o'clock tea, to hear it first-hand. Could you manage that?'

'You may have to carry me back, but I'll come even if I have to slide down on a tray.' They both laughed, remembering.

Beatrix put on a clean blouse and brushed and combed her hair. There was nothing like illness for pulling a person's appearance right down, her face was quite thin. The stairs were not so bad as long as she clung to the bannisters. She didn't know what she was doing this for, nothing Bertram said could make any difference.

Papa was pleased to see her in a muddled sort of way. He seemed to think she had been away. Mama enquired pointedly if she could manage to get upstairs as well as down. Beatrix accepted a piece of thin bread and butter and a cup of weak tea and watched Bertram making inroads on the scones.

He was in no hurry, parrying questions from Papa on what painting he was doing at the moment and how long he would be in

London. Mama confined herself to saying he was looking well, which seemed to surprise her. On finishing his second cup of tea, Bertram cleared his throat nervously.

'Beatrix tells me,' he said, looking at Mama, 'that you are opposing her marriage to William Heelis.'

Mama was clearly shocked at such a direct attack. Her eyes widened. 'I hardly think that is your concern,' she countered.

'Not my concern? The happiness of my sister!' He lost his nervousness. 'What have you got against William Heelis? According to report he's an upstanding member of society and won't beat her or make her scrub floors. Is it because he actually works for his living?'

'Surely it's obvious.' Papa had more or less caught up with what was going on. 'The man's only a country solicitor, land sales and conveyances, quite unsuitable.' He puffed irritably.

'Don't intend her to marry beneath her station in life, eh?' There was a satisfied sound to that statement that obviously alarmed both parents. 'Well let me tell you this then. I've been married now for getting on for ten years and not only that, I married a farmer's daughter.'

There was an appalled silence. Both Papa and Mama looked as though they had been suddenly exposed to a dreadful smell. Bertram was grinning wickedly and Beatrix wanted to cheer his resolution, though he hadn't quite had the courage to tell them that Mary was really the daughter of an inn-keeper. Still, it ought to serve.

Bertram hadn't finished yet. 'Also, as apparently you've not noticed, Beatrix is nearly fifty years old and can marry whom she wants. Come on now, admit you've been wrong and give her your blessing.'

Mama sat and looked at her hands, her face paler than usual. Papa rumbled and huffed, pink with annoyance.

At last Mama spoke. 'I still say it's not a good marriage and it's Beatrix's duty to look after her parents, but with Bertram's discreditable example in front of us I can see we shall have to let her go.'

Mama had nearly choked on the words, they had been said with bad grace, but at least they had been said. Beatrix felt dizzy with elation and weakness.

'I'm sure you won't dislike William,' she said, 'and will welcome him into the family in time.'

Mama merely closed her eyes and Beatrix got up with the

help of the chair arm. 'I think I'd better go back upstairs.'

'I'll help you old girl,' said Bertram, rising with alacrity.

With Bertram's arm supporting her, Beatrix reached the nursery without mishap. She subsided, heart pounding, into the armchair. 'O frabjous day! Callooh! Callay! – Are you chortling, Brother? You've every right to,' she said, beating a soft tattoo on her knees. At least she no longer felt like crying; all this excitement must have done her good.

Bertram took her hand and squeezed it affectionately. 'D'you know what I think did the trick? Not Mary, bless her heart, but my mentioning that you are getting long in the tooth. I truly believe that they both still saw you as a vulnerable young girl in need of protection.'

'From Willie?' said Beatrix, feeling stronger every minute in spite of being long in the tooth. 'It might be the other way round.'

It was clear, even to Mama, that Beatrix needed country air to convalesce and she arrived at Hill Top in April. She brought with her an invitation to Willie to spend a weekend at Bolton Gardens. He was shocked at Beatrix's wan appearance and horrified at the invitation.

'Stay with your parents? But what would I do? There'd be no golf or bowls and I don't know them at all.'

'That's the idea of the invitation,' Beatrix said, laughing at him, 'to get to know them. I could always take you round the South Kensington Museum.'

William thought she really meant it until he saw her face.

'Mind you,' he said, looking at her sideways, 'responding to popular demand, I've made it known amongst the Heelis clan that you will be At Home to callers.'

Beatrix was well aware of the threatening loom of Willie's relations, scattered around Hawkshead like almonds on a cake. So far she had not met them. She awaited the first arrival with apprehension.

Mrs William Dickinson Heelis, wife of Willie's partner in the firm, arrived on an afternoon of sunshine and showers when Beatrix was making another attempt to complete her *Pigling Bland* illustrations. This time she was sitting outside the sty, wrapped in a sacking apron and wearing clogs as being without laces, sketch pad on her knee and much inconvenienced by Esmeralda's squealing offspring.

Mrs William, an imposing presence, was dressed for calling. Her crisp starched white dress, black kid shoes and the organdie frills on her hat proclaimed this to the world. 'Oh my ears and whiskers,' Beatrix muttered and dropped her pencil on the muddy cobbles.

Eventually they were seated in the parlour, Beatrix minus the apron but she had found no opportunity to change her footwear. They explored the state of Beatrix's health, not a subject on which she liked to dwell, the state of the weather and the state of the garden, and all the time it seemed Mrs William couldn't keep her eyes off Beatrix's feet. Beatrix thought of explaining about Esmeralda's passion for boot laces, but it all seemed too difficult. Anyway, she was finding clogs very comfortable for farm wear.

At last Mrs William came to her ostensible reason for calling. 'William and I were so pleased to hear of Willie's engagement,' she said. 'It's time he was married. We are wondering what you would like for a wedding present?'

Beatrix would have liked to ask for the latest thing in incubators. She had found gas better than an oil lamp, but the new incubators, she understood, were much more efficient. Hatching them at Hill Top would be an improvement on Bolton Gardens.

'I really have no idea,' she said to Mrs William.

'Would a silver cream jug be acceptable?' asked Mrs William, rather desperately.

'No, no, I really don't think that would be much use,' Beatrix said, her mind on incubators, 'I believe I gave one away not long ago.'

Mrs William left shortly after that and Beatrix had a feeling that the visit had not been a success.

Her next visitor was Willie's landlady, his cousin Fanny Ann of Hawkshead Hall, known to the family as Fananna. She was large and rather jolly and her hat was decorated with artificial cherries which nodded as she introduced herself. The shining, bobbing fruit distracted Beatrix's attention.

'I beg your pardon,' she apologised, 'I didn't quite catch . . .'

'What would you like for a wedding present?' asked Fananna again, as though addressing a deaf mute.

Beatrix was suddenly exasperated.

'You don't really want to know,' she said. 'That's just an

excuse so you can call and see what odd fish Willie has hooked in his old age.'

To her surprise, Fananna roared with laughter, the cherries shaking as though in a gale. 'You'll do very well together,' she said. 'Willie is a bit of a shrinking violet; he needs someone who knows her mind to give him a push.'

Mrs Cannon, too, was inclined to dwell on the engagement until Beatrix changed the subject to that of incubators and young ducklings, but Mr Cannon had another preoccupation. He was having trouble with their new neighbour, a Mr Simpson.

'He won't fence, Miss Potter. Lets his sheep wander at will. Not Herdwicks o'course, some awkward cross between rough fell and Leicesters. All it needs is for one of his tups to get amongst our lot, then we'll have real trouble.'

Beatrix went back to London in June to get her parents ready for their summer vacation, which was again to be spent at Lindeth Howe. Willie accompanied her, repeating several times on the journey that after all, it was only for three days.

The weekend was not an unqualified success. Mr and Mrs Potter didn't say much and Willie told Beatrix they kept looking at him which made him nervous. Was he dressed improperly for London SW?

'You give them something good to look at for once,' Beatrix said stoutly, aware that it wasn't only her parents who were studying Willie in his good tweed suit. She'd seen unexpected flicks of apron strings now and then and even Mr Beckett wasn't keeping his eyes strictly on the horse's ears. 'Come on, I'll take you to see the Tower of London.'

'I've always rather wanted to see Madam Tussaud's,' said Willie hesitantly. 'Missed out on it somehow.'

They spent two happy hours among the waxworks, comparing some of the more notorious villains with the inhabitants of Sawrey and almost deciding they should live in Castle Cottage as Hill Top wasn't big enough, but Willie had a setback in the evening; he offered to teach his future father and mother-in-law to play whist.

Beatrix suffered for him as Mama explained, acidly, how Unitarians felt about playing cards. She then demanded a list of his other interests.

'Well, I like climbing mountains,' said Willie nervously, 'do a bit of fishing sometimes too and I'm a member of the

Hawkshead Bowling Club. Oh, and I like dancing, Morris dancing and country dancing.' He smiled his lopsided smile at her but only received another lecture, this time on the evils of dance.

The question of dancing also brought on his first quarrel with Beatrix. Willie didn't see what possible objection there could be to country dancing. He was fairly bristling about it.

'It's traditional, and the dances'll be lost if no one actually *dances* them. You'd enjoy them too. If you don't feel like taking up golf, you could join our country dancing team.'

'No, no I couldn't do that,' Beatrix said. 'I've never danced in my life. It wouldn't feel right at all.'

'Not even a children's class?' Willie asked. Beatrix shook her head. 'Well, you should have.' They were in the nursery and he paced about a bit in a caged sort of way. 'Ridiculous, the way you were brought up. I don't know what your parents were thinking of.'

'Probably about what was best for me,' Beatrix countered in a sudden uncalled-for rush of loyalty.

Nothing more was said on the subject and Willie left after lunch, rather silent.

# CHAPTER TWENTY-ONE

Beatrix followed Willie north two weeks later with her parents. They both found the journey trying, Papa especially so even though Elizabeth came with them and helped to carry the cameras. Mr Beckett travelled up the following day with the horses and carriage and his wife and the boys. Lindeth Lodge had been made ready for them.

It was almost a week before Beatrix could get away and meet Willie at Hill Top. Papa didn't seem to recover properly from the journey and it was only realistic to get a nurse, at least temporarily. Even Mama agreed to it. A note to Canon Rawnsley produced Nurse May from Kendal, who arrived by train with commendable despatch. She was a bustling body who spoke her mind and Beatrix looked at Mama apprehensively.

She was also apprehensive about her first meeting with William after their disagreement, only slight but their first, on the subject of dancing. She had decided that if it came up again she would agree to watch him Morris dancing, even though she wouldn't dance herself. In the deep gloom of the night she wondered if Willie still wanted to marry her.

She need not have worried, he never mentioned it. When they met, he was his usual placid and companionable self and Beatrix saw she was quite wrong to think he would ever hold a grudge, it was not in his nature. Still, he had done something unexpected. He had settled Mr Simpson.

'Cannon told me about the problem,' he said, 'and naturally I took it on. That's the sort of thing I can do for you, settle matters where there is a question of law.'

'The man was so abusive I wouldn't have thought the law or anything else would have settled him,' Beatrix replied. 'What did you say?'

'What did I say? Well, after he'd called me an interfering young jackanapes who poked his long nose into matters that weren't his business, I felt like saying quite a lot. In the end I told him the law required him to keep his fences in repair, and if this was not done his strayed sheep would be impounded. I also happened to remark that the market price for fat lambs was going up. Cannon told me he was hammering in new fence-posts the following morning.'

'In your position too!' Beatrix was slightly shocked. She'd never have thought it of him.

But Willie was unrepentant.

Beatrix's freedom to visit Hill Top did not last long. The regime Nurse May imposed was strict: a restricted diet, regular walks, no excitement, early bedtime. Her idea of excitement included photography and Papa soon reached a point where he could no longer endure the boredom of what was supposed to be his summer holiday. Mama had of course been against any such ridiculous rules from the start. They both insisted that Papa's improved health was in spite of, not because of, Nurse May's extraordinary ideas.

'When I ordered steak and kidney pudding for lunch, she would not let your father eat it, even though everyone knows it's a most sustaining dish, but insisted on him having *scrambled eggs*,' Mama told Beatrix indignantly on her second return from Sawrey, 'and she makes him sleep with his window open and with only two blankets on the bed, so I've had to move to another room to avoid pneumonia! She's got to go. Anyway, Papa is recovered, in spite of her efforts to starve or freeze him to death'.

Beatrix could see that Papa at least thought he was better, making plans for photographic excursions with his daughter. She wondered, as both parents seemed so unusually cheerful when the landaulette and the silhouette of Nurse May's disapprovingly straight back had disappeared towards the station, if she should leave home now, whilst the going was good.

Canon Rawnsley's parochial visit – parochial because any parishioner who had been under his hand for however short a time remained a parishioner for life – took place the following day. He arrived in good time for 5 o'clock tea, beaming at them all, including Elizabeth whom he nearly chucked under the chin but prevented himself at the last moment when he saw that Mama had her eye on him. He had a countryman's colour, bright eyes and was bristling with health.

He declared himself delighted that Nurse May had effected such a rapid cure and settled down for a good gossip, which he would have stoutly denied was his favourite occupation.

After everyone's health had been enquired into, he reported on the hydroplanes. 'There's no doubt we're winning. There have been questions in the House: "Does the Minister realise that war has already begun in the northern country of Westmorland, where hydroplanes are upsetting horses, capsizing pleasure yachts and causing trouble of all kinds up and down Windermere?" That sort of thing.'

'It doesn't matter what you do as long as you don't upset the horses,' quoted Beatrix. 'I'm sure that's a good line to take.'

Mama, who paid Canon Rawnsley the compliment of occasionally listening to what he said, raised her head. 'My dear Canon,' she said, 'there is far too much nonsense talked about preserving the peace and quiet of this area; in my opinion it needs livening up. These hydroplanes would certainly do that. The horses will get used to the noise and it gives people something to look at besides these green, monotonous hills.'

There were little puffing noises from the sofa and Beatrix wondered if Papa, who had been listening with one hand cupped against an ear, was going to support the peace and quiet lobby in defiance of his wife. She soon found he had other matters on his mind.

'You said,' he finally articulated, looking accusingly at Canon Rawnsley, ' "war has already begun". What d'you mean by that, eh! What other war are you expecting to break out?'

Canon Rawnsley at once looked much less cheerful, in fact rather anxious. He glanced at Beatrix as though for support.

'Nurse May,' she told him, 'thought reading the newspaper could lead to excitement and might affect Papa's blood pressure.'

Canon Rawnsley opened his mouth and shut it again; clearly he didn't know where to begin.

'Come on man, out with it.' Papa had hoisted himself into a sitting position.

'Not read *The Times* eh?' The Canon fingered his beard. 'What you've missed is the news that a week ago Bulgaria invaded Serbia, who brought in Rumania so Bulgaria had to retreat back to the old borders. The dispute isn't over yet and Rumania could always change sides, but the leading article said this was just a curtain raiser. The real war will begin when the great powers decide the right moment has arrived for them to take part.'

'What does that mean? Speak plainly man.' Papa was bouncing up and down.

'Plainly? There's little plain about anything to do with this

185

mess, but plainly Germany is pushing forward her naval and military preparations, Russia is building railways on her western borders, France has extended military service and Winston Churchill is commissioning dreadnoughts in every dockyard we possess. War will certainly come, the uncertainly is the alliances and the timing.' Canon Rawnsley was grim.

'The Kaiser, that's who's pulling the strings. See's himself as a world conqueror.' Papa looked more alive than he had for months. 'We'll show him – God for England, Harry and St George.' He looked round, as though for his regiment.

Beatrix rose quickly and went over to him; this would never do. 'Calm yourself Papa, *The Times* has made mistakes before.' She caught Canon Rawnsley's eye and he supported her at once.

'It has indeed and will again.' He put down his empty cup. 'And now I must be on my way. Time and tide wait for no man.'

He made his farewells and Beatrix went with him down to the hall.

'I'll never learn to keep a bridle on my tongue,' he said ruefully. 'I'm afraid I may have left you with difficulties.'

'Papa will forget in no time,' she reassured him, 'but what you said has confirmed a decision I had almost made: that is to leave my cottages and farms, those I have already bought and others I may yet own, to the National Trust. A war is only going to make it easier for people to lay waste to the countryside, they can always say it's in the nation's interest, and I have to agree that the Trust appears to make a good guardian. I can change my will if I change my mind.'

'You won't do that.' The Canon had no doubts. He took her hand in farewell, then bent and quickly kissed her cheek. 'You have great courage,' he told her, his eyes twinkling at her astonishment, 'and will use it well.'

The front door shut behind him, but it was a while before Beatrix moved and went back upstairs to the drawing-room.

She found Mama seated beside Papa on the sofa, poker-backed and grim of mouth.

'Of course it's impossible you should marry now,' she told Beatrix. 'War, invasion! You cannot leave us to be murdered in our beds by Russian cossacks.' There was a hint of triumph in that deep voice. A war was not too great a price to pay to keep her daughter at home.

'Surely you are exaggerating, Mama? There is nothing to say at the moment that the Russians would fight against us. They may even be our allies.'

Russians, Germans, Bulgarians – what does it matter? What matters is our safety. No, I've made up my mind. You simply cannot marry until the war is over.' There was an affirmative grunt from Papa.

Beatrix found, to her surprise, that her feelings were not of despair and despondency as on similar occasions in the past; instead she felt a profound irritation.

'No really Mama, you cannot get away with such a flyer. Whether I'm married or not will make no difference to your safety. In fact, with Willie in the family, a man of ability and decision, you will have more security. You'll have to make up your mind to it once and for all, because if you do not, I shall go regardless and Willie and I will not be there when you need us.'

It was the first time she had said 'Willie and I' and it was surprising what strength it gave her. She watched Mama's face and saw her eyelids droop in resignation.

Beatrix realised she would have to make the arrangements for her wedding herself. It would be altogether too much to expect Mama and Papa to undertake them. It would be quiet of course, probably at St Mary Abbot's, Kensington.

'Will you be hearing white, Miss Bea?' Elizabeth asked.

'Well no,' Beatrix said and saw Elizabeth's face fall. 'But a very nice expensive hat I think. Tell me, will you be happy with my parents after I'm married?' She was a little doubtful about Elizabeth at the moment, she seemed quieter these days and it would be better to clear the air.

'Yes Miss Bea, don't you worry. I can manage the house and Mr Beckett will be in charge of the horses and that. Between us, we'll keep everything right and tight.'

Beatrix still felt dubious, but Elizabeth sounded surprisingly firm. Of course there was always her unexpected hobby of collecting Persian rugs and it was odd but she and Mama seemed to have come to a reasonable understanding and now tolerated each other with equanimity.

Beatrix was feeling much stronger by the time the letter arrived from Fruing Warne, though she still had difficulty with the hill from the ferry to Far Sawrey. He wanted to come and see her.

'I haven't been to Warnes' office since last autumn,' Beatrix said remorsefully to Willie. 'That must be the trouble, with lots of things to settle and discuss and to pay the money they owe me. He can't stay at Hill Top though, there's only one bed. I'll have to find him a room in the village. He'll need meeting off the train.'

She wrote to him accordingly.

Willie couldn't meet the train, he had to be in court. Mr Cannon wasn't available, the vet was coming to one of the cows. There being nothing else for it, Beatrix borrowed the trap and Molly and drove over to Windermere to meet the train herself. It was a showery day so she wore an old felt hat, draped a sack over her shoulders and wrapped her legs in a rug.

The train was in when she arrived and she could see Fruing, more like Norman than Harold, looking despondently at departing carriages and automobiles. He was in his city clothes, black and white striped trousers, a black frock-coat and a top hat, causing heads to turn and young girls to giggle. Beatrix pulled her hat over her eyes and watched him walk over in her direction.

'Tell me, my good man,' he said, 'is there a conveyance available to take me to Sawrey?' Then Beatrix took off her hat and turned towards him.

She told Willie afterwards that she'd done it because he looked so out of place and silly and he should have known better than to dress like that for a country visit. Really Fruing had taken it very well, though he'd further annoyed her by exclaiming at her courage in driving alone in this wild country. He had got rather wet when the heavens had opened on their way up Ferry Hill and his top hat had suffered.

'He looked like a drowned aldermanic beetle,' Beatrix continued, 'with his gold watch chain across his front, and he didn't at all like the Lake District. He said we were sadly lacking in civilised amenities. I wonder if Norman would have felt the same?'

Willie didn't comment on the point but wanted to know Fruing's reason for coming all this way.

'He said he hadn't wanted to put what he had to say in a letter – I wonder if he thought that would constitute evidence which could be used against him. In fact, he said I had been quite right to worry about Harold's muddles, he wished they had taken me seriously long ago. It appears Warne's finances are in turmoil. So much so that he asked me to forego my royalties for the moment, and could I see my way to finishing my new book and starting another as soon as possible? He was quite peevish about the length of time it is taking me to finish *Pigling Bland*.'

'They want the money in quickly to hush up any scandal,'

said Willie. 'Lombard Street to a china orange it'll come out anyway. These things always do.'

'I'm not quite such a good catch as I was, Willie,' said Beatrix.

'No,' he agreed, 'but I'll not throw you back.'

'I've promised the book for the end of September,' she went on. 'Esmeralda's piglets have not all been sold yet. I shall start again tomorrow. But the sooner I cease being Beatrix Potter, writer and artist, and become Mrs Heelis, farmer, the better I shall be pleased. When shall we get married?'

'October's a good time,' said Willie. 'Beginning of the farming year.'

Beatrix took her parents back to London on 24th September, finding it tiresome to have to come away when the building of the extension at Castle Farm, where she and Willie had finally decided to make their home, was just getting interesting. She had, to her great relief, got rid of the revised proofs for *Pigling Bland* the previous week. She had sent Willie a sketch of the last illustration in the book, where Pigling Bland danced Pigwig over the hills and far away.

'Not precisely a likeness,' she wrote on the bottom of the drawing, 'but we can at least follow in their footsteps.'

# EPILOGUE

———— • ————

The marriage of Beatrix and William Heelis was a happy one, though it was tested almost at once by the impact of the First World War. Beatrix had to manage her farms with boys and old men, giving help herself where she could: William was deprived of his younger clerks.

Rupert Potter died early in 1914 and Bertram in 1918. Mrs Potter made her home in the Lake District at Lindeth Howe, with Elizabeth as her housekeeper.

After the war Mrs Heelis continued to buy property, finally convinced she could safely leave it to the National Trust. She died in 1943, and her husband eighteen months later. Her bequest to the Trust amounted to 4,000 acres and many houses and cottages. This was a most important gift, not only for its size but for what it represented. Mrs Heelis's concern to protect the landscape became Trust policy for the Lake District as a whole.

Her ashes were scattered by her head shepherd, Tom Storey. He was charged with secrecy as to where he put them by Beatrix herself. 'She said, whatever I did, to tell nobody.' The farming world of Cumberland and Westmorland agreed with the shepherd who said 'Aye, it's a bad day for farmers' at her funeral. The Trust, too, had lost a friend.

The continued popularity of Peter Rabbit and friends would have pleased but surprised Mrs Heelis, who did not have a high opinion of her own abilities. Generally speaking, she would have been better pleased by the success of the National Trust, which now protects over one-third of the Lake District.

Today's increased sales of her little books and people's greater awareness of the need to protect the countryside only serve to underline the practicality and foresight of Beatrix Potter, naturalist, farmer, writer and artist.